Dedication

For the princes who let themselves be saved by the princess.

JA HUSS

PROLOGUE

Rook

Day 1,110 in Captivity
Six Months Ago
Wayne, Illinois

Thirty-one days.

That's how long it takes my face to heal.

I watch the girl in the mirror, looking for marks. She tilts her head this way and that, lifts her chin, stretches her neck for any sign of fingertip-shaped bruises, and then she sighs.

They are all gone. I can see a tiny scar on the edge of my lower lip, but it's not as bad as it could've been if Jon hadn't rigged up a rudimentary butterfly bandage so he didn't have to take me to the hospital. It should've been stitched, but it wasn't.

My pack is waiting on the floor of the bathroom. I wasn't sure if today would be the day. I tried last week but there were still a few purple splotches on the skin under my eye and the lip was scabbed.

It's been torture waiting to heal. And I kept thinking—what if he does it again? Before I heal? Then I'll be stuck here even longer.

But enough of that. It's healed now and I have an appointment. I take one more look in the mirror and give myself a little pep talk. "You're going to live, Rook. You're going to *live*. You might not have the best life, but it will be better than this one. No matter how bad it is at first. Things will get better."

I really believe it too. Before all this mess with Jon—that's what he calls it, the mess—I was what some people might call an optimist. A half-full kind of girl.

I think I can be that girl again.

I think I can.

My suitcase contains all my worldly possessions. It's not much really, just some clothes and trinkets. A few softcover books I never finished, and some crap that meant something to me at one time or another, but no longer matters.

I just want to leave it all behind. Every bit of it. But I don't want Jon to have anything of me. I want to leave this house and leave no trace of myself.

It's impossible, I'm not delusional. I'm all over this place. I picked out the dishtowel hanging on the stove. I found the dishes at an antique store not far from here. I'm the only person to ever have used the oven. And I'm leaving behind an entire room of things I can't bear to look at.

But I can't change any of that. I can't erase the imprint I'm leaving here.

All I can do is remove the few very personal items I have and stuff them in this suitcase.

Jon left the car keys today. And a list of errands he wanted me to do. Go to the store, buy his favorite foods, pick up a package at the post office—he was pissed about that, that it had to be picked up instead of delivered. But it was his fault. I couldn't exactly open the door with my face all purple.

I take one more look down the hallway to the last

door on the left. It's closed. It's always closed.

I hope it stays closed forever because I'm so tired of thinking about it.

The suitcase is very heavy since it contains all the things I'd rather throw away than leave with Jon, but I manage to get it in the backseat of the Toyota, then plop myself down in the driver's seat and put my pack on the passenger side.

I'm remarkably calm for a girl who is about to run away. I expected my heart to beat wildly, like the last time I tried to leave.

I didn't make it that time. But that was two years ago now. He's made a mess of me so many times since then and I never tried to run away again, so I guess he figures I'm beat. He's won.

The car protests with backfires and clouds of smoke when I turn the key. I just press the gas until it gets over it. It will work today, I know it will. I'm not worried about the car breaking down at all, and typically I worry about that even if I'm just going to the supermarket in town.

Today it doesn't matter.

I pull out of the driveway and never look back.

The first thing on my checklist is to ditch the suitcase. I have no use for all that crap in my life anymore. My pack contains two extra day outfits, seven pairs of underwear, one pair of pajamas and some personal hygiene items.

I pull up to a dumpster just inside the Chicago city limits, then lug the suitcase out of the backseat and throw it down on the ground. There's a few homeless people sleeping nearby so I call out in a friendly voice, "Free stuff in this suitcase. Take whatever you want."

Most of them just stare at me looking pretty miserable. But a few get up and mumble out a 'thank you.'

I shrug and get back in the car and weave down a number of streets filled with cars and people walking. Going places and generally being busy on this Monday morning.

Monday is the perfect day because Jon can't work from home on Mondays. He has to go into the office downtown and work on the servers and stuff at the police station. So even though I won't answer his calls all day, he won't be able to figure out what's wrong until he gets home tonight. By then I'll be long gone and he won't be able to find me easily. His thing is computer forensics, so he's like a god in the virtual world. But I don't do anything virtual these days, so that's a total dead end for him. I have cash in my pocket that I've been stashing away, little by little, down in the basement for years.

And my bus ticket isn't even purchased yet, so he can't track me that way.

I park the car in a trendy neighborhood far away from the bus station and check the mirror one more time.

I smile. My lips pull back from my cheeks and I look like a skeleton. I've lost a lot of weight, probably fifteen pounds, and skinny is in my nature, so right now I could probably stand to gain at least twenty to fill out my frame. I smile again and try not to see my life in my eyes.

This time I look almost OK. When you ignore the fact that my soul is crushed and my eyes really are a mirror inside. I don't look so bad.

But like the car, it doesn't matter today. I'm not worried about how people see me. If they see my fading bruises, or my cut lip, or the lost, tragic look in my eyes— I do not care. I exist alone in this world as of today.

There is just me.

The smile stays on my face as I enter the beauty salon.

And when I come out two hours later, I'm someone else. There's no sign of the limp blonde hair I've been dyeing since Jon took over my life. The tragic eyes are only half full of sadness and despair, the other half is hope. My hair is as close to its natural brown-black as you can get and not look fake and I changed into my other outfit before I left. All the ladies in the salon made a big deal out of me because I told them I had a special first date tonight and they chuckled and smiled and congratulated me and told me to 'go get him.'

What I left out was that my first date was with myself.

I end day one thousand one hundred and ten sitting on a Greyhound bus heading to Las Vegas. It's a two-day trip and I've been sitting in this seat for less than half of that and my back already aches and my legs are going numb.

But I don't care.

It's nice to meet me again and I can't wait to get to know me better.

CHAPTER ONE

Rook

**Six Months Later
Denver, CO**

The music pounds in my ear as I force myself up one more aisle of steps at Coors Field. This song always gets me trying a little harder. I hop the long step, then take a stride and pump my legs to go up two steps at once. I can't do this very long, I'm still no Ford when it comes to running stadiums, but I almost make it to the top before I have to slow down and then finally stop.

I look for Ford, but he's doing the lower sections today. Just a blur of a black shirt running much harder than me up his current set of steps. I jog in place until the song winds down and realize I've used up all my energy. So I stop and enjoy the view. This is why I come to the upper section these days.

The view. These mountains are gorgeous and I never get tired of looking at them. I'm off to the far right of first base. I'm not a baseball person, so I have no idea what that area on the field is called. Right field? I dunno. I'm not on the field anyway, I'm up in the stands, so it hardly matters.

The only thing that matters is that I can see the mountains and the way the reflected sunrise from the east lights them up all pink. Sometimes when Ronin and I are up there for the weekend or just for a ride, I have to pinch myself, that's how pretty it is.

Colorado changes once September arrives. One minute you're grilling outside and the nights are pleasant, the next it's freezing-ass cold. Well, fifties and sometimes forties, anyway. Too cold to hang out at night in shorts anymore.

But the new crisp air feels spectacular on my sweaty skin right now. In fact, I get a little chill because I'm starting to cool down. I enjoy the relative quiet for a few minutes. The traffic down below is pretty loud, but it's tempered by the ever-constant wind whistling across my ears. Colorado should be nicknamed the Wind State because it's a regular thing.

Life is so weird. I still can't get over how much things have changed for me since I stepped off that bus six months ago. I have a lot of money. Well, maybe not a lot compared to Ronin, but to me, a million dollars is too much to even comprehend. STURGIS will pay out at just under six hundred and fifty thousand dollars, plus the fifty grand I had from TRAGIC, plus the money the guys took from Jon when they set him up. I've got over a million, actually.

And I've bought nothing since before the STURGIS contract started besides food and gas and stuff like that. Not one thing. Not one article of clothing—I have way more clothes than I need. Not a stick of furniture—Ronin purchased all my furniture. Not even a car. Although this is gonna change very soon. I'm just too content to think about spending right now. I've never been a shopper and money has not changed that in me.

"Why did you stop?" Ford has made his way across the stadium and into the upper level while I was daydreaming. He's even carrying burritos and drinks.

"I'm done. Besides, I wanted to enjoy the view. It's our last time here, Ford."

He smiles. He does that a lot these days. And not just at me. I'm not one hundred percent sure if this is normal, but I'm guessing not. September has rolled in and everyone in my new little family is suddenly a lot happier.

Elise is pregnant, so she's one of those glowing moms-to-be. She's tiny everywhere but her stomach where she's just getting her fourth-month baby bump. No wonder she was so crazy all summer worrying about Clare. She was just as surprised as the rest of us when she did the pregnancy test the day we came back from Sturgis. Good thing Elise is not a partier or she'd probably be insane with worry because her mothering instinct is already kicking in. Antoine is beside himself with pride. He even asked her to marry him but she said, and I quote, "After twelve years I refuse to accept your proposal knocked-the-fuck-up."

He's still working on her, but she hasn't taken his ring.

Ronin is happy too. He's in charge of the GIDGET contract, which is not erotic modeling. Well, not really. It's a retro pin-up catalog shoot for a new lingerie company. They aren't really new, they're some subsidiary of another huge lingerie company, hence the cash flow for this kick-off.

Spencer is back up in Fort Collins doing his thing. But I'll see him tomorrow when Ronin moves me up to the shop for filming of the first season of Shrike Bikes for the Biker Channel.

Ronin and I talked about this decision *ad nauseam* after Sturgis. I won't go into the boring details, but he was managing the GIDGET contract so it was only fair that I got to do the show with Spencer because they start at the same time. It's perfect really. Our last flirt with this crazy world of modeling, then on to vague new things.

We haven't gotten that far yet, so I'm not sure what that means other than not what we're doing now.

"Here," Ford says, handing me a water and my partially unwrapped burrito. I take it and dig in. "We'll find something to take its place when we get up north. Don't worry."

"Hmm," I say with my mouth full. "I don't see what, Ford. That place is in the middle of nowhere. And winter is coming."

He smiles at the film reference. "Snowshoeing. Cross-country skiing. Extreme croquet."

I spit out some eggs as I laugh. "What. The. Fuck. Is. That?"

"It's croquet, but not." He sighs. "It's all relative, I guess."

"Sounds like my kind of game, actually. It's for stoners, isn't it? Like Frisbee?"

Ford laughs. "Maybe. We can skip the extreme croquet then. I'll figure something out. How's school coming?"

School. I'm in school. Sometimes I have to pinch myself, that's how excited this makes me. Ford, ever the stealthy hacker genius that he is, rigged my mandatory placement test for the community college up in FoCo and got me registered for fall semester. It's all online, so it's not really life-changing like if I was living on campus at Colorado State, which is the big FoCo university, but I'm stoked. I'm taking basic shit. English composition, History of Western Civ, biology, and pre-algebra.

Yes, I'm a total math loser, but what can you do? One

baby step at a time.

"How's math, in particular?" Ford asks, like he's reading my mind. "I know you hated that I put you in a non-credit class, but it was the right decision, wasn't it?"

"Yes," I reluctantly admit. "I'm barely keeping up to be honest. It's confusing for me. I'm not a math girl."

"Well, luckily you need very little of it for film school, so don't dwell. Just do your best."

Ford is very supportive of my academic pursuits. *Very* supportive. It makes me wonder sometimes. It's not like Ronin isn't supportive, he is. He wants me to follow my dream. But Ford is supportive in a different way. Like he's invested in it or something. Like his success is dependent on mine. And that gets me thinking back to what he said a few months ago. About how patient he is. About him giving me the tools I need to fix my life, so I'll stop looking for Ronin to do that for me. He wants me to be strong all on my own. Not need anyone.

I like that about Ford. It's like he trusts me. Like he's got faith in me.

It makes me have faith in myself.

"How come you don't have a girlfriend, Ford?"

"What makes you think I don't?"

"Oh," I reply, embarrassed. "Do you?"

He looks away. "I have… women." He looks back, smiling. "But they're not girlfriends."

I'm not even sure what to say to that, so of course I choose something totally inappropriate. "Are they… whores?"

He laughs. "No comment." And then he takes a big bite of his burrito and shuts that conversation down.

"Clare's coming home tomorrow." I'm not sure why I fill in the silence with that tidbit of information—

"You're nervous about meeting her."

—but apparently Ford has a pretty good handle on my psyche these days. "Yeah. I still think about what you said, you know."

He shrugs. "I'm not going to say any more about it. Ronin's your boyfriend, you like each other. That's all that matters."

I stare at him for a few more seconds and let this sink in. "Good, that means you've lost interest in me and all that shit you said last summer about wanting me to leave Ronin is over."

He laughs. "We're friends, right? I'm happy with how things are going between us. It's perfect actually."

Hmmm. That's weird. In fact, I'm weird right now. I shouldn't be asking him this stuff but I can't help myself. "Because you're... what? Emotionally incapable of intimate relationships? This friendship is as far as you go? There's nothing after this but the physical act of sex?"

"Yes, yes, and yes. You missed your calling. You should've been a psych major."

"I cheat. Ronin told me about... well, he told me why he was so insistent on me not talking to you."

"And do you agree with my diagnosis?"

"Not really," I say, shaking my head. "You're a bit on the strange side—"

He laughs again, his eyes darting around the stadium, like he's thinking about this.

"—and I'm guessing you really are some scary smart genius. I totally see that. But you've done a lot of very nice things for me, Ford. And I never asked for it. I'm not always nice back to you, but I hope you know I really, really appreciate it."

He drops the smile now and stares hard just past my

head, like he's thinking. I hold my breath as I wait for him to say something and when he finally begins to talk, it's soft and low. "We fucked Mardee up pretty good. We were all tight—Mardee, Ronin, Spencer, and me. A sort of unit. Even though Ronin and I never got along well, it was different when the four of us were together. It was... just different. And you stunned me last summer when you asked me that question, Rook. I didn't know what to say."

"What question?"

"Who was I chasing." He lets out a long breath. "Her. I'm chasing her. I'm trying to catch up with all the mistakes we made. It's funny how you take people for granted." He looks me in the eye for this part. "We took her for granted. We used her, we..."

I wait him out, patient, like he is with me.

He takes a drink and swallows hard before continuing. "Ronin blames himself for not paying attention to her, and Spencer blames himself for bringing her around the drugs, but we all played a part. You two really have nothing in common, but every time I look at you, I see her. And it just..." He stops to shake his head. "I just want you to succeed so badly. It feels good to watch you grow stronger."

I'm not sure what to say. I knew this Mardee girl weighed on Ronin's conscience, but it seems to go much deeper than that. There's a lot more to this story than they've told me, but Ford was right about something else he told me last summer. I'm a keeper. A secret-keeper, just like they are. And I'm not sure I want to keep their secrets as well as mine. I'm not sure I can handle that right now.

So if these guys do have more secrets, they can keep them. I'm totally OK with that and I take my chance to change the subject before I learn something I might not want to know. "I am getting better, though. And you're helping me. All three of you are helping me, actually. You with the running and school, Ronin with trust and relationships, and Spencer with the jobs. I'm so lucky to have you guys."

"I'm enjoying you too, Rook. You've taught me a few things as well."

I choke down a snort. "Like what?"

He begins to talk, but stops the words at the last second. His gaze sweeps across the baseball field below, then rests back on me. "Emotions have been... very difficult for me. It's true what Ronin said. I wouldn't say I have none, or that I'm incapable like my father thought. It's not that I *don't* or *can't* feel things like that. It's that I don't want to. I just don't care about people." He throws up his hands. "That's my dirtiest secret and now you have it. I just don't give a fuck about people, I really don't."

I can't help myself because these personal conversations with Ford are not common, so I ask. "Did you care about Mardee?"

"I did," he says with a sigh.

"And she preferred Ronin?"

He's the one who almost snorts this time. "Don't they all?" He looks over at me. "Don't you all prefer Ronin?"

I rest my elbows back on the concrete step behind me and then stretch my legs out. "You're a nice-looking guy, Ford. So is Spencer. I'm not sure one could actually choose between the three of you. You're all good catches. Equally desirable in different ways."

He screws up his face. "How is *Spencer* desirable? I have never understood what girls see in him."

I laugh. "Well, he's like a big fun-loving goof-ball, but powerful and dangerous at the same time. He's the bad boy girls fall in lust with and don't mind taking orders from."

"And Ronin?"

"Ronin's just hot." I grin over at him. "He's the player all the girls want to settle down with. But he's nice too. If Spence is the bad boy, then Ronin is the good guy. The knight in shining armor, like you said."

"And me?"

I don't look at him this time, but I can feel his stare like it's heat. Waiting. "You're... predictable."

He belts out a laugh. "Well, I appreciate the ego stroke, Rook. Thank you." He gets up and starts to walk down the stairs.

"I wasn't finished."

He stops but keeps his back to me.

"Not predictable as in boring or repetitive, but predictable as in safe. Even though I'm always adjusting when I'm with you, reevaluating things about myself and... you. You're like an open book, Ford. What you see is what you get. So I'm not sure why your father thought that about you, I'm not really qualified to think too hard about it and make a better observation. But I'll just say this. The reason I like you is because you're honest. I know what I'm getting with you even though you keep me guessing. Because I always know that when you give me something, it will be good and you're only thinking of what's best for me. Ronin and Spencer are not better-looking than you, that's for sure. You guys are just desirable in different ways."

He turns around and smiles. "Good to know. Ready?"

I shrug because I can see through his act now—he avoids talking about himself in personal ways most of the time. He'll tell me all about his college days, his jobs, professional things like that. But he hides from the emotional stuff, the things that cause him to feel too much. Not everything, mind you—he opens up every once in a while—but that open book has closed for today and I know this is his signal that talking is over.

I'm OK with that because I, too, am patient.

CHAPTER TWO

Rook

There are a ton of girls milling around the building because Ronin is having an open casting call for the GIDGET models. I'm actually relieved I'm not GIDGET. Not that there's just one, he needs like a dozen of them, I think. But I'm so over modeling, it's not even funny. I can think of hundreds of jobs I'd rather do right off the top of my head. Like rodeo clown. I'd rather be a target for a raging bull than be a model.

The girls are here early to line up and they wind around the corner and spill over into the back lot. They are all dressed up, full make-up, heels, and they look cold. I'm still warm from my morning exercise, but I can feel the chill in the air. And just looking at their shoes makes my toes sad. I'm so glad I'm the new parts girl for Shrike Bikes. I get to wear jeans, and hoodies, and sneakers.

I totally got the better end of the deal.

Ford and I walk towards the parking lot as per usual and he gets annoyed at a girl who is standing too close to his vehicle. He always parks in the same spot in the back of the lot, just off to the left of the back door. He just got a new car—well, I'd never really call it new, but last week was the first time I've seen it. He used to drive a sporty little black Beamer but then he showed up with this…

thing. "I liked the old car, Ford."

He's just about to open the door when this comes out and he stops to look back at me. "Really? Why?"

I crack a smile and so does he. "It suits you. This circa 1986 Bronco is just all kinds of wrong."

"I needed a truck for winter. I still have the BMW, I just parked it in my mom's garage."

"You have a mom?" I laugh as the words come out.

"You thought I was a demon spawned from hell?"

I nod and laugh again. "I might buy a car. I'm gonna get something totally inappropriate for winter. Like a VW bus."

"Or a convertible. I could totally see you in a Roadster."

We both stop for a second. I'm sure the irony isn't lost to the armchair psychologist in him. I just compared myself to a beaten-up old has-been and he compared me to a classic beauty. I smile. "Yeah, I love those. But I'll probably end up with a truck too. It seems that's the vehicle of choice around here."

Ford nods in agreement. "What time are you and Ronin driving up tomorrow?"

"Well, I think Clare is supposed to get here tomorrow around noon, so we should make FoCo early evening, maybe? I'm not sure."

"OK, see you then." He turns back to his hideous truck and I notice that there are a lot of girls in the back parking lot now. They're all staring at Ford and me. I make my escape to the back door, punch in my code, and then take the stairs up to the fourth floor.

There's lots of people here today even though it's a Friday. Typically Fridays are dead, but it's open casting. Ronin already hired two models who have worked for

Antoine before. And Billy is the only male model. But since they're doing a catalog shoot with hundreds of clothing articles, they need a lot of girls. Plus, once the shoot is over they're having a special fashion show in LA for the kickoff just before Christmas. It's kind of a big deal for the models. A career-making kinda job.

I wave to Ronin across the studio, but don't stop and chat. He's busy talking to Roger, who is the main photographer for this contract. Antoine is officially on hiatus so he and Elise can keep an eye on Clare when she gets home from the clinic.

She was up there at that treatment center for four months and she's barely out of the woods. My mom was a crack addict, she never did heroin that I knew of, so I'm not all that up on the consequences of that particular drug. But after hearing about Clare's struggle this summer, I just can't understand why anyone would even try that shit once. She had a terrible time. It made her slightly insane for a while. And she was in a lot of pain, I know that for sure because Ronin left some literature out in the living room once and I read it. The withdrawal from heroin is so bad, so painful, that most people just can't do it.

Clare is lucky. She has Antoine, and Elise, and Ronin. And they're all very rich. She got the best treatment money could buy. She was sequestered up in the mountains, away from all negative influences, and she was dragged through the program by people who love her until she could manage the commitment herself. It's a miracle she got this far and we had a very serious conference call with the treatment facility yesterday about what she needs to do going forward. They've finally weaned her off the methadone, which is a long-acting opiate that alleviates the pain of withdrawal without getting her high.

Her last dose was two weeks ago and the doctor insists she's done very well, but it only takes one slip-up. Just one and all that hard work will be for nothing. She'll always be addicted to opiates, she can never take them without risking the possibility of withdrawal pain. "She will never," he stressed, "be normal again." The drug has changed her forever. She will always be tempted to take it, remembering the euphoria of the high and not the pain that comes after.

It scares the shit out of me just thinking about it.

I punch in Ronin's apartment code and head to the shower and then peel off my clothes and start the jets.

Clare's lifelong addiction issue scares me for two reasons. One, of course, is that it will be so difficult for her to stay clean. I feel sorry for her and I really do want her to succeed. But even more than that, it scares me because it practically guarantees Ronin a girl who will need him forever. And even though Ford won't bring it up again, I'll always be wondering if I'm just a project for Ronin. If I'm just a broken girl who needs a knight to save her.

I'm not broken. In fact, I've never felt so together in my entire life. I have everything going for me. I've got money, a cool job, friends, a place to live… I have it all. And I'm pretty sure my damsel-in-distress moments are over.

So if that was the reason he liked me, I'm gonna figure this out pretty fast.

I'm not convinced that Ford's characterization of Ronin is correct. I mean, Ronin has said over and over that he thinks I'm strong and brave and I'm not getting the liar vibe off him. Not at all.

But still.

I'd rather know sooner than later if this is the case. I don't want to ignore the warning signals that things are going off track and then wake up three years later and realize I wasted my time—it's over.

I check the clock and realize I have to get downstairs to help out with the casting, so I pull on some jeans, a t-shirt, and a little zippered hoodie just in case I get cold. I slip out into the hallway and see Antoine and Elise standing down at the end of the hall in front of their apartment.

"Rook!" Antoine calls. "Ellie is going back to bed. Can you check the girls in today?"

I walk over to them and look down at Elise. "What's wrong?" So far she's had a pretty easy pregnancy, but she's practically green this morning.

"Just queasy, that's all. I need to go back to bed for a little bit, I'll come help later."

I take her hand and pat it gently. "I can do it, Elise. Just go rest." I turn to Antoine. "Ronin and I can handle it, Antoine."

"Are you sure?" he asks doubtfully. "There are hundreds of girls already lined up."

I shrug. "Well, it's a casting call, not anything life-threatening. We'll manage. Just go relax, you guys."

I don't have to say it again—they are outta there. I smile as I go downstairs. The front door is still closed but everyone is already busy. Ronin and Roger are chatting over some notes when I walk up to them.

"Antoine said I can check the girls in since Elise isn't feeling well."

Ronin turns to me quickly. "What's wrong with her?"

I take his hand. "She's fine, just morning sickness." I smile up at his worried face. I think it's cute he worries over Elise so much. He's really gonna be a fantastic uncle. When Elise told us after we came back from Sturgis Ronin was so happy he could hardly contain his excitement.

"You sure? I'm new at this baby stuff, I worry about her."

"Antoine's with her. If she needs help he'll come tell us."

He thinks about this for a few seconds and then puts his arm around me in a casual embrace. "OK. Billy!" he yells. "Show Rook how to check in girls up here and you can do first cut downstairs."

Billy nods and I kiss Ronin real quick and head over. Billy is fussing with a laptop that is set up near the door. He points to it. "OK, Rook, it's pretty simple. When they come up you check them in in groups of five. We put out an international casting call, so we will have hundreds of girls outside today. I'll choose which ones can come up for a group interview and give them a number bracelet." He points to the computer. "Then you fill in the form with their names and stuff, then hit enter. Ronin and Roger will get it over at the set"—he points to the large black partition segregating us from the interview section of the studio—"and they'll send you a message when they want you to send them over. Then it's just lather, rinse, repeat. Got it?"

"No problemo," I answer back.

"OK," Billy says, checking his phone. "It's five minutes to nine now, so I'll go start choosing and then send them up one at a time. Check them in as they come because pretty soon there will be a lot of girls lining up on the stairs."

I salute and he heads down to the street level. The computer is set up on a tall cafe table and there's a stool for me to sit on. But I take advantage of the silence and wander into the kitchen and grab a cup of coffee from the massive automatic machine, then make my way over to the computer table and wait for the first girl to arrive.

It takes five more minutes before the main door whooshes downstairs and the first girl's heels click up the stairs. I bet she is a nervous wreck. I know I would be. I picture myself as I made my first trip up these stairs and I barely recognize that girl in my memory. I'm lost in my own recollection of weakness and fright when the girl comes into view.

I'm not sure what I expected, but this was not it. The girl is a few inches taller than me, which is saying something because I'm five foot nine, and her hair is long and naturally blonde. It's got streaks of brown in it, like people pay salons hundreds of dollars to replicate, and her eyes are a striking blue-green. Blue-green. Who has blue-green eyes? She is so beautiful I'm almost speechless. I swallow. "Hi, I'm Rook and I'm gonna check you in."

"I'm Océane," she says. Her accent is French. I have to turn away to stop the sneer. What did I expect? Antoine has beautiful girls walking around here every day. I'm one of them, actually. But even though Billy said they put out an international casting call, I guess I just expected Denver girls to show up. I take a deep breath and start checking her in, trying my best not to worry about Ronin being around all these beautiful women for the next few months while I'm up in the middle of fucking nowhere prancing around in my t-shirts and jeans, picking up parts for Spencer's bike shop and playing extreme croquet in the snow with Ford.

It only goes downhill from there. One extraordinarily beautiful girl after another walks up those stairs. Billy knows what he's doing sorting the wheat from the chaff, because they are all stunning with a capital S. I'm still mulling this over, half-heartedly checking in girls as they come up the stairs and sending them into the studio in groups of five, when the freight elevator dings.

We hardly ever use the freight elevator. Most of the time everyone just takes the stairs because the elevator is slow and clunky. So this ding actually makes me stop what I'm doing and turn around just in time to see a thin blonde girl exit with a man in a suit. It takes me a minute to recognize her because of the cute outfit and lack of make-up. She's wearing pink sweatpants, a white tank top, and a cropped pink zippered jacket to match her pants. Her fresh face is glowing, her eyes are bright, and she is the picture of health. Her long hair is tied back in a ponytail and she looks like she's about to model for Victoria's Secret *Pink* line. She walks past me, never even looking in my direction, and the white letters splash across her ass. Yup. *Pink* all right.

"Who's that?" someone asks from behind me.

She disappears behind the tall black partition wall put in place for the interviews and I can hear Ronin's roar of delight.

"Clare Chaput," I reply absently in a whisper. "That's Clare Chaput."

CHAPTER THREE

Ronin

GIDGET is the first project that Roger and I are working on exclusively. The first project where Antoine is not involved at all. So everything is just slightly more important than normal. At least for me—I'm a perfectionist ninety percent of the time and I've been obsessing over this contract since I won it a few months back. If I play my cards right I might be able to make a go of fashion marketing. Not that Rook and I need the money. Work stopped being about money a while back. I've lived in money for a dozen years now and at least half of those years I was earning a significant amount on my own just from modeling. The con jobs don't even factor into my bank account bottom line because it sorta creeps me out.

Stolen money. We stole all that money. Ford, Spence and I ruined more than one family over it and I do feel a little bit guilty about that. People's children should not have to suffer for the misdeeds of their parents, but we had our reasons.

I don't touch that money. It's in so many different trusts and offshore accounts I might not even know how to find it all again, should I ever want to.

I laugh at that internally as I pretend to listen to the

group of girls in front of me. Ford would know how to find it. We might hate each other most of the time, but he's got his skills, and manipulating money and keeping track of bank accounts is one of them. The three of us made a pact after that last job. No spending any of our new money until we all had careers that would justify the lifestyle change and avoid any scrutiny, because I'll be honest here, we barely got away with one a few years back. It was a technicality really. Rules of evidence worked in our favor.

There was no paper trail because we were strictly virtual criminals, but one detective got nosey with a computer that was not part of the crime scene and he found a teeny-tiny nugget of info which led to something Ford had taken great care to hide. But because the detective had no warrant, meaning he'd accessed that computer illegally, nothing he got from it was admissible as evidence when the grand jury was asked to indict us.

We walked away free and clear and that little bit of info was sealed and not given out to the media, but the cops know what we did.

And they are patient. They watch everything, I'm sure.

Which is why we're working our asses off. We're patient too, and besides, all our cons, and that one in particular, were for revenge, not paying bills or vacations.

Ford, Spencer, and I all have the same work ethic and that's one of the things that bind us so tightly. Each of us has been given opportunities through luck or paternity, and we never took them for granted. We're professionally successful because we work hard, not because we steal. I don't need to work, I have a shitload of honest money saved up, but I will be working once Rook and I leave this life behind because sitting on my ass is not an option.

I scroll down the laptop screen as the next group of girls walks in. So far there are maybe one or two who might fit with what we're looking for. Tall and thin are a given, but beyond that I'm looking for fresh. Exciting. Clean-cut. And wholesome—it's a retro pin-up type shoot, after all. We like to use pouty and depressed girls for the dark erotic shoots because they sell better, but this is a catalog shoot. Lots of bright artificial lighting is a must so the girls typically at the top of my model list are not really suitable.

I look over this group, absently smile at them as Roger does the interview, then we dismiss them and I choose no one. "Did you like any?" I ask Roger.

"Nah. Next."

I'm just about to message Rook so she can send the next group when another girl walks into our makeshift room. It takes me a moment to recognize her because I haven't seen her in over a month, but once I do my happiness is immediate.

"Clare!" I get up and scoop her up in a big hug. "We're supposed to pick you up tomorrow!" She squeezes me tight as I lift her and everything just melts away. I put her down and hold her out at arm's length so I can look her over. "You look so good, sweetie!"

She sighs and then flashes me an embarrassed smile as she blushes. "Thanks. Hey, Roger, long time, eh?"

"Yeah," he says, standing up and coming over to her. He plants a kiss on her cheek and pulls her into a hug. "You really look great, Clare. Really great."

"Do Antoine and Elise know you're here?"

"No, I wanted to surprise you guys, I wanted to—"

I grab her hand and pull her towards the stairs. "Oh,

you're gonna make them so happy, Clare, come on!" I drag her upstairs, totally ignoring the guy she came in with, punch in the code and rush her into the apartment. Elise is lying on the couch with her feet in Antoine's lap. It takes them a moment to recognize Clare too, but both sets of eyes go wide when it kicks in and Elise jumps up faster than she should for someone with morning sickness. She flings her little arms around Clare and hugs her tight.

"You sneak! We were gonna pick you up tomorrow!"

Clare starts crying as Antoine joins the group hug and then pulls her into his arms and buries his face in her hair. "I'm so glad you're home. So glad you're home."

Clare is like a new person. I just stand there and shake my head. I can't remember her ever looking this good. Ever. She's put on at least ten pounds, her hair is sleek and her blue eyes are bright and alert.

How long has it been since I saw her clean?

Years. It's been years since this girl looked healthy.

I just smile at them as they chat and Elise and Clare wipe away tears. "Oh, Rook! You have to meet Rook, Clare." I jog through the door and stand at the top of the stairs. "Everyone—take thirty, please. Clare's home!" I hear a smattering of claps from the regular staff and take a deep breath and let the happiness wash over me. *It worked*, I think to myself. *We fixed her. She looks better than ever. It worked!*

"Rook!" I call down. "Come up here, Gidge! You have to meet Clare!"

Rook smiles and sets down her clipboard, then pushes the girls outside the door and closes it before walking slowly over to the stairs. I take her hand once she reaches me and let out a long sigh. "Did you see her come in? Doesn't she look great?" I don't wait for an answer, just tug her into Antoine's apartment with me and spread my arms wide. "Rook, this is Clare. The *real* Clare," I add. "Not that psycho bitch you saw in the dressing room that day last spring."

Clare swats me on the arm. "I deserve that, but I'd rather not be reminded."

I pull her into another hug before she greets Rook, then lean down and kiss her head. "I am so happy, you have no idea!"

She swats me again and pulls back as she offers her hand to Rook. "I've heard a lot about you, Gidget." Clare winks at her and when I look over at Rook she's blushing.

Rook extends her hand out and shakes it. "It's so great to meet you, Clare," Rook says. It comes out polite and sweet, like all her words. But I detect something underneath. She can't be jealous of *Clare*. Can she?

Clare turns back to Elise and Antoine and they talk excitedly in French. When I look back to Rook she's frowning. "Hey, English only when Rook's here, guys. She can't understand and it's rude."

"That's OK, Ronin. I don't mind."

This is a lie, but I'm not about to push it here. I pull her close and then lean down to kiss her. "Let's get back to work." I look over to Antoine and nod. "We're still on for tonight?" He nods back and I smile down at Rook again. She's uncomfortable with Clare, I can tell. Maybe jealous, maybe even intimidated.

"What's tonight?" she asks.

"Oh, just dinner at your favorite French restaurant."

She moans and follows me out the door. I stop at the top of the stairs. "You don't want to go fancy with me tonight? I'll pick you out a sexy dress from the closet." I waggle my eyebrows at her to try and play innocent, but she's irritated on two fronts now. My choice in restaurants and insinuating I get to choose her clothes.

It takes all my self-control not to laugh at her, but I manage because she's right where I want her. So I say nothing, just drag her back downstairs and drop her off at the front door and then take my place back on the other side of the room with Roger.

Yup. I've got her right where I want her.

CHAPTER FOUR

Rook

The rest of my day goes like shit. I check in hundreds of girls. Hundreds of beautiful girls who make me look like some homeless person living out of a garbage can in my zippered hoodie and my last year's jeans.

I'm not kidding either. I know I'm not ugly. Hell, I'm pretty enough to get two major modeling contracts, so that's not what this is about. It's not about me, or my degree of pretty. These girls are drop-dead, can't-take-your-eyes-off-them, stunningly beautiful—gorgeous.

They have perfect skin, toned bodies, designer clothes, professionally applied make-up, and exotic accents. Almost all of them have some sort of accent, even if it's just Southern Belle Sweet or Valley Girl Annoying. None of them sound the same.

And then, of course, there's the really exotic girls. The ones from Asia and Australia and Europe.

I wonder if my barely-there Chicago accent qualifies as exotic?

I snort quietly to myself. I'm pretty sure that's a big fucking no.

And if all this wasn't enough to make me feel super insecure and plain, Clare is here.

Clare. The first beautiful person I encountered the

day Luck changed my life. The one girl who commands Ronin's attention like no other. Not even me. Sure, he shows up and saves me when I need it, but if Clare and I had an emergency at the same moment, I'm just not sure he'd pick me every time.

I sigh and send the last group of girls over to Ronin and Roger.

These girls look tired and worn down. It's past six now and they've been standing around for the better part of twelve hours. They must really be in denial because there's no way Ronin and Roger, exhausted and sick of looking at girls and reading resumes, are even remotely interested in these last five girls. But maybe they like the girls enough to keep their names on file for something in the future. I guess if you're desperate to be discovered as a model, this is one way to do it.

Less than five minutes later Ronin comes out from behind the walled-off partition stretching his arms as I let the sad group of girls out and then make sure the door clicks to indicate it's locked. A knock scares the shit out of me and I open the door again.

"Delivery for Chaput?" the man with a clipboard says.

"Um…"

"That's us," Ronin says. He signs the paperwork and points over to the kitchen or maybe the terrace. "Over there is fine, thanks." And then the freight elevator dings and Ronin has me by the arm and he's leading me upstairs.

"What about my dress?" I ask as we flash past the dressing room.

"I told you, I got you covered."

I scowl at him. "I seriously thought you were kidding. You're not kidding?"

"Trust me, Rook." But I'm not sure I should, because his face does not look trustworthy, it looks... *devious*. If my silence bothers him, he doesn't show it, just pulls me down the hallway to our apartment, unlocks the door, and whisks me inside.

"What's going on?"

"Wanna have living room sex or kitchen sex?"

He winks at me and I let out a long breath and laugh. "What?"

His hands slide around my hips, dipping down to caress my ass a little through my tight jeans, then slip under my shirt. "Or patio sex?"

"What's wrong with shower sex?" I ask, smiling. *What's gotten into him?*

"We have shower sex every day, let's spice things up."

I blush a little because it has gotten a little predictable lately. Ronin has been cautious with our sex life all summer over all that Jon stuff, but I'll be honest and admit that I prefer the sexually adventurous Ronin over the sexually cautious one any day. "Well..." I say, dragging out the word. "What do you have in mind? And how long do we have before we have to meet everyone for dinner?"

He leans in and kisses me, sliding my zippered hoodie down my arms and letting it drop to the floor. I never know what I'm in for when he gets in the mood. Sometimes he acts like he's starving for my lips, desperate and wanting and rough.

Tonight it's like he's afraid of breaking them, that's how soft and tender he is.

I like it and I kiss him back just as tenderly, our tongues twisting together as he lifts up my shirt. He pulls back for a moment to slip it over my head and then resumes the kiss as the shirt is discarded. One hand cups my breast and then reaches behind to get rid of my bra while the other one unbuttons my jeans. "Kitchen or living room?" he breathes into my mouth.

"Right here," I reply as I lift his t-shirt up—dragging my palms against his muscular back—clear his head and drop it in the pile of clothes at our feet. He pushes me a little until I take a step back. The back of my knees bump up against the leather couch and I am forced to sit down, coming eye to eye with his hard thickness through his jeans.

I smile up at him.

He smirks down at me.

I go for the button on his jeans but he gently takes my hands and pushes them away. "No, Gidget. Not tonight." He pushes me back on the couch, unzips my pants, grabs them by the belt loops, and pulls them down, taking my panties with him.

He looks down on my naked body with hunger. Like he's never seen it before. He licks his lips and kneels down.

"What are you up to?"

"It's present time," is all he says as his head dips between my legs. He lifts one leg up and pushes it towards my shoulder and his lips find the dent behind my knee.

I laugh when he sucks and nips the tender skin there, and then arch my back because holy fucking shit, I had no idea that spot was so, so, so… erotically sensitive.

I close my eyes and moan as he nips just a little bit harder, making me immediately wet.

And then his fingers are inside me. Fucking Ronin always did have magic fingers. What he does with those fingers, oh, God. I could write books. I try my best to calm down, but it's very, very difficult to ignore the way he makes me feel. Just as I'm about to get it back under control his tongue joins the party and I can't help it, the orgasm explodes against my will.

When I open my eyes and look down at him he's grinning so big I have to laugh. "What?"

"You," he whispers and lets out a sigh. "You are the hottest fucking woman I've ever laid eyes on. I saw hundreds of girls today, each one prettier than the last. But I compared each and every one of them to you, Rook. And not one—" He stops to look me in the eye as he stands up and takes off his pants and boxers, then pulls me to my feet, sits down where I just was, and places me in his lap. I drape my arms over his shoulders. "Not one of them even came close to measuring up to you, Gidge."

I blush as all my insecurities melt away.

Like instantly.

I lean down and kiss him, another tender one. He responds in the same manner, not hurried or desperate, but slow, and patient, and soft. "I am so in love with you, Ronin Flynn. So very, very much in love with you."

"OK, wait," he says with more urgency that is necessary. I have a little panic attack thinking he's gonna say he's not in love with me anymore, but that melts away when he cups my face and looks me in the eyes. "I can't call you Rook Walsh anymore."

I laugh. "What?"

"I can't say it without feeling sick. So what's your last name?"

"Corvus," I say in a whisper. "My name is Rook Corvus."

He smiles, like he's in on the joke, but he keeps it to himself if he is. "Miss Corvus, I am so far beyond in love with you, I can barely function. I want to marry you. Like yesterday. But I know that's not gonna happen just yet, so

I just want you to know, I can wait." He studies my face as I take all this in. "I will wait."

CHAPTER FIVE

Ronin

Even though Rook and I have had quite a bit of downtime over the past few months, it's not enough. I wish for endless days of doing nothing but making love, feeding her fruit, and sleeping with my arms wrapped around her.

Right now we're both spent from the mind-blowing sex. Her cheek rests on my shoulder as I lean my head back on the couch. "I could fall asleep right now."

"Let's stay home," she mumbles into my neck. "I'm too tired to get dressed up and go to dinner."

"We can't skip this one, Gidge. It's our last dinner until next weekend."

She moans but doesn't lift her head. "I'm gonna buy a car and commute to Fort Collins. It's not even that far."

"I'm one hundred percent on board with that." And then I smack her ass cheek playfully and make her squeal. "Come on, let's take a shower real fast. It'll wake you up so you can enjoy the evening."

I stand up, still cupping her close to me, and she reluctantly untangles herself and kisses me on the neck. "Don't get me the duck this time, OK? Maybe pasta."

I laugh. Poor Rook. "Don't worry, I promise, you'll enjoy dinner."

She livens up in the shower when I wash her, but it's

hard for her to get excited when she thinks she's being forced to wear a dress she'll probably hate and eat food she knows for sure will make her hurl.

I almost feel bad. But not quite.

She's sitting on the bed wrapped up in a white towel, just moping, as I pull on my tux trousers. "The dress is in your closet, Gidget. And it doesn't have legs, so it won't come to you."

She makes a face at me and then hoists herself up and walks into the closet. I slip my crisp white shirt on and wait for it.

Silence.

Little itty-bitty tip-toe footsteps behind me.

My grin is huge as she drapes her arms over my shoulders and breathes her words heavily into my ear. "What is that absolutely gorgeous gown doing in my closet, Larue? That's not something you wear to dinner, no matter what kind of food they serve."

I turn around and look down at her. "No? Well, you must be the expert, so tell me… what kind of event warrants a gown like that?"

"A Cinderella ball," she coos in my ear.

"Oh, fuck, Rook. Do that again and I'll never let you out of the apartment tonight."

"Fat chance of that now! I'm wearing that damn dress. I'm not sure what you've got planned, but whatever it is, I'm going."

She skips away making happy squeals and calling out guesses about where we're going. "A fundraiser?"

"Nope," I say as I button up my shirt.

"A private jet to… well, shit, there's no classy cities close to Denver, so… Albuquerque?"

I laugh. "Only Bugs Bunny goes to Albuquerque."

She snorts for real at that remark. "That's funny." I tuck my shirt in and go for the bow tie. "Somewhere in the mountains?"

"Try again."

I grab my suit coat and slide it on, then check myself in the full-length mirror. There's no way I'll be able to live up to how beautiful Rook will be tonight, but it will have to do.

"Zip me," she says quietly from behind.

I turn and take her in. I didn't pick this dress, Elise did. In fact, Rook has no idea, but it was made especially for her by a fashion friend of Antoine's. We've been planning this night for more than a month. It's a floor-length strapless white gown with the slightest mermaid shape to it. Not enough to make her look ridiculous, just enough so that the smooth fabric hugs every curve on her body and flares out near her feet. And Rook has all the right curves in all the right places. She's nothing like the skinny models who came through here today and I love everything about her shape. The tail drags just enough to make her look like she's floating when she walks, but not enough so that it will cause problems in a crowd.

"What's the occasion, then?" she asks coyly. Clearly she knows what the occasion is, but she's fishing to see if *I* know.

"The occasion? I don't need a special occasion to take you to the ball."

"So it is a big event?"

"Yes," I say as I turn her around and slide that zipper up her back. I lean in and nibble behind her neck. "Leave your hair down tonight, OK?"

"Yes, sir," she says with a wink as she pulls back.

But she's not getting away that easy. "You can't *yes, sir*

me and then expect to walk away without a reminder of what's to come later." My hand reaches behind her neck and I press her whole body into mine, then kiss her, raking my fingers up into her long dark hair and fisting it a little as she moans and throws her head back. I know she likes some of the dominant stuff we do in the bedroom, but I don't try it often. It took me all fucking summer to get over what her ex did to her as a teenager. But that awkward feeling is beginning to fade. And I'm not sure it was ever a real problem with her, so maybe tonight she'd like to do something fun.

"I hope that's a promise, Mr. Flynn."

When she says my name like that it takes my breath away. I want her to be my Mrs. Flynn so bad it makes my heart ache, but I refuse to pressure her. I want her to come to me when she's ready. "Miss Corvus, don't ever doubt me." Her blue eyes sparkle when she looks up to me and for a moment I can actually picture our beautiful family. A whole gang of little blue-eyed cherubs running around.

It makes me sigh.

"What are you thinking about in there, Ronin? I see the wheels turning."

I slip my arm around her waist and dip her backwards, making her squeal. "You, that's all." I lift her back up and smack her butt to end the flirting and get us back on track, because we are already fashionably late and people are probably tired of waiting.

She goes into the bathroom and chats to me non-stop about the dress and her make-up, which she applies as she talks. My phone buzzes and I check it, then text Antoine back and let him know we're coming in five minutes.

When she's done with her make-up she fluffs up her damp hair with the blow dryer, making it cascade down her back in loose raven curls, and then pulls a brush through it. Her feet slip into the white satin shoes and she looks over to me and smiles. Rook hates heels and if she had her way I'm sure she'd be wearing those old-ass red Converse with the holes in the toes. So I made sure her shoes for tonight are comfortable ballet flats. She turns her back to me so I can clasp a necklace around her neck. The only time Rook wears jewelry of any kind is when I put it on her. Otherwise she won't bother. I hand her some earrings to match the necklace and she puts them on and turns to the mirror.

"Wow. I look great."

I laugh. "Yeah, you really do, Gidget. You clean up nice."

"I almost feel like a bride, wearing this white dress."

"Don't taunt me with that image, please." I take her hand and lead her out of the apartment. "But I'd be more than happy to pretend this is our wedding reception if you like."

"OK, spill it. Where are we going?" We walk down the hallway towards the stairs. "Why's it so dark in here?"

"I dunno, but you better hold my hand a little tighter so you don't fall down the stairs."

We get to the bottom without killing ourselves and we're just walking past the terrace when I notice the light out in Rook's old apartment. "Who's in your place?" I ask.

"What?" she asks, craning her neck to see outside. "Huh. I have no idea. Maybe Ford's in there doing something?"

"Let's check it out." I urge her to follow me over to the terrace doors and punch in my code to open the door. "After you," I say, waving her forward.

"It's dark—" The words are just leaving her mouth

when the whole place lights up. Every cherry tree is sparkling with white lights.

"Surprise!"

I laugh when she jumps back at the shouts. And then everyone appears from the various alcoves and nooks. Rook's hand goes up to her mouth. "What's this?"

I pull her close as she takes in the scene. Everyone we know is here. Spencer and Veronica, Clare, Ford and his… *woman*. Antoine and Elise, all the camera and sound crews from the Shrike Show, Director Larry, Billy and his girlfriend, Roger and his wife and a few of the other photographers, the Chaput models, and all the salon girls and their husbands.

Every man is wearing a black tux and every woman is wearing a white dress.

"A black-and-white affair for my Gidget. Because Rook, you are one batshit insane chick if you think you can have a birthday around here and not be embarrassed with a huge over-the-top production!"

She cries.

And I hug her close as everyone comes over, smiling and laughing at putting one over on her and making her tear up with happiness.

She turns and hugs me hard, then dips her mouth to my ear. "Ronin Flynn, you are my forever guy. I'd just like to say that right now. You are my forever guy."

"I fully plan on holding you to it, Gidget. One hundred percent. Now let's have some fucking fun with our family and friends."

CHAPTER SIX

Rook

I'm living in a fairy tale.
Seriously.

The entire terrace is something magical. The cherry trees are awash with soft white lights, the late September air is crisp but not cold, and for once, there is not even a hint of wind. I just look around and take it all in as the musicians play a soft string piece. I burn the sight, the sound, and the smell into my memory for safekeeping. Because one day, when life is hard, or ugly, or depressing, I'll be able to think back on this night. Even if I never have another moment as special as this for as long as I live, I will be OK because I will always have this memory.

Ronin's arm tightens around my waist and then he pulls me in close, turning my body so I'm pressed against his chest. He takes my hand in his and we dance.

I don't even know how to dance like this, but it doesn't matter. I just drop my head on his shoulder and let him lead, my feet making small steps as he whispers in my ear. "Do you like it?"

I don't even look up because I can't bear to lift my head from the place on his shoulder where it fits perfectly. "I love it, Larue."

His chest rises a little with his chuckle. "I have a gift

for you too."

"Isn't this party the gift?"

He kisses me on the head and pulls me in so close, we are like one person. "Hardly, Gidget. A party isn't a gift, it's a celebration. Mine is with all the others."

I do look up now. "What others?"

He points over to a table near the door and sure enough, there's a pile of pretty presents. "Oh, wow. Why did you make them bring presents?" I complain on the outside, but inside I'm clapping like an idiot and screaming *presents, presents, presents!*

"I didn't make them, Rook. They just wanted to."

I'm so happy I could cry, but I don't want Ronin to get the wrong idea, so I squeal instead. "Let's open them now!"

He laughs. God, I love when he laughs. Those blue fucking eyes sparkle and his whole face beams. How did such an amazing man fall for me? I don't get it. "Not now, Gidge, I'm trying to monopolize your time and keep that creep Ford from cutting in."

"May I cut in?" I laugh as Ford's voice comes from behind me. "I promise to give her back."

Ronin smiles down at me. "I dunno, Ford. She's looking pretty content right now."

I peek back at Ford and smile. "Oh, absolutely, Ford. Because I want to know all about that date you brought. Like every single detail."

We all look over at her at the same time. She's... older. Mid-thirties, older.

I turn to Ronin. "I need that story. Come save me from His Weirdness in five minutes."

He hands me off and Ford slides in next to me without even breaking the little shuffling dance Ronin and

I were doing. "Is she the… *girlfriend?*"

A smirk from Ford. "I told you, I'd never call them girlfriends."

I look at her again as Ford turns us on the patio. She's tall, blonde, thin, and wearing an elegant white dress that goes just past her knees but hugs all her curves. Her hair is piled into a sophisticated up-do that even Josie would envy. "What's her name?"

"She has no name."

I laugh. "*Ford.*"

"I'm serious. I never get their names."

"Is she a call-girl?"

He scowls. "No, I don't pay for sex, Rook."

"Hmmmm. I'm not sure what to think."

"I told you, I do not give a fuck about people. I wasn't kidding. I use them, they use me. Everyone is happy."

"But you're not using me."

"Of course I am. You're filling the friend role for now."

I look up at him and he winks.

"I'm not sure if you're serious."

"I am serious."

My thoughts are racing as we continue to spin slowly.

"But just so we're clear, I do like you and I'm oddly drawn to what you do with your life. I'm not sure why, but I feel like I need to participate in it. So, I'm sorry, but you're stuck with me."

I shake my head as Ronin comes back. "OK, I can see him morphing into psycho Ford in real time, so that's enough."

Ford drops my hand and backs off. "I have a present for you tonight, Rook. But I have another one for you as well. I'll give it to you tomorrow at Spencer's place."

And then he just walks away.

I look over at Ronin and he just sighs. "I give up. I can't predict him, I can't control him, and I can't compete with him. He's *your* weirdo friend now, Rook. I wash my hands."

I lean up and kiss Ronin's soft lips. He responds with his twisty tongue and I melt a little. He does this to me every time. "Ford *is* weird. He says he doesn't even know that woman's name."

"Well, that I believe. I'm not sure how he even gets them to participate in his—" Ronin stops before he completes the sentence. "Never mind, I'm not sure I want to go there." And then he literally shakes his head and grabs me by the waist and pulls me close again. "I had the caterers prepare the perfect dinner for us tonight. Guess what it is?"

"Snails and goose liver?"

He laughs. "You peeked!"

I lean up and kiss him one more time because his lips are like the siren's song, they call to me, they blind me to everything around me. "I don't care what you ordered me tonight, I'll eat it because you want me to have it."

"Ah, that's a good little Gidget." And then I squeal as he spanks my ass, drawing the attention of all the partygoers.

My cheeks go hot and I turn back to Ronin. "I will have to punish you for that later, Larue."

"Promises, promises."

The terrace is sprinkled with round tables and real white linen tablecloths set with so many utensils I get a little overwhelmed. But Ronin leans in to my ear as he slides my chair in and whispers, "You can slurp your soup with the butter knife if you want, Rook. No one gives a shit, so stop thinking about it."

Veronica is two chairs down on my left and her boisterous laugh fills the night air. "Too true, Ronin. No one here gives a fuck what fork you use, Rook!" She leans past Spencer who is next to me, picks up my champagne glass, clinks it with her own, and then thrusts it towards me so I'm compelled to take it. "Cheers, sweetie. Since you're not trying to steal Spencer from me, and I *did* take a bullet for you a few weeks ago"—everyone groans at her over-exaggeration—"I think we'll be friends."

And even though Veronica scares me a little with her perpetual smoking—which isn't even real, she only smokes e-cigs—and her over-the-top self-confidence, I feel warm inside. I like Elise and Josie, but they have been besties for a long time so there's not much room for a new girl who's a lot younger than them. I'd like to have my own package deal, so maybe Veronica and I can be like that. We're closer in age, she's twenty-two and I'm twenty now. Plus, she lives up in FoCo, and I'll be close by at Spencer's place. I'm sure she'll be around a lot, so making her my new BFF is probably a smart idea.

Our table has Ronin and me, Veronica and Spencer, and Ford and no-name. We're going boy-girl tonight, so I'm in between Spencer and Ronin. Ford's woman is on Ronin's right, so that puts Ford across from me with Veronica on his right. Everyone seems to be ignoring Ford's date and I sorta feel bad. "So," I say, loud enough to draw her attention. "I didn't get your name earlier."

Her eyes sweep past me, over Spencer and Veronica, and then rest on Ford.

Ronin leans in. "She's not allowed to talk, Gidge."

And this is when I notice the thin diamond choker around her neck. At first glance it looks like a piece of jewelry with a little charm on it. But... it's not.

It's... a collar.

"Hmmm. Well, that's interesting." I look over at Ford and he looks pretty proud of himself. "Should I drop it?"

All the guys chuckle as Ford nods, then Veronica takes over. "She's a pet, Rook. If you make her break the rules Ford will have her bark for us, and as fun as that sounds, I'm really not up for it tonight. So just pretend she's not there."

"Okaaaaay. I'm ready for dinner."

The waiters arrive and begin placing silver domed plates in front of us. Ronin stands just as they finish and taps his glass with a spoon. "A toast for Rook." He pulls me to my feet and when I look around I get a little embarrassed with all the attention. Every face has turned to me. "Rook." Ronin brings my attention back to him. "Four months ago you literally appeared on my doorstep. And the minute I saw you, I knew—" My heart flutters for a second and I have to take a deep breath because I'm not sure what he's gonna say. "I knew"—his voice softens as he looks me in the eyes—"that you were something special."

The whole terrace erupts into a collective, "Awwwww."

"And this party is just a way for all of us"—his arms spread out towards all the tables—"to show you how much we care." And then he leans down and kisses me, whispering "I love you," as he pulls back. "Cheers!"

Everyone cheers as Ronin and I take our seats and then Spencer cries out, "Let's eat!"

I lift the silver dome off my plate and bust out laughing. "Ronin Flynn, you are a sneak."

But he's *my* sneak, and I love him for it. Because on my plate is the most delicious-looking cheeseburger I've ever seen, nestled on top of a giant mound of French fries.

CHAPTER SEVEN

Rook

"What are you laughing about?" Ronin asks later as his hands slip around my waist and slide down to rub my stomach.

I'm standing over by my old garden apartment looking down at the people on the street. It's Friday night, so it's really busy. I turn to face him and casually drape my arms over his shoulders. "You know me pretty well, Larue. I thought for sure dinner would be something funky and French."

He chuckles. "It was either salads with chicken on them or hamburgers. And guess who made the final decision?"

"Um, the pregnant lady over there stuffing her face with strawberry shortcake?"

"That'd be the one."

We both watch Elise chew and chat with Josie at the same time. Antoine is also watching her from across the terrace and you can just tell he's dying to say something to her about talking with her mouth full. He hates that. But his hand scrubs his scratchy chin for a moment and he thinks better of it. Wise man.

"I'm falling hard for you, Rook. I hope you know that."

I look up at this incredible man and I have no words for what I feel. I'm not falling for Ronin, I'm laid out flat on my face. He is the perfect man. He's put up with so much from me. He's stood by me when I insisted on making mistakes, and planned an entire con job so that Jon would get his karmic payback. He deserves so much more than the indecision and distance I've given him over the past few months.

"I told you a while back that I'd like to belong to you, Ronin. *Someday*."

His hand cups my face and his thumb traces the curve of my chin.

"I think someday has come and gone because I think I've always belonged to you. From the very first moment we met in the stairwell, I wanted you. And even though it took me a while to understand my feelings, I guess I'm better late than never."

He laughs and pulls me into a hug. "I'll take late, Gidget. I'll take late."

Clare and Ford walk past us and then enter the garden apartment. It just occurs to me that the lights have been on inside there the entire night. "What's with those two?" I ask Ronin.

"Exit interviews for the pilot. Ford figured he'd have all of us together tonight, so why not do interviews. Two birds kinda thing."

"Oh." No one told me about any exit interview, but shit. No one tells me anything unless I ask. Maybe I should start asking? "But why Clare, then? She wasn't in the show."

"Well, technically she was. Since you were the female star and I'm your boyfriend. And I kept leaving you to go see her."

"Wait, so all that's gonna be in the show?" Oh, fuck. That sucks. I guess I shouldn't be surprised. Most of my angst came from jealousy of Clare. I just didn't think she'd be quizzed on it at the end. "Did you get interviewed yet?"

"Ford said I'm last. He needs your reactions first or some shit like that."

"He's setting us up. We should refuse to do them, Ronin. I'm not gonna do it. My contract is over, isn't it?"

He squeezes me tight. "Did you get paid yet?"

"You know I didn't."

"Then it's not over, Gidge. Ford likes you, he won't set you up. Just answer his questions. Lie if you want. No one cares. It's a stupid reality show."

But that's not true. Ford *would* set me up. Ronin never knew the extent of our conversations while he was busy with Clare last summer. Ford never came out and said he wanted to date me, but he did hint around to wanting *something* from me. I'm not really sure what, especially after this morning's conversation about his girlfriends. Not to mention the collared pet he brought with him to my party.

Ronin and I wander back into the crowd and chat casually with people, me leaning into his chest and his arms wrapped around me. He talks with Spencer and Veronica and I nod my head pretending to pay attention, but I'm focused on the garden apartment. The curtains are sheer, but I can't see any movement in there. He must be interviewing her in the other room.

Clare comes out and Ford calls for Spencer. Veronica claps for this and then looks over in my direction after Spencer walks off. "I get to be interviewed too, Rook! Because I saved your life and took a bullet for you!"

"Cool!" I say, but I'm still thinking about my private conversations with Ford. What if he brings them up on camera? What will I say? I didn't do anything wrong, I never cheated or anything. But Ronin might see my omission of facts as lying. We circulate around the terrace, talking to different people. I watch Veronica go in after Spencer. Then Antoine, then Elise. Ronin still seems so unconcerned, but by the time Ford dismisses Elise and looks over in my direction, my nerves are shot.

I look up at Ronin but both he and Spencer are laughing hysterically about something. I look back at Ford.

He beckons me with a finger.

Fuck.

I break away from Ronin and he pats my ass and says, "Have fun, Gidge."

CHAPTER EIGHT

Rook

I walk slowly over towards my old apartment and give myself a little pep talk. *He's not gonna trap you, Rook. He's not interested like that, he said so this morning. He sees us as friends only.*

"Ready?" Ford asks as I approach.

"How come you didn't tell me about the interview this morning?"

He waves me inside and then closes the door behind us. "Yes, I should've said, 'I'll see you tonight at your surprise party where I will conduct your exit interview.' Besides, my payoff in this friendship is getting to watch you react to me honestly."

I don't even know what that means, but it sounds very personal. Almost sexual. I look back at him for a moment and catch him smiling as I enter the bedroom. He's got two plush red chairs set up across from each other and two tripods with cameras. One facing each chair.

"Are you on camera, too?"

"For this interview I am."

My heart pounds in my chest. "Why?"

"Sit, Rook, and relax."

I take a seat and he follows, leaning forward in his

chair as I lean back. He rests his elbows on his knees and steeples his fingers under his chin.

And waits.

"What?" I ask. "What are you doing, Ford? Don't get weird with me, please." I look nervously up at the camera.

"It's not on yet, Rook."

"Well, turn it on and let's go."

"I'm making you nervous?"

"You know you are. Why didn't you tell me about this? What are you gonna tell Ronin? I thought we were friends."

"There's nothing to tell Ronin. What could I possibly tell him that he doesn't already know?"

"Know? He knows you told me you were trying to make me not need him? So you could, I dunno, swoop in and claim me as your pet, like that woman out there with the collar? Did you tell him *that*?"

"Do you want to be my pet?" he asks seriously.

"No!" I scoff. "No! I'm not in the least bit interested in becoming your fucking sex slave!"

He goes silent again, watching me as the grin creeps up his face.

I shudder. "I'm counting to five and then I'm leaving. One—"

He stands and moves toward me, his leg brushing against my dress as he reaches behind me to flip the camera on. The heat of his touch makes me dizzy for a moment. He steps back and then turns on the camera behind him before taking his seat. "Did you enjoy being Spencer's canvas, Rook?"

"Yes," I say truthfully.

Ford leans back and retrieves a clipboard on the small table next to him. "What did you enjoy about it? Oh, and talk in complete sentences, so the audience understands the question without having to hear me ask it."

"Well, I had a good time working with Spencer. It was a little weird at first because I had to model with him, and that was... confusing because I was just starting to date Ronin. But once that part was over and Ronin was my partner, everything went real well."

"Why did Ronin make it better?"

I squint my eyes at him but hold my tongue. I refuse to let him bait me on camera. I refuse to allow him to get ratings because I'm uncomfortable. In fact, I think it's my turn to make him uncomfortable. "Everything was better with Ronin because he knows my body. He's got a very personal relationship with it. So having him touch me and position me and kiss me for the photo shoots was easy. It felt good and I didn't have to worry about making him jealous."

"Did the shoots with Billy and Spencer feel good?"

I walked right into that, didn't I? "The photo shoots with Billy and Spencer were erotic, that's for sure, but not like they are with Ronin."

"And what did you think of our running routine?"

"I loved it, to be honest." Ford smiles and my heart rate increases when I realize Ronin will see that smile on TV next spring. "Running with you every morning was—well, I wouldn't call it fun, but I would call it helpful. I liked getting up early, and believe me, that was a huge change for me. But I like the feel of dawn. When things are just getting ready to stir and life is still on pause from the night before."

Ford stares at me for a second, a look of contemplation on his face. "That's a very poetic way to put it." Then he chuckles and moves on. "Tell me more about the shoots and the painting, Rook. And then you can be finished with the camera work. Just say whatever you want, I'll have it edited down."

"OK." I swallow, a little relieved at that. "Well, Spencer is incredible. His talent is beyond words. My favorite painting was the tattoo woman because he painted all his tattoos on me just like they were on him. And his own body art is exceptional. I've never seen tattoos planned out like that, it's not just a front piece or a sleeve, it's a whole upper-body piece. The birds—oh my God, even if my name wasn't Rook, I would fall in love with them. And the final painting at Sturgis was like the greatest gift I could ever ask for. I told him that this was the best summer of my life, and I wasn't kidding. I learned a lot about myself this summer." I stop and smile because he's smiling now.

"What else made you happy, Rook?"

"Modeling with Ronin in costume," I say, blushing. "He was that sexy Elvis and wow. And actually, Billy was a pretty hot cowboy, too." I shrug. "I loved it. I probably shouldn't have loved it, I should probably be embarrassed about what I did for money, about having Spencer paint up my body like that, not to mention the photographs and the rally show. But I'm not embarrassed about it. I'll never forget this summer. I'll never regret being Spencer's canvas, and I'll never regret becoming a model for Antoine Chaput."

Ford stands up and turns the cameras off again and then sits back down.

"That's it?"

"That's it for the questions I want on film. But I have a few more for you, Rook."

I gulp some air. "Ford, let's not, OK? Let's just leave

it here."

"No," he says firmly. "I have a few questions for you and since the Biker Channel wants me to have two roles in the full season I want to get this out in the open."

"What two roles?"

"Well, I'm still producer, but they want me interacting with you guys like I did in the pilot. So I'm a character now as well."

"Oh." I'm pretty sure this is bad for me. And I'm also pretty sure Ronin does not know this yet.

"So my first question is, why did you run with me all summer? Was it because you loved the exercise or because you did it with me? And no lies, Rook, I'm not interested in lies."

"Ford, please. *Please* don't ruin this for me. I love Ronin, I like you too, and I'm not sure what those feelings are, but I love Ronin. Don't mess it up."

"Why would I go out of my way to make you happy only to do something later to cause you pain?"

I shake my head. "I don't know. You're playing with me, you're messing with my head, you're—"

"I'm not, Rook. I'm not playing with you at all. Every intention is sincere, I promise."

"But I'm seeing Ronin, I can't—"

"I can't either. Do you know why I brought that woman here tonight?"

I swear my heart stops for a moment. "Why?"

"Because I wanted you to see me and maybe accept me for who I really am. I'm not a good guy, Rook. I'm not even close to a good guy. I want you to succeed, I want you to be happy, and that happiness will never come from me. I just want you to know that what I am doing, these little things—like reading to you, the exercise, bringing you breakfast, talking—it's the only way I know how to care."

A lump starts forming in my throat, my face goes hot, and I can feel tears. Actual tears starting to form. I have to breathe deeply for several seconds to shut down my body's visceral reaction to his words.

"And," he continues, "I want you to know that I care about *you*. I care enough about you to leave this conversation here in this apartment when you walk out that door and go back to Ronin. I want you to make your dreams come true and I'll do whatever it takes to help you. That is the only way I know to express… love. But I will never kiss you."

I look up and meet his gaze.

"I will never do anything physical to ruin what you have with Ronin. I would just like you to *talk* to me. Be honest when I ask for it, trust me, and be my friend. Is that too much?"

A little laugh comes out at Ford's question. "Of course not. I'd love to be your friend, Ford."

He pulls his hands back and smiles. "Good. Then we're done here. Just send Ronin in, I won't keep him long."

"I thought you wanted me to talk about Clare?"

"Why would I make you do that?" He grins and that chin dimple appears. "Why would I make you talk about her? On this night, of all nights? I only want you to be happy, Rook. If I had information you needed to know about *anything*, especially about Ronin being a lying, cheating piece of shit, believe me, I'd just tell you straight up. He's not, by the way. Ronin is a pretty straight shooter despite being the most convincing liar I've ever come across. I am not playing games with your feelings, I'm not trying to trap you and force you to interact with me or fuck up your relationship. I want you to *want* to be my friend. I want you to *want* to trust me, and come to me for help. I have no desire to corner you into doing anything. I just want to be the safe guy, like you said this morning. The person who will point you in the right direction and you can feel comfortable taking my advice."

"A friend."

"Yes. A friend."

I let out a deep breath. I can actually picture myself doing all those things with Ford. I like Ford. And if I don't have to worry about him making a move on me, I like him even more. "Thanks, Ford. I'm not sure why you're so interested in helping me, but… I'm glad you are."

"So we're straight with this now? No more weirdness?"

I nod. "OK, yeah. We're good."

"Great. Happy birthday, Rook. Next year we'll finally get to take you out in public and celebrate like grownups."

"Asshole."

But I laugh on my way out.

Yup, Ford is one weird dude. I'm just glad he's on my side.

CHAPTER NINE

Ronin

I close the door behind me as Ford pulls the blackout curtains across the front window of Rook's old garden apartment. "We're gonna throw in here, or what?"

Ford glares at me under his slanted brows. "I'd win that fight."

"*Riiiight*. Rook came out happy, what'd you say to her?"

He takes a seat on the couch and beckons me to the chair across the coffee table. I follow suit and ease down into the overstuffed chair.

"I told her I consider her a friend and if she needs anything, she's welcome to come to me for assistance."

"Uh-huh. That's all?"

"You don't trust her?"

"I don't trust you, Ford. I see the flashes of insanity inside your brain that pass as ideas and I'm worried that you've decided to make Rook your next victim."

He folds his hands in his lap and leans back a little more, giving off an air of being totally comfortable in this setting. "I'll be truthful, Ronin. I like her. A lot. Maybe more than any person ever. I'm not sure why, maybe because she's unavailable, maybe because she refuses to put up with my shit, maybe because she listens to me when

I give her advice. I'm not sure, but it hardly matters why. The fact is, I like her and she likes me."

I start to say something but he puts a hand up to stop my words.

"I think we both know what that sick fuck was doing with her. And if you're still delusional I'll spell it out for you. I recognize her behavior. She hides it pretty well, but she's quite easy to control once you know her triggers. I manipulated her all summer when we went running. They were all unconscious reactions, of course, and if I pointed it out to her, she backtracked and did everything in her power to prove she wasn't under my control. She was something to Jon, but a girlfriend wasn't one of them. Not from his point of view, anyway. What really happened?" He lets out a long sigh. "Well, we won't know that until she's ready to tell us. And that might be never, that might be tomorrow. We just can't know."

I have to swallow to keep my dinner from coming back up. I guessed this too, but Ford is seriously involved in that shit, I'm not. BDSM is just a game to me, it's something I play at. To Ford, it's a lifestyle. And if he says Rook displays all the characteristics, then I'm gonna have to defer to his expertise. I feel it to be true anyway.

"She will never admit this to you because she has yet to admit it to herself."

I lean back in the chair and rub my temple a bit. My head fucking hurts.

"She needs serious help. She needs a lot of time. And she needs a lot of freedom. I know she likes you, maybe even loves you, but if you keep her too close she'll fall back into the same patterns. And do you really want to get her by default?"

I pinch the bridge of my nose, trying to make the

shooting pain go away.

"She's running blind right now. She wants to do something, anything to erase what she was. So to prove to herself that she's not the same girl who put up with that life for three years, she's ready to jump on just about every opportunity that comes her way."

"I'm not breaking up with her."

Silence.

I lift my head and look over at Ford. "I'm not gonna do that. I'll back off, I'll give her space, I'll support her decisions, but I'm not breaking up with her."

Ford shrugs. "I'm not asking you to. She'll check out soon, though, Ronin. Write this down. She's not ready for you. She's not ready for anyone right now. What she needs is to start over. She needs to figure out who she was before Jon came along if she's to have any hope of figuring out who she is now."

"Is that your professional opinion, then? We done here?"

"Not quite. That ex-boyfriend is in town."

"Who?"

"Wade Minix, a boy from her childhood. Spencer said she lived with him as a teen in a foster family. This guy was her first boyfriend, or love, or something. His mother got worried when the relationship started getting serious and sent her back into the system. After that her status as ward of the State of Illinois goes cold. I figure Jon picked her up soon after. Before the Minix family she was in twelve other foster families."

"Yeah, she told me this part. Not good ones, either."

"Not good is an understatement. Almost of all them have been stripped of fostering privileges." Ford gets up and grabs a folder off the kitchen counter, then takes his seat and opens it up. "Rook Camille Corvus entered the foster care system at age five when she was found wandering the streets of Chicago barefoot in the middle of January. She didn't speak to anyone for months and when she finally gave up enough information to determine who her mother was, it was too late. The woman had OD'd and was already a cremated body in an unmarked grave. I could go on, but if you use your imagination, I'm sure you can fill it all in. She never got involved in drugs, prostitution, had any illegitimate babies, or did porn." He stops to laugh. "Until you guys, that is."

"Fuck. You."

Ford smiles one of his evil grins. "Sorry, I couldn't resist. But as I was saying, Wade Minix is in town. He hasn't contacted her from what I can tell. I saw him wave at her at the show up in Sturgis. He followed her all over the strip the day of the show. Then ended up standing in the front row that—"

"What? How come you didn't tell me this?"

"Because Rook never responded to his wave and never made any move to reach out to him. She ignored him. But I'm telling you now because he's back. And I think she should reconnect with Wade."

"Yeah, I'm sure you do."

"Well, Ronin, he's gonna get his chance to speak to her no matter what you do. Face that fact. He's here, he's here to see her, and he's not leaving until he does. So you might as well just embrace it. Because you can't stop it, that's for sure. And if you make a big deal about it, she'll just do it anyway. And she'll break up with you because you forced her to make a choice."

I hate it when Ford's right. "So I'm just supposed to sit down and shut up? That's what you're saying?"

"Yes. This is not about you, it has nothing to do with you, in fact. She likes you, that's for sure. Otherwise she'd take that money, buy herself a car, and be on the road to anywhere but here. Because that's just how she works. I call her type the Leaver."

Ford and his fucking labels. "Yeah, I think you're right about that. She's got no fear of the road. I could tell that immediately. What kind of teenager gets on a bus alone knowing she'll be homeless when she steps off? She's not afraid to chuck it all and start again."

"Exactly. And I'll go one further. She told me she had no intention of getting off the bus in Denver. She was on her way to Vegas but she thought fate was sending her a message via *South Park* and got off on a whim. No plans, no home, no money, no friends, and no prospects. She stepped into the unknown because of a fucking cartoon. Now she has all of those empowering things and more, how hard would it be for her to just leave now? If you pressure her, she's gone."

I hold my head in my hands, trying to stave off the headache with a last-ditch brow pinch.

"Just give her some freedom, Ronin. I'll keep an eye on her up at Spencer's place."

I get up and walk to the door, then stop. I don't turn and say it to his face, but I say it just the same. "Thanks, Ford. And dude, just so you know, I'm sorry. About… Mardee." I don't wait for an acknowledgment, I just plaster a smile on my face and walk through back into Rook's birthday party.

CHAPTER TEN

Rook

"Did you have a nice birthday, Rook?" Ronin unzips my dress and I wriggle out of it, just an itty-bitty bit drunk. He laughs as I wobble. "I'll take that as a yes."

Once the dress is gone all I have on are my panties. I watch helplessly as Ronin hangs the gown up. "This was the best birthday of my life. And thank you so much for the camera. You did not have to do that for me. But I love it. I'm gonna start filming tomorrow and I'll never stop. Ever."

That camera is like something else. It looks like a mini-version of the cameras the film crew use for the show. I have no idea how to use it but how lucky am I? I have a film team at my disposal to teach me. I smile at this as Ronin guides me over to the bed and pushes me until I sit down. Once I get some momentum going it's hard to stop and I end up lying all the way back.

"I'm drunk," I say, laughing.

The lights go out and then Ronin's bare skin slips up next to my own. "I know. It's a good thing we had mind-blowing sex before the party." He nuzzles into my neck and pulls me close to him, just like he does every night. "I love you, Rook. I hope you know that."

I sigh into his perfect muscular chest and then trace

my fingertips down the length of his stomach. "I know that."

And that's it for Rook. My night is over.

I wake early, dying of thirst. I swallow down my cotton mouth and disentangle myself from Ronin.

"Where're you going, Gidget?" he asks groggily.

"Water," I croak.

I get up, slip on a dirty t-shirt draped over a chair near the window, and pad out to the kitchen and grab a bottled water. I gulp it all down and then fill it back up with the tap water and do it again. My gaze wanders over to the dining room table and I spy my presents. I have no memory of carrying them upstairs, but here they are.

I got a bunch of stuff. Some clothes, girly hair accessories, and some sapphire earrings from Elise and Antoine. A journal and two tickets to the opera from Ford and his pet. Spencer gave me a custom-painted black leather biker jacket with zippers. It has Gidget painted down one arm and Blackbird down the other. Like each of these men have made a claim on me. The back of the jacket is a giant blackbird logo with the words *Shrike Fucking Bikes* painted inside a red circle that surrounds the bird.

Even Veronica got me a gift. A gift certificate for a free tattoo at her shop up in Fort Collins.

But it was Ronin's gift that touched my heart.

The camera. A camera I can make movies with. I open up the box and start unpacking. It's got interchangeable lenses. I don't know a whole lot about camcorders, but I do know that it's not normal to be able to change lenses on them. Which means this camera is a BFD. When I check the clock it's only five fifteen AM. I do a search for my phone and find it on the little table over my the front door, and then call Ford.

"Miss Corvus, we do not have a date this morning."

I laugh. "I know, Ford. But I'm looking at my camera that Ronin got me and I want to start filming now. I have things to capture before I leave this place. Can you come help me set it up?"

"Did you charge the battery last night?" he asks with doubt.

"Um, no," I say, disappointed.

"OK, well, I'll grab a camera and bring it to you. How's that?"

Happiness overtakes the disappointment. I guess he's serious about this friend stuff. "Thank you."

"Meet me on the terrace in fifteen minutes."

I wash up, change into some jeans and one of the Shrike Rook shirts Spencer made for me, and then pull on my red Converse shoes. I keep waiting for these things to fall apart, but they never do. They have holes in the top near the toe and there's even a little hole in the bottom of the left one. So my feet totally get wet in the rain. But I don't care. Besides the backpack I left my last foster home with, these ratty shoes are the last thing I own from my life before Jon. I take it as a sign that the old me is still around. Somewhere.

By the time I get to the terrace Ford is ready. He's got a camera like mine upstairs and he's pointing it at me as I walk towards him.

"You're up, Rook. I'm your cameraman. Say what's

on your mind."

"Oh, now I'm nervous." I giggle. "OK, well, I just want to show…" I stop and take a deep breath and start again. "I just want to capture what's happened to me. What this place did for me and how it all started."

"All what started, Rook?" Ford asks from behind the camera.

"The journey back." He says nothing to this, just waits for me. "The journey back to myself." And then I point to the swing. "And it all started right there." I walk over to the swing and take a seat. "It started under these trees last spring. When they were filled with flowers and they smelled so incredible, the scent was almost overwhelming. And the very first night I spent here at Chaput Studios Ronin pushed me in this swing." I look up at Ford and he's smiling. I lean back and kick my feet out in front of me, pumping my legs to gain some momentum to push myself in the swing.

"And then he started asking me personal questions and I jumped off." I jump and land on my feet this time. "That was my very first night in the garden apartment. That's how my new life started." I take Ford over there and we go inside and I sit in each room and tell the camera some memory about it. Afterward we go back out on the terrace and he shoots me standing with a view of Coors Field behind me and I talk about our running.

We go through the whole studio. We hit the two-story-tall windows where I had my test shoot with Antoine, the dressing room where Ronin gave me all those clothes, and the salon where Elise washed my hair. Then make our way upstairs where a sleeping Ronin jumps up in surprise when we enter the bedroom.

"What's going on, Gidge?" he asks, still groggy.

"I'm recording my life here with you for posterity, that's what." I jump into bed with him and Ford sets the camera down on a chair and walks away.

"I'll see you two this afternoon. That camera is still on, Rook."

Ronin tackles me and rolls me over on my back. "You're trying to make a sex tape with me?"

I laugh. "No! I just want a little film of us in private. That's all."

"Mmmm," he growls. "But in private we do lots of naughty things, so that means right now we have to be sweet."

"I like sweet."

"Me too," he says, nipping my earlobe until I squeal. "I'm gonna miss you real bad, Gidget. I'm gonna go crazy down here thinking about you up there with Spencer and Ford."

"And I'm gonna go crazy up there thinking about you down here with Clare and the GIDGET models."

"There's only one Gidget for me and that's you."

"And I belong to you, Ronin Flynn."

He flops back and pulls me onto his chest. "God, I want to hear you say that again."

"I belong to Ronin."

His lips find mine, kissing me softly, his hand slipping inside my t-shirt to tickle my stomach. "And I belong to Rook."

CHAPTER ELEVEN

Ronin

"How?" Rook asks me with a totally sincere expression on her face. "How will I ever survive until Friday afternoon without you?" Her fingers dance along the arm of the new couch I bought her, along with all the other furniture in her little basement apartment. "I'm gonna be bored to death."

"You won't be. Spencer and the guys will keep you busy. Besides, I bet Veronica will be here all the time."

"Unless Spencer gets sick of her because he's got commitment issues," she sneers.

I finish up with the surround sound set-up and then grab the remote to check it out. The TV comes on and I flip through the guide until I see a movie she might like. *"Yippee-ki-yay, motherfucker!"* blares from eleven strategically placed speakers in her large basement apartment in Spencer's farmhouse.

Rook turns quickly. "Bruce! Oh, I love Bruce. And this *Die Hard* is the best!"

It's the second one and I agree. "See, you forgot about me already."

She saunters up to me and wiggles against my leg, making me laugh. "You're the one who hooked up the movies. All I need is a popcorn machine and I'm set."

"I'll put it on the list, ma'am."

"You can't call me ma'am and not jump my bones, Mr. cute-total-stranger-cable-guy-who-just-showed-up-to-hook-up-my-surround-sound."

"I jumped your bones twice today already. But if you need it again I'm happy to oblige." I wink at her. "Ma'am."

"Will you miss me?" she asks, suddenly insecure.

"More than you'll miss me, that's for sure. You have Ford and Spencer, they're already friends, so it's not like you'll be alone. I have no one."

She snorts. "That's not true. You have *Clare*."

"I can't hang out with Clare. What do we have in common? Nothing."

"You're her boss now, right? She's the main Gidget model?"

"Yeah, but she needs that job, Rook. She needs to stay busy until she's confident that she won't slip back into her old habits. If you're jealous, you should save yourself the angst because I'm not interested in Clare. At all. She's like a fucking sister to me now."

Rook wraps her arms around me and whispers, "Thank you. I just needed to hear it one more time."

I kiss her sweetly. "You're welcome. Now walk me up, because I have to get back to Denver and you need to settle in. I guess there's a big party planned for tomorrow with all the Shrike cast members, so that will be fun, right?"

"Yeah, I guess."

We walk up stairs and meet the guys in the living room.

"Hey, you leaving already, Ronin?" Spencer asks from the kitchen. "Not gonna stay for the Let's-Embarrass-Rook welcome dinner?"

"Ha, ha, Spencer," Rook says as we walk past.

"No, I gotta get back. Roger and I have casting bullshit tomorrow. We need to sort through the audition pics and figure out if we can fill up all the spots for GIDGET."

"Don't strain yourself, Ronin," Ford says dryly from the dining room where he's messing around with a tablet. "And don't worry about Rook, I'll take care of her while she's here."

"Ford—"

"Relax, Larue," Rook interjects as she rubs my arm. "He's messing with you. Come on, let's go outside, I have a gift for you."

She tugs on my hand and when I look at the expression on her face I know she's up to something, so I follow. "What's that look for? You're being sneaky?"

We pass by her Shrike Rook bike as we walk to the truck and I catch her eyeing it with longing. "You gonna ride that thing, you think?"

"Absolutely. I can't wait."

"Hmmm, I'm not sure about that, Rook. It makes me nervous. Don't ride it alone, OK? Make sure you've got Spence or one of the shop guys with you."

I lean back against the truck as she pushes herself into me and purrs in my ear, "You worry too much, Larue. I'm a big girl. I'm only gonna ride it for a few weeks before it starts snowing. Besides, I have the Shrike truck to hold me over until I figure out what kind of car I want."

"And that's another thing—"

"Don't start with me! I'm buying my own car, I already told you that."

I lean down and kiss her gently. "What were you gonna give me, Gidget?" Her hands slip under my t-shirt and chills ride up my body. "Fuck, I'm gonna miss you."

"Well," she coos in my ear. "I'm gonna miss you too. But the gift I'm giving you before you leave is my heart."

And then she turns her bright blue eyes up at me and I feel it.

I'm not a romantic, I'm really not. I believe in love and all that shit, and I like to make girls happy with presents and careful attention as far as sex goes. But this is something else entirely. She makes my heart ache. Literally. My chest feels like it's gonna be ripped apart from the longing, that's how much I love this girl. "I'm totally taking that gift, Rook. And I'm never giving it back, so please don't ask for it."

"I'm not sure where we're headed, Ronin. I have to be honest about that. I know you're ready to settle down, but I'm not there yet. So I hope you're patient with me. I just started school and parts of it aren't fun, so maybe I don't have what it takes to get a college degree. But I need to figure that out. I might need to go and do all that stuff before I'm ready to settle. Will you be OK with that?"

"Gidget, I'm ready to stand back or step in. You just tell me which one you need and I'm there."

"Just love me, because I love you. I really do. And tonight, when the reality of today sets in and I have to crawl into that cold bed alone, I'm gonna cry my eyes out."

Awwww. I lean down and feather little kisses across her lips. "You better call me if you do. In fact, you can call me any time you want and I'll be there, OK? You need me to drive up, just say so. You need to come down for a day, just show up. I don't care what time it is, what day it is, or what else I'm doing. You're my life, Rook. You're my future, but I'm not in a rush, babe. I'm not. I can wait, so just do your thing, OK?"

She kisses me and the whole world disappears. Just blips out of existence for me. When she kisses me there is nothing but her tender lips and my pounding heart. There is nothing but the buzzing of her essence coursing in my blood and penetrating my soul. There is nothing but us.

"We're an us," I say impulsively and she giggles into my mouth.

"We're definitely an us."

I gather her face gently into my cupped hands and tip her head up. "If you need me, Rook. I'm here, OK, babe? I'm here. You can come to me with anything."

We hug one last time and then I reluctantly get into the truck and drive away, my eyes flickering between the road in front of me and the beautiful girl waving goodbye in Spencer Shrike's driveway.

I hope Ford is wrong, I swear. Because I might die, that's how bad this makes my heart ache. I might die if she checks out on me and walks away.

CHAPTER TWLEVE

Rook

I watch Ronin drive off and suddenly my stomach is twisting into billions of knots. This is probably a mistake. I have so little confidence in what I'm doing with my life, and now that he's gone and I'm here all alone, every decision feels like the wrong one.

"You coming inside? Or you just gonna stand outside and cry?"

Ford is over by my bike. He's wearing jeans and a Shrike Rook t-shirt, which I'm hoping Ronin didn't notice because that's weird. "Why are you wearing that shirt? To piss Ronin off?"

He looks down at his shirt, pretending to be surprised. "It's a blackbird, Rook. It barely looks like you at all."

And then he flashes me that chin dimple and I laugh. "Save it, you're a horrible actor. Besides, the blackbird has blue eyes and the fucking shirt says Rook right across the top."

"Yes, but that's the name of the bike. This one in fact." He smiles smugly as he points to my bike.

"Whatever."

"I have a present for you, come inside."

Ford doesn't wait for me to agree or watch to see if I follow, he simply turns and walks off. And even though I know what that means, I follow anyway. It's not like I really have a choice. I have to go back inside at some point. Might as well do it his way and get a gift out of it. I end up in the great room that connects to the kitchen. Spencer has been cooking all freaking afternoon and it smells awesome. Ford is back at the table flipping through a stack of papers.

"Hmmm," I mumble as Spencer hands me plates and silverware.

"Hmmm, what?" Ford asks, not bothering to look up at me.

"I live with two guys. I never really thought of it that way, but it's pretty clear now."

"We promise not to walk around naked too much, Blackbird."

"Or bring stray pets home." Ford smirks, still concentrating on his work.

"Set the table, Rook, and get the drinks. I won't card you because it's your first night, but just remember I'm doing you a favor and you owe me."

I shake my head and pass out the plates and silverware and then get us three beers. Spence only has one kind and it's from the microbrewery in FoCo, which is kinda cool. "I might regret staying here with you guys. Ford, get your shit off the table, we're eating now."

"See, Ford. Told you, she's already bossin'."

Ford stacks up his stuff and puts everything but one large yellow envelope over on the living room coffee table. "What's this one?" I ask, pointing to the thick package.

"Your gift. But let's eat first."

I look over to Spencer as he sets the basket of bread on the table and then goes back to get the spaghetti. "Don't get excited, Rook. It's not something cool like a motorcycle. I mean, he gave you opera tickets last night for fuck's sake." Spencer practically snorts. "His gifts are as lame as his personality. No wonder he has slaves instead of girlfriends."

And then Ford glares at Spencer so hard I wonder if it might come with a growl.

"Sorry," Spencer says quickly, looking over at me. "Sorry, that came out wrong."

I swallow and try to ignore the awkward moment by grabbing some bread as Spencer dishes out pasta on my plate. "Well—here we are," I mumble into the silence.

"Yeah, well, let's toast. Rook, I knew you were my blackbird when I first laid eyes on you"—I blush a little. I didn't expect something personal—"and I was right. You were the perfect model for my paintings and you're gonna be the perfect addition to my new show. I'm so glad you talked that caveman boyfriend of yours into letting you come join me here. I'd kiss ya, but something tells me you liked it a little too much when we did that last summer, so I'll spare you the embarrassment of fawning all over me and keep it professional." He winks and I laugh.

"I still don't see it," Ford mumbles. "How? How is that desirable, Rook? If I were toasting I'd say—" He clears his throat. "To Rook, the girl who got back up. The girl who never looks back. I hope you find your dream and it's everything you ever wanted."

"Awwww, Ford."

"And to the end of her first failed fucking marriage because it's official! May you never have another!" We all shout "Cheers!" together and clink bottles. I knew Ford was working on it, but he never said anything about it happening so soon. "Annulment, Rook. Like it never happened. You are hereby legally a marriage virgin."

"Thanks so much, Ford. Is that what's in the envelope?"

"No, that shit's over there in the living room. This," he says, holding up the envelope, "is your future."

I hold my breath for a moment and then let it out. "What's in it?"

"Everything you'll need to apply to CU Boulder and an interview with the film department head."

"What?" I'm stunned. "How? And why? I'll never get in so soon, Ford. I'm not even done with one semester. And I might suck at this college stuff, I'm not doing well in math, so maybe—"

"Stop," Ford says in a serious voice. "You'll be fine. I've already chatted with the higher-ups and they're giving you life credit for the reality show work. That's enough to declare film your major. You *will* have to actually get in. But really, Rook, if I did all this, do you think I'd leave you hanging?"

I shake my head. He never would, I know this to be true.

"I've got a lot more in this envelope but we'll do that later this week."

"Good," Spencer says through a mouthful of spaghetti. "Because this school shit is boring the fuck out me. Let's talk about bikes. Or tits."

"How did I get here? We're *Three's Company*. Spencer is airhead Chrissy, Ford is intellectual Janet, and I'm pretending to be gay so I don't notice that you two are roommate eye-candy."

Spencer looks over to Ford. "What the hell did that have to do with tits?"

Ford just shakes his head and laughs.

God, I love these guys.

CHAPTER THIRTEEN

Rook

After dinner Spencer goes out to the shop to work on his bikes and Ford kicks back on the couch, setting up my camera, as I do dishes. Every other word out of his mouth is 'fuck'.

"How's it going in there?"

"Fuck."

"You don't have to do that, you know. I can ask one of the camera guys tomorrow."

He grunts in response.

"You know, I think that white thing on the floor by your foot is actually the manual."

He looks up at me slowly and screws up his face, then goes back to pretending to not need said three-hundred-page book on the floor.

Typical man.

"Tell me what this school stuff is about, Ford. I'm starting to freak out a little. I'm not ready for that. I'm barely making it in math and—"

"I hired you a tutor, stop worrying," he says as he messes with a camera lens.

"What tutor?"

"At the community college. Mondays, Wednesdays, and Thursdays at seven PM. Just show up, I already set it up and he'll show you exactly what to do so you pass the tests."

I'm staring at him over the bar that separates the kitchen from the living room. "Him who?"

"Um—" Ford gets up and grabs the envelope and shuffles though the paperwork. "Gage something. He's a senior in engineering. Sounds like a real nerd, which means he's perfect." Ford goes back to the camera gear and snaps in the battery. "There, I think it's ready now. But *you* will need to read the manual, otherwise you might as well be using your iPhone to make movies."

I start the dishwasher and go plop down on the couch next to Ford. "Thank you. I'm so excited about this. I'm gonna start making movies like now."

He puts his arm around me and gives me a squeeze. "You're gonna be good at this, I can tell. You wanna go shoot Spencer in compromising positions and then edit the shit out of it to make him look stupid?"

I lean over and kiss Ford on the cheek. It's impulsive and he almost has a small freakout before he shuts it off. "Sorry, didn't mean to make you uncomfortable, but you're awesome."

He disentangles himself from me and gets up, pulling me up with him. "I enjoy it, Rook. Being with you feels normal. I should be thanking you."

We grab all the gear and spend the rest of the evening fucking around with Spencer in the shop. We even get him to lip-sync that *Bad to the Bone* song into a socket wrench. And by the time I get back to my basement apartment I'm feeling a lot better about my decision to come up here and live with Spence to do this show. My phone beeps an incoming text just as I settle back on my couch and turn on the TV.

My heart flutters a little as I read the text.

Dear Rook (AKA Gidget),

I've never had the urge to write a love letter but I'm lying in bed, looking over at your side, wondering if I can somehow change your mind about this whole deal and talk you into coming the fuck home. (I'm a selfish asshole, I know.) But I get that you need this so I'll just say this instead: I felt like I was leaving a piece of my soul behind the moment I left. And every second that passes, I miss you like that, times a million.

Love,
Ronin (AKA Larue)

I press call under his name and he picks up on the first ring. "Ronin Flynn, you are like a door."

He laughs. "It was that touching, huh?"

"Not a window where you can see through to the other side and be sure of what's coming. But a door, still closed and leading to every opportunity imaginable and requiring a leap of faith that the risk is worth it. You are my doorway to endless possibilities and I'm ready to take that risk."

I can hear him swallow on the other end and when he's done his words rumble out in his deep, sexy voice. "Rook, I'm not a risk, I'm a sure thing. You're the only girl I want to build a future with. Ever. You're the one, Rook. The love that only comes around once in a lifetime and I refuse to settle for anything else."

He's perfect. Simply perfect. "I love your love letter, Larue. It made me sigh like a schoolgirl."

"Well, you *are* a schoolgirl, right? I think I'm gonna

have to go looking for a little tartan skirt and some knee socks. Dress you all up in a sexy outfit this weekend."

"If you do that, I might have to be bad on purpose, Mr. Flynn."

"Don't tease, Gidget, or I'll spank you."

"You promise that so much and never come through. I hardly get excited about it anymore."

He guffaws this time and I can practically picture his gorgeous smile lighting up his electric blue eyes. "I can't fucking wait until Friday."

I giggle a little as I picture our Friday. "I might just ditch class early, Mr. Flynn."

"And that will earn you two spankings, Miss Corvus."

"Promises, promises."

***

After Ronin and I hang up I read the text over and over again. A letter. It's sorta old-fashioned and sweet. I look over at the camera and the idea that started this morning with saying goodbye to my latest journey through life with a wrap-up of Chaput Studios gives me another one. I set up the camera on the small kitchen table, sit down in front of it, and turn it on. I take a deep breath and begin to talk.

"Dear Rook at age fifteen. Your life is not over. Wade Minix was not your one. I wish you'd stop crying and being depressed and just make yourself get over it, because I'm Rook at age twenty and I know better. I know that your one is waiting for you five years in the future and his name is not Wade. I wish I could warn you to stay far, far away from that diner where you meet Jon. I wish I could warn you that moving out to that house with him in the country will be the biggest mistake of your life."

I take a deep breath and then continue.

"I wish I could tell you what to watch out for, when to say no, when to walk out, and when to never look back. But I can't. Because you need to do all those things without my help. You need to learn all those lessons. You need to experience all that fear and pain and desperation. You need to see all that stuff. Because at the end of all those bad things, there is a sweet and gentle man named Ronin Flynn."

The tears start to flow down my face as I allow myself to feel a small fraction of the emotions I've bottled up in the name of survival since I left Chicago.

I get up and turn the camera off and take another deep breath.

I'm ready.

I'm ready to accept what happened and let it go. I'm not quite sure how I'm gonna do that and I'm not quite sure what will happen when I confront the past and take a good hard look at all those memories. I just know that I'm tired of pretending that girl is not me. Ronin deserves a girl who is whole. He's done so much for me that I owe him this. I owe him a whole girl who can accept his protection and love without constantly being afraid she'll make the same mistake twice.

CHAPTER FOURTEEN

Ronin

After Rook and I hang up I lie on the couch and halfheartedly watch *The Last Samurai* as I think about making love to her this morning. She's definitely getting more adventurous, but I still feel the need to be careful with her.

A knock brings me out of the daydream and I jump up and jog over to the door. It can only be one of three people. Clare, Elise, or Antoine. That's one thing about living in a secure building. No unexpected visitors.

The door lock clicks as I open it and Clare is smiling at me from the other side of the threshold. "Hey, what's up, little chick?" She's wearing some pink shorts and a white tank top, looking totally cute.

"Can I come in?"

I throw the door open wide. "*Mi casa* and all that shit, right?"

She laughs. "Right." She eyes my outfit now. I'm only wearing a pair of baggy black sweatpants cut off mid-thigh and her gaze lingers on my bare chest a little too long. I clear my throat and wave her over to the couch. She takes a seat in the middle so I plop down next to her and put my arm around her shoulders. "You came to hang out and watch movies? Or you have something on your mind?"

She looks up at me with those blue eyes of hers and I can't help but smile. "I just needed to say it in person, that's all. When I'm not high, or crying, or a total mess in all the other ways in which I'm normally a total fucking mess."

I squeeze her a little. "Say what?"

"Thank you. I really mean it, Ronin. I know you put up with a lot from me last summer. I was a total pain in your ass and I probably made your life more difficult than it needed to be. So I'm sorry for that."

"Hey," I say, taking her chin and lifting it up so she has to look at me. "You're family, right? I love you. You're part of me now and I'm not gonna let you give up. I never understood what that drug was to people, but I know now. After watching you struggle and go through all that pain, I know. But you're a fighter, Clare. And I have an idea about what you're feeling, so just put those doubts out of your head. You're gonna make it. You're over the worst and now it's just maintaining, right?"

She swallows hard and leans back against my chest. I automatically sit back into the couch cushions and pull her in next to me.

"You're a good guy, Ronin. I totally messed up when I blew it with you back in high school."

"Yeah, well. Bygones, OK? Don't dwell on my silly high-school crush. I'm happy with how things shook out. You'll find the right guy, Clare. You're fucking beautiful, and smart, and French."

She laughs and then turns her head up to look at me. "But—maybe, if things don't work out with you and Rook, you might give me another chance?"

I laugh a little. "Well, I hate to disappoint you because I'm gonna marry Rook. But I promise, if things go bad, I'll call you first, OK?"

Her fingertip traces along my lower arm and sends a chill through my whole body. "I miss you."

I push her off and get up because this is not gonna happen. "I'm tired, OK? I gotta get some sleep so Roger and I can get everything ready for the test shoots on Monday. Maybe you can help us choose the girls, eh? You have a good eye for that, right?"

Clare drags herself up from the couch and walks off slowly, not turning back until the front door is open and she's about to walk through. "Everyone can see she's a mess, Ronin. She's not gonna stick around."

Clare pulls the door closed behind her before I can object so I just stand there, holding my breath as I internalize those words. Ford pretty much said the same thing. *She's checking out, Ronin.* That's what he said. And even though Clare knows nothing about Rook, she's right. Rook *is* a mess. She's looking pretty good on the outside, but the stuff she's covering up on the inside is another matter. I grab my phone off the coffee table and press Spencer.

"Yeeeello."

"Yello? Dude, you sound like a fucking eighty-year-old grandpa."

"And your point is? Grandpas are cool, everyone loves a grandpa."

"Pfft, obviously you've never been to the Chaput family compound in France."

"I hear that papi of yours is a real killer."

"Yeah, like literally. He ran over the baker last month with his fucking bicycle. There were baguettes everywhere, made the guy sprain his ankle. He's lucky he's not in jail."

Spencer laughs. "OK, well, what the fuck do you

want? I got nothing to tell you, really, Rook seems fine. We had dinner, she did the dishes because I cooked and you know Ford, he's not about to lower himself to do domestic work. Then they came out to the shop and filmed me with her new camera, trying to bait me into saying something stupid so they could edit it down and embarrass me. She's OK."

I let out a long breath. "I dunno, Ford said—"

"Why the fuck, Ronin—after all these years, after all the bullshit between the two of you—why the hell are you even wasting one fucking second on what that asshole has to say about *your* fucking girlfriend? I mean seriously."

"Because he's been noticing some really fucked-up signs, Spencer. Stuff that only he would see, stuff that makes me sick to even think about."

"Oh."

Silence.

"Yeah, *oh*. And I have to say, now that he's put it out there, I can sorta see it too. I think she needs real help, Spence. She pretends like none of those years with Jon Walsh ever happened. Or actually, maybe she's not pretending. Maybe she's legitimately blocked it out and she can't remember? And Ford said she's gonna leave. He doesn't think she'll stick around."

More silence.

"Spence?"

"Yeah, I'm here. Just thinking is all. God, I fucking hope he's wrong. Do you think he's wrong? It was just your run-of-the-mill abusive relationship, right? I can't even think about that other shit."

"I want to believe he's wrong too, I really do. But I don't think he is. I mean, Ford knows. And they are very close right now. He spends a lot of time with her. She trusts him. They might, in fact, be BFFs or something."

It's Spencer's turn to let out a long breath. "Well, maybe she needs a new best friend? I'll call Veronica and see if she'll invite Rook to hang out. Plus, she's got that coupon for a free—"

"Spencer, do not tat up my girl, OK? I like her the way she is."

"Yeah, well, I'll call up Ronnie and see if she'll take her shopping or something. Rook needs girlfriends anyway. It's not good for her to hang out with so many guys."

"Yeah, tell me about it."

"I'll keep my eye on her. I think Ford's gonna—oh, hold on, here he is—"

There's some shuffling sounds as the phone is passed to Ford, then some muffled talking.

"How can I help you, Ronin?"

"I'm not sure. I'm just worried about her."

"She seems fine for now. She was in a good mood tonight. She's in bed. I'll wake her up early to run stadiums in town, and she's got the party tomorrow night, and schoolwork. Her days will be full. She might just settle down and be fine."

"Or she might not."

"Right, well, we'll have to wait and see. I'll do my best to see if I can persuade her to seek help, but it's touchy. She won't put up with a lot of pushing from me. She walks away angry."

"She walks away from everyone. Including me. I can't push her either."

"So why are you?"

"What choice do I have? Just let her hold it all in until it explodes?"

"I told you about Wade. I think she should talk to him. Maybe that will spur her in one direction or another?"

Silence from me now.

"If she chooses him, then there's nothing you can do, Ronin."

More silence from me.

"She won't choose him, though. I've spied on him, sifted through all his online records. He's not her type anymore." He waits a few seconds to see if I'll respond, but I don't. "Well, it's been fun. Here's Spencer."

"Yeeeello."

I laugh a little. "You're a dumbass."

"Hey, if it'll make you feel any better, I'll go kiss her goodnight for you."

"Asshole. OK, I'll check in tomorrow."

"Later, Larue."

The line goes silent before I can respond to Spencer's dig.

Nothing I can do. Ford is right, this is all about her and there's just nothing I can do.

CHAPTER FIFTEEN

Rook

I'm up with time to spare the next day. I throw on some black yoga pants, a black running tank, a Shrike Bikes zippered hoodie, and my running shoes. Ford lives above the shop, so I grab my camera and head down the driveway to see if he's awake and ready.

Spencer has all his doors coded like Chaput Studios so the crew and other employees can get access when they need to, so I punch in my code and walk through the shop reception area. This is where I'll be working. Answering phones, making appointments for clients to Skype in with Spencer and place a custom order, driving around town picking up and dropping shit off.

Your basic receptionist-slash-delivery driver position.

Right now the shop has eight bikes in progress. Spencer and another guy named Ryan build the custom bikes, while Fletch and Griff make the showroom bikes. Customers are allowed to ask for modifications, so they do a little custom shit too. What Ford will be doing here is beyond me. As far as I know, he doesn't build bikes. But he's been known to surprise me before. He lives upstairs above the shop in another apartment. I walk to the far end of the work area, picking my way between half-built bikes and tool chests, then climb the steep steps.

I knock.

I hear a faint, "Come in," from behind the door.

"Ford?" I call back as I open the door.

"You're early," he says through a mouthful of toothbrush. He's wearing a pair of old jeans that hang low on his hips, exposing his happy trail because he has no shirt on.

Hmmm. Ford is not a bad-looking guy. He's all muscle, but not the same way that Spencer is. Spencer is bulky and buff. Ford is lean and taut.

Taut. What a great word. I laugh internally at that, then realize I laughed externally as well.

"Stop staring at me. I never stared at you when you were prancing around naked all summer."

"I didn't prance! And I'm not staring," I reply, blushing. "I was comparing your body to Spencer's."

He walks back into the bathroom to spit and rinse. "How do I stack up?" he asks, walking across the hallway to his bedroom to change.

"Umm—" I shouldn't even go there.

He peeks his head around the corner and tugs a black shirt on. "Well? You can be honest because let's face it, I'm much better built than Spencer." He ducks back into his room and I laugh.

"Well, you're certainly more full of yourself."

"Right. That's a good one. I'm humble compared to Spencer." He comes back out into the little living room with his shoes and sits down on the couch. His jeans are gone now, and replacing them are his usual black running pants. "Why do you have that camera? Is this gonna be your thing? You're one of those film students who records every moment of their life?"

I shrug. "Maybe. What's it to you? I'm eager, that's

all."

He looks up from lacing a shoe and smiles. "Yes, I can tell."

I'm not sure if that was innuendo or not, so I change the subject. "Where are we going, anyway?"

"CSU Football stadium. It's southwest of FoCo, but there's a back road we can take from Bellvue, so it shouldn't take too long to get there. It's a scenic drive, that's for sure. So you can film that if you want something nice for B-roll."

"I love it when you talk film to me, Ford."

He smirks up at me as he finishes up his shoes. "You're not allowed to be this happy at five in the morning. I will train that smug smile right off your face in about twenty minutes, you wait."

He grabs his keys and one of those trendy running jackets and we hop down the stairs and walk outside to his Bronco. I get my camera ready just in case there is something pretty to shoot for B-roll. You never know when you'll need a shot of Colorado back country.

We drive in silence—well, that's relative because this hunk of junk is not exactly quiet. But neither of us mind letting the rumble of the engine fill the silence. I just watch out my window, filming the scenery. We go right through Bellvue and come out on an empty road south of town. It takes us past a lake on one side and a bunch of university buildings on the other. "Research stations," Ford says, pointing to the buildings. "Horsetooth Reservoir," he says, pointing to the lake.

A few miles later the stadium comes into view. We have to go past it and double back on another road to get there, but it really didn't take that long. "Wow, there's a lot of cars here. They must have quite the AM training program."

"Homecoming weekend stuff," he explains. "But we've got permission as long as we're out by eight."

"How do you get permission for all this, Ford?"

"Money," he deadpans. Then he looks over at me and laughs. "How else?"

"You have to pay for us to run? Did you have to pay for me at Coors Field?"

He ignores me and pulls the Bronco up to a security guard at the parking lot entrance, then reaches into his jacket pocket and flashes two ID's. The guard waves us through. "Money," he says again, looking over at me this time. "And hacking skills."

I'm not sure if he's serious, so I leave it. Because I'm not interested in his hacking activities or anything else Ford does with Spencer and Ronin as part of their 'business'.

I hide my camera under an old jacket that Ford hands me from the backseat and then we head over to the stadium entrance. We pass several more security checks. Each time Ford flashes those badges and each time we are waved forward. Ford seems to know where he's going so I just follow. We come out in the stands, about halfway up, like we used to at Coors Field.

"OK," Ford says once we get inside and choose a spot that's not being used by other runners. "I will slow down for you. From now on, we run together. But I won't slow all the way down, you need to meet me halfway. So you have to actually push yourself. No more slacking off."

"Well, that's no fun. I'm a moper, remember? I come to shuffle."

"Your shuffling days are over, Rook. And I'm sick of your moping. From now on, you're training with me. So keep up or I'll find ways to make your life uncomfortable."

"Ha! Like how?" I cross my arms in front of my chest in defiance and before I can even process what he's doing, he leans forward into my personal space and slips his hand under my hair behind my neck, drawing me close to him. His touch affects me immediately and I flush with heat. I can probably count on two hands the number of times Ford has actually *touched* me, and most of them have happened in the past few days. His mouth dips down to my ear, his breath hot against my skin, and for a second I think my heart will actually stop from the shock of it all.

I swallow.

"Like this, Rook." Ford's soft words vibrate into me. "I like you. I'd like to show you how much, actually. I'm being a gentleman to make life easier for you, but believe me, it's not really in my nature to be so accommodating. I typically just take what I want."

A shudder erupts as his fingertips drag lightly across the back of my neck. He pulls away smiling. "So keep the fuck up or I'll make things very confusing."

And then he turns and takes off running up the stairs.

What the hell just happened?

But I don't have time to think because he's already halfway up this aisle. I follow, running hard for a second to try and catch up, but once I match him he slows a little so that I don't have to exert myself too much. He continues to adjust our pace like this, running harder for ten or twenty seconds, then slowing down for a minute or more.

And I realize something.

Ford knows me. He knows exactly what I'm capable of at my current fitness level. He recognizes the sound of my breathing when I'm getting winded, as well as the sound of it when I'm too comfortable.

He pushes me to do better and try harder in just the right way.

Not too fast, not too slow.

But just right.

We run this way for almost an hour. Much longer than we normally did at Coors Field. That was always thirty minutes or so. I'm starting to lag behind severely, and no amount of threatening me with uncomfortable sexual touching will make me keep up, so he slows to a walk. "We'll do two sets like this, then we can be done."

I wait for my hard breathing to slow and my heart rate to come back to normal and then I figure I *have* to say something. Because the entire run, all I thought about was how his hand felt on the back of my neck. "Are we playing again, Ford?"

"Playing what?"

"Are you gonna try and make a move on me? I thought we were friends?"

"I thought you said you trusted me to do what's right for you?"

"Yeah, as a friend, I do! But that was before—" I'm not sure what the hell that was back there so I don't even have a word ready to describe it. Ford doesn't offer any help, in fact I can sorta see him smirking out of the corner of my eye. "I think you just came on to me."

He laughs, then stops and stands in front of me, forcing me to look at him. "Believe me, Rook," he says with a serious expression. "If I was coming on to you, you'd have no trouble recognizing it." He turns and continues walking.

"So I should just—what? Ignore that exchange back there?"

"Just keep up in training, Rook. And you'll have nothing to worry about."

I stop and throw up my hands. "OK, I'm done then. I'm out." I turn around and start walking down the stairs.

He follows and when he gets alongside me he jumps down several steps and cuts me off. He starts walking back up, which makes *me* almost fall, but he grabs my arm and then lets go when I'm steady again. "So that's it?"

"What's it?" I ask, annoyed.

"That's your boundary? I can push you to run past your current endurance level just fine. You adjust and work harder without one complaint even though I doubled our running time and had you gasping for breath on four occasions. But when I push emotionally, you shut down and run away immediately. You know, I'm the guy who supposedly has no emotions, I'm the one who's supposed to be incapable of feeling. I'm the one who doesn't give a fuck about people. But you, Miss Corvus, are really giving me a run for my money. You want to play as long as you're in control, right? You stare at my chest then freely admit you're checking me out to compare to Spencer. So I might ask you the same question. What are you doing with *me*?"

"You said we were friends. I was joking about Spencer."

"You spend time with me why, Rook? Because I'm your friend? Or because you like this game we're playing? You say you love Ronin but you argue and rebel against all his good advice, yet you do almost everything I ask whenever I dangle the smallest carrot in front of your face. Why?"

"I just want you to be my friend."

"That's not an answer to my question. Answer the question."

I get flustered for a second and don't have anything to say. "Why do I like you? Is this what you're asking? You need me to stroke your ego a bit, Ford?"

He laughs. "Hardly, Rook. I just want the truth from you."

"I just need a friend. I want you to be my friend."

"I am your friend."

"But that back there was not what friends do, Ford. It *did* confuse me. I already have a boyfriend. We're in love."

"Yeah, a boyfriend who's desperate for me to figure out what the fuck is going on inside that messed-up head of yours because he's terrified you'll walk out on him if he asks you himself."

"What? You assholes are talking about me? He's asking you for advice and you make a move on me?" I shake my head and start walking off again, but this time Ford grabs my wrist.

"Stop!" he commands.

I stop.

And then I realize what he just did and attempt to yank myself free. But each time I struggle he pulls me closer until I'm pressed against his chest, fighting off tears. He leans down again and whispers in my ear. "I was wrong about you, Rook."

I swallow and look up at him, meeting his gaze.

"You're not inexperienced, are you?"

My heart is ready to jack itself right out of my chest and I try my hardest to break free, but he holds me tight and close.

"You're not inexperienced, you're submissive. You just spent the last few years unconditionally following orders, didn't you?"

"You have no idea—"

He grips my wrist hard enough to cut off my words and make me cry out. "I'm the guy who brought a *pet* to your birthday party, Rook. Don't fucking tell me I have no idea."

I turn off. That's all I have left, I just turn off. I stop struggling as my eyes glaze over. I concentrate on a point out on the sidelines where a cheerleader is doing tumbling moves. A few of her friends join her and—

"Look at me."

"Fuck you."

He lets go of my wrist and I lower my head and count the seconds to see what he's up to. When I get to ten and he has nothing to say, I jump down the stairs and head for the parking lot.

CHAPTER SIXTEEN

Rook

My face is hot and it takes all my willpower to prevent the tears from coming out with the anger and frustration. Ford is weird. I need to stop this. Ronin was right, he's got emotional issues. Or lack of emotion issues, I'm not quite sure. Either way, I think I'm done with Ford. I reach the Bronco and yank on the door handle to get in and realize it's locked.

Of course it's locked, you idiot. Your eight-thousand-dollar camera is in there.

I lean against the door and watch Ford walk towards me across the parking lot. When he reaches me he says nothing, just pushes his key into the lock and then opens the door.

I climb in as he goes around to his side and does the same.

He sinks back into his seat and I turn my head and watch the various groups of people bustling around the stadium.

"You ran."

I shake my head. "I'm done here and I'd like for you to start the fucking truck and drop me off at Spencer's."

He lets out a sigh. "Too far, then?"

I look over at him now. His face is expressionless, just

passive, like this isn't some monumentally fucked-up moment in time for me. "So you're fucking with me? Is that it, Ford? Your job here is to rip apart my brain and do what? Use me up and spit me out like the rest of your pets? Am I a pet to you? Your project? You know what's fucking funny? You say Ronin's the one with the hero complex, but from what I can tell, that's you, Ford. Ronin doesn't fuck with me like this, he just accepts me for what I am."

He laughs. "Is that right? Do you have any idea what Ronin *does* in our little partnership?"

"I do not give one fancy fuck about Ronin's part in what you guys do together."

Ford looks away and sighs. "I'm sorry, then, OK?" He looks back over at me and waits a few seconds to see if I'll respond. But I keep silent. "I didn't realize it would affect you like that, OK? I'm sorry."

I continue to stare out the window. "Whatever. You know exactly what you were doing, so save it. Just take me home."

"Rook, I swear, it was a little harmless flirt, that's all. I didn't realize you'd get all…" He stops. "Well, I don't really understand what happened, actually. Do you *like* me? Like that?"

Oh, my God. I am so completely fucking humiliated. "Just take me home."

I catch him scrubbing his hand down his face from the corner of my eye, like I'm frustrating him. "OK, I'll start then. How's that? Because I really didn't mean to have this conversation with you, like ever. But since I've unleashed it—maybe unconsciously, maybe not—I'll just say it."

Holy fucking shit, he's gonna go there.

"I want you. I have it pretty bad, in fact. I knew the fucking moment I saw you come into Antoine's office that day we went out to dinner. I went out of my way to make sure you were sitting next to me. And you, you… you just… there was just something about you that drew me in. I had no idea what it was. At least back then." He stops and swallows and then looks over at me and stares hard, straight in my eyes. "But I do now. I know what it is that draws us together and I think you do too."

"I'm not talking about this."

He ignores me and continues. "I'd never make you cheat on Ronin, Rook. I'm not like that at all."

"Take me home."

"But you'd make my year if you admitted to me that you feel this too."

"Oh. My. God! Shut the fuck up and take me home!" I shout it and I expect some reaction to this lapse in emotional control, but a laugh isn't quite it. "Why are you laughing?"

"You do like me, don't you? Enough to leave Ronin? Not that I'm asking," he adds hurriedly. "I'm not asking you to do that, OK. I'm just—"

"You're just playing with me, right? You think you've guessed something about my past and that gives you the right to mess with me? Play concerned friend, take me running and then flirt and make me uncomfortable. Get me to spill my guts and then stomp all over my feelings and rub it all in. That's what you're doing, right?"

"Rub all what in, Rook?" he asks, confused.

"The fact that you could dangle that teeny-tiny carrot in front of me and I'd jump."

"Do you like me?"

"Of course I like you. Why else would I spend so

much fucking time with you?"

"Do you *want* me?"

I take a second to think this through because this question is much harder to answer.

"Do you, Rook?"

"No, Ford. I don't." I look over at him and let my defenses drop a little. "You have this power over me, you make that rotten carrot look like spun sugar. And I've been there already. I know it's an illusion. I'm not looking for that kind of relationship again, OK? But..." I'm not sure I want to say the, rest, so I stop and chew on my nail as I watch the people in the parking lot.

Ford stays silent for a while, but there's no way I'm getting out of this now, so when he pushes I'm not surprised. "But what? Just tell me, Rook. If you want me to keep it from Ronin, I will. I won't tell him any of this."

I continue my silence, my mind racing with what Ford is asking me to admit. I'm not sure I'm ready to do that, in fact, I might never be ready to do that. But I need to tell him something. I swallow down my fear and turn to look at him. "If you were to ask me to leave with you. To just walk away from all of it. The show, Ronin, school... all of it."

He raises his eyebrows in surprise.

"I'd go. Because you're right, there's a part of me that finds that dominance shit attractive and you control everything. Every encounter we have, you are always in charge. So that draws me in, and I'd go if you asked because you... you know how to make me *want* to do what you ask. And giving in to what I was is so much easier than taking control and becoming something else."

Ford huffs out a laugh and turns in his seat to stare out the front window.

"But if I actually did that, you would ruin my life."

He looks back, any pleasure he got from my revelation instantly gone.

"You'd ruin my life because there's a huge difference between you and Ronin, and regardless of whatever insecurities you have about your looks, that's not what's different, Ford. You're plenty good-looking. You practically sweat sex, and there is something very frightening, yet compelling about you that makes me want to… to give in to you—to *submit*." I throw up my hands. "There, was that what you were waiting for? That word? Fine, you can have it, consider it a gift. It changes nothing for me, because the difference between you and Ronin is that you're looking for the girl I was and he's looking for the girl I want to be."

I wait for him to respond but he's the one who looks away now.

"Yes, you have it in you to compel me to do a lot of things, Ford, simply because you know the right way to ask for it, you know how to manipulate my emotions because of the way I was tr… tr…" I search for another word because that one just won't come out of my mouth. "You know how to manipulate me because of how I was *treated* in the past. But if you did decide you wanted me, you'd get that other Rook and you'd be stuck with her forever, because regardless of what you think, I *did* save myself back in Chicago. I did it once, but I'm not sure I could do it again. And I'm not saying you're anything like Jon. Maybe you treat that pet of yours nicely. Maybe she even loves you and maybe I would too, but I'd never have it in me to walk out again. Being with you would be a total surrender for me. You would *ruin* me."

He thinks about my words for several seconds and

then looks over to me. "I'm so sorry."

"For what?"

"For what I said and did earlier. I was just having some fun with you back there. It really was just a flirt. I never expected it to make you feel like this. I do like you and if you wanted to be with me, I'd be in for that. I would. But I don't want that other Rook." He stops to sigh and look out the window for a few seconds before continuing. "I want nothing to do with that Rook and I'd never be able to live with myself if I dragged you backwards and made you surrender. I'm into your potential, I love your strength, and I'm in awe of your struggle to overcome these things in your past and be a new person."

"I'd rather die than go back to being that other girl, Ford. I'd rather die. I need Ronin's gentle hand and I need to make these mistakes because I had all my choices taken away from me back in Illinois. I had no free will at all. So to answer your question about why I refuse to accept Ronin's good advice, it's because he gives me the *choice* to refuse. He lets me be me. And he stands by me, even if he's unhappy with what I'm doing. I need that so *badly* right now. I need all this freedom but I also need to know someone will set me straight when I stumble. And that someone is Ronin."

We sit in the silence for a while, his eyes darting back and forth as he takes his turn watching people in the parking lot. And then he abruptly shoves the key into the ignition and starts the engine. "Would you like to go see the math building at your little college so you know where to meet your tutor tomorrow night?"

I huff out a breath. "Yeah, sure."

"And then we can take a drive down to Boulder and look at the university, it's not that far. I'll show you the new building they have for film studies. It's a great facility."

Fucking Ford. "Sounds like a plan, let's go."

"Well, first we have to get breakfast bagels." I release the built-up tension as a laugh and look over at him. He's smiling at me. "Because this stupid fucking CSU stadium has no open concession stands for its early-morning trainees." He pulls the Bronco out of the parking lot and looks over at me. "We miss Coors Field already, don't we?"

"Yeah, we do." I pick my camera up from the floor and turn it on, recording some B-roll of the drive as Ford talks about application deadlines for CU Boulder and summer internships.

Ford and I have a lot in common and one of those things is denial.

We do denial well.

In fact, we're exceptionally good at denial when we do it together.

I like that about Ford and I have a feeling he likes that about me too.

CHAPTER SEVENTEEN

Ronin

"I think these girls will be a good fit."

Clare leans down over my shoulder, her hair brushing past my cheek as she touches my arm with one hand and rests the file folder gently on the desk in front of me. I look up at her and she smiles. It's not seductive, and believe me, I know that look well. She's never done sexy shoots like the other models, but you don't need to be naked to have bedroom eyes. This is not her being seductive. And even though she said straight up the other night that she was still very much interested in having a relationship with me, the typical game-playing I could expect from the old Clare is missing.

"Thanks," I tell her with a genuine smile. I flip through the folder and look at each girl.

"I chose seventeen, do you want me to set them up for test shoots this week?"

I shuffle through the resumes. All these girls are beautiful and they are all experienced. "Yeah, we'll probably keep at least twelve, just in case someone doesn't work out. Nice to have back-ups. And make sure they understand the contract before the test shoot, OK? I don't want any surprises. Find out if they have any… issues." I try to be gentle, but she knows what I'm saying. If they're on drugs, I'm not interested. "And make sure to tell them about the scale. Billy's in charge of the closet and the girls for this shoot."

"Got it," she says, then dips down and pecks me on the cheek real fast and skips out of the room.

Watching her makes me happy these days. She is so pretty. Her blonde hair is long and lush, her eyes are blue and bright, her body is curvy instead of rail thin, and her skin is glowing. She's not the girl I knew back in high school, not at all. She's better. "Hey, Clare?" I call out before she gets too far away from the office door.

"Yeah?" she asks, turning around.

"I'm glad you're home."

She beams at me and lets out a long sigh. "Me, too."

I kick my feet up on Antoine's desk and think about Rook. I know she's running with Ford—this is a habit I've come to accept, even if I don't like it. She likes him, it's clear. But how far that affection stretches, I'm not sure just yet. Her attitude towards me hasn't wavered. She's always interested, she's always happy to see me, and her playfulness has only increased since the whole Jon thing before Sturgis.

But I'm desperate for more from her. I'm desperate for something more permanent. And I do understand that it's totally selfish of me to expect her to give up her dream to make me happy, so that's something I'd never ask her to do. But it eats away at me. Her lack of permanence. It's like she's fleeting, like she's a moment. Something that comes and goes. I want marriage, I want kids, I want everything I never had as a child, and I want it desperately.

But I want her more.

I will wait, that was not a lie. I'll wait forever if I have to.

"Elise is back!" Clare yells from the studio.

I jump up from the desk, rush out to the studio and wait in front of the elevator with Clare. It dings pathetically just before the doors open and Elise and Antoine appear.

"Well?" Clare exclaims.

"I told you, they won't know for another month. This ultrasound was just to check on things."

"Oh, please! I happen to know for a fact that they can tell at seventeen weeks. My roommate Jamie from rehab was pregnant, so I heard all the scary details of bun-baking while I was up there."

Elise smiles coyly. "Well, the tech did give us a hint."

"What is it?" Oh fuck, I'm so excited I can barely stand it.

Elise defers to Antoine who lets out the biggest fucking smile I've ever seen on that asshole's face. "Boy," he laughs. "It's a boy!"

"Ahhh! That's great!" We high-five and then clap each other on the back, then look down at Elise, who is frowning. "A girl would be good too! But it's a boy, so hey, what can you do?"

"I'm just happy it's OK. I'm so stressed out. I'm tired, my feet hurt, my back aches, and I'm not even five months yet. I don't think I'm a very good mother."

I look up at Antoine to see what this is about but he's got a strange look on his face. "Oh, come on, Elise. It's normal to be all those things when you're pregnant, right, Clare?"

Clare's about to shrug it off, but she catches my look. "Oh, yeah, Ellie, mothering is natural, right? You'll be a natural."

But I can see Elise's mind whirling as these words

sink in. Our mom was not a natural. She was pretty terrible at it, actually. And she picked a bad dude to have babies with, hence the whole beaten to death and prison sentence outcome. I take Elise's hand and tug her towards the stairs. "Come on, I'll watch girly TV with you if you want." She smiles at me and lets me lead her away. I steal a look back at Antoine as we walk up the stairs and he mouths 'thank you' at me.

"Let's watch at my place, sis. I have a better TV and besides, you never visit me at home anymore."

"I'm sorry, Ronin, I'm a bad sister too."

"*Please*. This is definitely hormones talking." I punch in my code and unlock the door, then wave her into the living room but she heads straight to the bathroom. I plop on the couch and kick my feet up on the table, then flip through the DVR and find some Ellie shows. She likes all the typical shit that I'd normally never be caught dead watching, but this is how I spent my childhood. Sticking to Elise's side like glue as we navigated our way through a very fucked-up home life. She had a little TV in her room and six nights out of seven I was in there sleeping with her instead of my own bed. We'd watch Jenny McCarthy and *Jackass*, then the Top Model show later, after Antoine took us in. It was kind of a joke, right? Since we lived with Antoine and half the time I had famous models taking me on tours around foreign cities and Elise was in a position to make and break careers with a whisper in Antoine's ear.

She had wanted to be a model, even though she's so small. She knew the high fashion stuff was a no-go, but the erotic stuff didn't have those kind of requirements. And that's how she ended up here. Well, Antoine had a much smaller studio over in North Denver, so that's where Elise dragged me that afternoon, about six months after our family disintegrated. She was so nervous and I was only ten years old, too young to understand what she was about to do for money. So I was just scared. And when Antoine came to get her from the front room Elise started to tremble and I just flipped out and refused to let her go with him. I tried to fight him, in fact.

I can laugh now, but I was so fucking afraid for her. I thought for sure this guy was gonna do something horrible, why else would she be so scared? And then I'd be alone, totally alone.

But Antoine let me come back into the studio and he took so many pictures of her that day—fully clothed—that I fell asleep on the floor. The next thing I knew, I was being homeschooled in India while he photographed important people and used Elise as his make-up artist.

It was surreal how Antoine changed our lives.

When we came back from India he bought this building. We lived in a high-rise apartment during the renovations and I had private tutors because every few months we'd pack up and go somewhere else. I've been to more countries than I can count. And we always did fun tourist stuff when we were there, even though I could tell Antoine hated all that shit. He took us anyway.

I tell myself he's not like a father to me, or a brother. And that's true. Because there isn't a word to describe how much Antoine means to me. Father just doesn't cut it because my father was such a bastard, I'd never saddle that moniker on the guy who literally saved me and my sister. Antoine is like… like a best friend more than anything else.

When the building renovations were finally over three years later, Elise and I grew accustomed to this life and forgot all about the violence and fear we left behind.

That's when Antoine enrolled me in Saint Margaret's for the end of eighth grade and I met Spencer. Ford was already in high school, so I didn't meet him until the next year when Spence and I started ninth grade. Antoine, Ellie, and I still traveled, but not as much. Things settled down little by little, and pretty soon Antoine was just... sorta famous. I'm not even sure how it happened. He was well-known in certain circles before this transition, but at some point he became someone you had to book a year in advance to get your fucking picture taken. That's when all this contract shit started. And that's when I started modeling seriously myself.

I'd been discovered way back in India. Everywhere we went someone wanted a picture with me in it because, well, I was a handsome fucking devil, what can I say? But when I was almost seventeen I was approached by big-name designers. Jeans at first, then underwear, then sportswear, and once I turned eighteen, some of the more tame erotic shit. Then the woman who was running the closet got pregnant and quit. So I was in. After that the FIRE contract came up and they wanted Clare and me to model together, but Clare opted for fashion and glamour contracts and signed with an agency that took her all over the world for the next two years. And she came back an anorexic addict. So the girl I ended up doing that FIRE contract with was Mardee.

Mardee.

You know when you see a group of guys and they have the token girl? The tomboy who they never see as a girl, so she gets a pass into their inner circle? Well, that was Mardee. The little sister in our con circle. Spence, Ford, and I were only doing stupid pranks back then, not the major hacking we did later. And we used Mardee for a shitload of small-time money-grabs. I liked her, sure. But Ford *really* liked her, and Mardee and I were a little bit drunk one night... so. Yeah. We did the drunk fuck and were too young to understand we were supposed to back away gracefully the next day. She wanted to give modeling a try and Antoine actually thought she was perfect so... the rest is history.

I've spent the last few years trying to understand all the mistakes I made that year, but even after all my recent hardcore introspection, I'm still not sure I could have changed things. I could've let Ford have her, but I'm not convinced she would've listened to him if he told her no modeling because the girl could only be described as a whirlwind. She blew into our little group and twisted us all up, then left all the damage in her wake.

And all four of us participated in it. It wasn't just her, it wasn't just me, or Spencer, or Ford. It was all of us. We got caught up in the shit and the shit kicked our asses.

Us guys share that regret and I suppose that's what keeps us so connected. Her death mixed with the knowledge of how much power we have as a team. How much damage we're actually capable of. Because after Mardee died, we wielded that power to the extreme for the better part of a year.

Until we conned the wrong guy.

The bathroom door opens and I drag myself out of the past. Elise comes back with red eyes and a sniffly nose. "What's wrong, Ellie?" I asks her softly. She drops down next to me and I wrap her up in my arms and pull her close. "You're just emotional because of the pregnancy. Don't cry."

She cries harder.

I should know better. When you tell a girl not to cry,

they really think you're telling them to go for it.

"Tell me," I say in French, because French is the language of Antoine and our charmed life with him. It's a reminder that we are good, and happy, and normal. "You can tell me, Elise. I'm a good listener."

"I'm gonna screw up this kid, Ronin," she replies in English. "I have no idea how to be a good mother."

"Oh, come on." I tsk my tongue at her. "You're just being silly now. And you know what?"

She looks up at me with her red and watery eyes. "What?"

"You did a pretty good job with me. You raised me since I was a baby. You changed my diapers and fed me and made sure I took baths and brushed my teeth. When people used to ask who my mother was when I was a kid, I'd always tell them you. It kinda freaked some people out once you got to be a teenager." She stops crying for a second and huffs out a half laugh. "You know exactly what to do with a baby because you've already done it with me. And barring that one near-grand jury indictment, I came out just fine."

She laughs for real now and I know I've won.

"You'd be a good father too, Ronin."

"Yeah, I really would." I kiss my sister on the head as she wipes her tears and settles down. "I'm looking forward to being a father, actually. And your new guy will be the perfect *petit garçon* to practice on."

We watch a bunch of *Vampire Diaries* shit for the next couple hours and she tells me the whole story, explaining every freaking detail of Stefan, Damon, Elena and what the fuck ever. I try to listen, but I'm too preoccupied with daydreams of baby girls who look like Rook to do more than give her an obligatory nod every once in a while.

CHAPTER EIGHTEEN

Rook

My life has gone from fast and fabulous to dead-ass boring in one week. Last week I was Rook, super naked model for Antoine Chaput and the human canvas for Spencer Shrike's amazing artwork. Now I'm a receptionist who has no idea how to subtract negative numbers and requires a paid tutor even though she is twenty fucking years old. The phone rings and I pick it up. "Good afternoon, Spencer Shrike Bikes, this is Rook, how can I help you?"

You see? This is my new life.

"Yes," I say back to the person on the line as I click through the bike production schedule on the computer. "We have a Skype conference scheduled for next Monday at ten thirty AM mountain time."

I make appointments. I pick up tailpipes from the chrome guy down in La Porte and painted frames from the body shop in Fort Collins. Sometimes, if my day is really exciting, I also swing by the upholsterer's shop in Loveland and grab a bike seat or two.

"Great, I'll call you five minutes before the meeting and we'll get your bike in production," I say enthusiastically to the guy on the other end of the phone. "Thanks!"

I hang up the phone and turn back to the shop. Ford's presence startles me because I didn't hear him walk over. "What's up?" I ask.

Ford's job here is still undefined. I'm not sure why he's on the show, let alone what his purpose is in Spencer's shop. But no one cares what I think. I'm a fucking receptionist now, so I have to make coffee, and take sandwich orders for all these men, and when we have person-to-person meetings with important people who are gonna be on the show—we've got famous bikers coming out of the fucking walls already and we've only taped two days—it's my job to flirt with them.

"I need to go to town. Need anything?"

"Do I need anything? Yeah, you know what I need? A life, that's what I need. Can you pick one up for me?"

Ford scowls at me. "Why are you such a bitch today?"

I sigh. "I have to take a test for math by tomorrow and I'm still confused. Plus, I'd like to go see Ronin early, but fucking Spencer has some guy coming in for the show, so they want me here until six tomorrow. So how am I supposed to get to Ronin's early if I'm stuck here until six and I have to take a test after?"

"Cheat on the test and tell Spence to fuck off." He shrugs, like that's the most stupid simple answer in the world.

"Cheat? That's real nice, Ford."

"That's why I hired that tutor in the first place, Rook. I never expected you to actually *learn* the shit. When he called Monday night and said you didn't want him to take the tests for you I was appalled by your morals."

I laugh a little. "I'm not against working the system, Ford. Seriously, I'm not some high-and-mighty moral fuck who looks down on people who take shortcuts or whatever. But if I am gonna screw up my karma with underhanded tactics, I'm gonna do it for a subject that is not pre-fucking-algebra, OK? I'm gonna do it for biology or the real algebra class I have to take next semester, the one that *counts*."

"OK, I see your point for that one, but you can still tell Spencer to fuck off."

I laugh again. "What are you getting in town?"

"An apartment."

"What? Why? You're gonna move out?"

He smiles coyly as his eyes dart around the shop. "No, not exactly. I just need a place. A place that's not here."

"Uh-huh. For that pet of yours?"

"No, I'm trying something different now."

"Get the fuck out of my reception area. I'm busy."

He walks out the front door laughing.

I shudder and try to get that image out of my head. I can't stand to think of Ford with these girls. It makes me sick. He knows this too, and I think he likes making me uncomfortable with the notion of his personal life.

Or maybe it's all in my head. Ford probably doesn't give one shit about what I think of him.

I check the clock and it's almost six, so I shut down the computer and clean up my desk so it looks presentable for the cameras. They're not here today, but they will be tomorrow because that important biker dude is taping his show. My phone buzzes just as I'm about to throw it in my purse and I read the text from Ronin.

Working late. Call you tomorrow.

I don't text back because that's the second time this week he said that and it's pissing me off.

This job sucks. The money is good, ten thousand

dollars an episode, but do I really need another hundred and twenty thousand dollars?

I shrug to myself. It's a lot of money to most people. Hell, it's a lot of money to me, but it doesn't mean much when I have plenty of money these days.

I slip on my Shrike Bikes leather jacket that Spencer had custom-made for my birthday, grab my purse and backpack, and peek around the wall that separates my area from the shop. They are all busy behind the glass, laughing and joking as they work. These fucking guys love their jobs. They stay until all hours—hell, they practically live here. I push the door open and the noise of men leaks out. "Hey, I'm taking off, Spencer. I have to meet my tutor, OK?"

All of them wave but only Spencer calls out a 'goodbye.'

Yup. I'm no one special here, that's for sure.

I walk up the driveway to my Shrike truck, throw my bag and purse onto the passenger seat, and climb in. I do love this truck, though. Although I'm careful not to speed on the road into town. That deputy who busted me for speeding is always on the lookout. I think he wants to date me though, not write a ticket.

I'd rather get the ticket. So I drive the fucking speed limit all the way into Fort Collins. And let me tell you this, living thirty minutes from town sucks. I hate it. La Porte is not very far, but that place has nothing, it might as well be Bellvue. It takes even longer to get to my community college because it's all the way on the south side of FoCo, so by the time I make it to the math building, grab all my shit, and haul myself across the parking lot, my tutor Gage is already waiting for me outside.

"We gotta go somewhere else tonight, Rook. Water

pipe broke and there's a massive clean-up going on in there."

Gage is kinda hot for a nerd. He doesn't have those stupid black glasses and he doesn't wear a pen protector in his pocket, but he's definitely a nerd. I know this because I asked him what he does on the weekends yesterday and he said study. He's in some special engineering department down at CU Boulder, not regular building stuff, but like robots or mechanical hearts or some shit like that.

"Well, where can we go? I'm not familiar with this area, Gage, sorry. You'll have to pick."

"There's a coffee shop with wireless down the street. We could go there."

"Great," I say as we make our way back to the parking lot. "I'll follow you."

I have a better parking spot than he does, so I reach my truck first. He eyeballs it with a weird look on his face as he walks past. Probably wondering what I'm doing with a Shrike Bikes vehicle. It's pretty conspicuous, this truck. I really need to buy a car of my own so I can blend in.

I pull the truck out and look around to see what he's driving. There's only one car on the move and that's an old-ass light blue Camaro. He waves at me to follow and we pull out.

The coffee shop is busy and loud when we walk in, but Gage points to the back where there's doors separating a section from the main room and a sign that says, *Study Area*.

We're the only people in there, but he picks a table in the corner to get away from the noise in the other room.

"OK, here's the deal. That guy who hired me for you called earlier and said you need to take that test tonight so you can leave town tomorrow. So we're gonna pull up the test, you can do it yourself, but if you have a question, I'll be here to answer it."

"That's cheating."

"It's an online math class, Rook. Everyone is cheating. It's open book, anyway. What's the difference?"

"I just don't want help. I'd rather you check my work that I did last night and explain where I went wrong. I'll take the test tomorrow night like I planned, my boyfriend down in Denver will wait and Ford can just butt the fuck out of my life. It's none of his business, and just because he's the one who pays you doesn't mean you have to listen to him. I can pay you myself, you know. I don't need his money."

Gage is staring at me with another weird look.

"What?" I ask.

He laughs. Like loud.

"What?"

"I knew it!"

"Knew what?"

"Ford? The guy who hired me is Ford Aston, isn't it?"

"Um, well, I don't actually know his last name but—"

"Rich, pretentious asshole?"

I laugh. "Yeah, that's him."

"And you drive a Shrike Bikes truck because you're working for Spencer Shrike?"

"Yeeeahhhh…"

"Please tell me the guy you're meeting in Denver tomorrow is not Ronin Flynn. *Please.*"

"Why?" My heart starts beating super-fast at the mention of Ronin's name. "He's my boyfriend, why?"

"Are you from here?"

"No, what's that got to do with anything?"

He shakes his head as he laughs, then huffs out a long breath of air. "Well, I'm sorry to be the one to tell you this, but your friends are bad fucking news. And if I were you, I'd get as far away from them as you possibly can because they committed a high-profile murder a couple years back and walked away free and clear on a technicality."

CHAPTER NINETEEN

Rook

I blow through the doors of Best Buy on College Ave on my way home from tutoring and before the greeter guy can ask me what I need I bark out, "Laptops?" I'm already moving down the aisle he's pointing to before he can get the words out. Back in computers another kid wants to help me so I manage to say, "The best laptop you have, *now*."

Ten minutes later I'm cruising back down College, my mind racing with wild imagery of my friends committing murder. I need to do some serious research and a phone browser just isn't cutting it. Hence the laptop purchase.

I played it cool with Gage earlier. "Oh, that," I snorted. "I know the inside story, it's nothing."

I'm pretty sure he saw through me because I'm a terrible liar, but it was all I had in me. My head was spinning the whole time. I told him I'd do the test tonight on his computer if he left me alone so I wasn't tempted to cheat. I did take the test, but I definitely failed. That's because the only thing on my mind was the fucking search page I pulled up and was glancing at on and off while I was trying to subtract negative numbers.

How the fuck did I never think to Google these guys? How? After all I've been through, how the hell did I not even once get curious?

Because Gage was not lying. I found an article almost immediately, but I didn't want to leave a search history on his computer, and I don't have my own computer at Spencer's, I just use his.

So manic shopping spree through Best Buy at eight forty-five PM was in order.

I do not even know how I got myself back to Spence's house, but here I am, sitting in the idling truck in the driveway.

The outside light goes on and Spencer peeks out the door. "Hey, comin' in or what?"

I turn the truck off and grab all my shit and go inside.

"What's all that?" Spence asks as I struggle with all the bags. I got an extra power cord and a battery and pretty much everything else the salesman said I needed just so I didn't have to fight with him about it.

"Just a computer, you know I should have my own, right? I'll need it for class." I smile and make my way towards the stairs. "Well, I'm beat and we have a big day tomorrow, so I'll see you in the AM. Night, Spencer!"

"Night, Blackbird," he calls out softly to me. It's like he knows. Something's off with me.

Shit, shit, shit.

But when I get downstairs to my apartment and look back, he's not following me, so I push through the door and dump all my shit on the new couch and then start tearing into the bags. An hour later my computer's up and running and connected to the house wireless.

I wonder if they can see my browsing history remotely?

I'm a paranoid freak because of Jon. But I don't have the patience. And besides, what would they do if I found out? I mean, seriously? They have to know that I'd stumble onto it eventually.

I plug their names into the search bar and I swear my heart skips when I see what the headlines actually say.

Brutal Slaying by Local Golden Boys

Boulder Seeks Grand Jury Indictment of Aston, Flynn, and Shrike

Golden Boys Walk!

I lean back on the couch after reading more than two dozen articles and let out a long breath. "Well, Rook. You sure can pick them."

What should I do? Should I leave? Should I confront Ronin? Should I ignore it?

I run through each one—it would be stupid to just leave. I could, I have plenty of money, but these guys have been very good to me. And Ronin's never lied about anything before. He told me all about Mardee and he admitted that they set Jon up. And I can't confront them. I'm not a confrontational person, it makes me sick, actually. I can't even imagine doing that.

So ignore it?

How? How can I ignore the fact that some millionaire businessman up in the Boulder hills was brutally killed a few years ago and my fucking boyfriend and his BFFs are the ones who were accused?

And the article says straight up the DA had the evidence but they couldn't use it in court because they obtained it illegally.

But this is Ronin, Rook. Do not overreact.

I clear my browser, cookies, and cache just in case.

Just in case what?

Shit, I'm doing it again! I'm acting like I was back in Chicago with Jon.

But I shut the computer down clean all the same, then

take it in my room with me as I sit on my bed.

The bed that Ronin purchased for me, along with all the other stuff in this apartment. It's way more than ten thousand dollars' worth of stuff. The TV, the surround sound, the furniture, the kitchenette supplies.

But he did lie to the police about Jon. And he was quite convincing. They left me alone all afternoon before asking for my statement. I didn't need to lie, actually. Everything I said in my statement was true. Ronin said he saw the threatening texts on my phone, but I never saw them, and that's what I said. But then Ronin was right there next to me, saying he hid them from me so I wouldn't get scared.

The cops never even blinked at his lie.

And Ford hired Gage to help me in math and enrolled me in college. He's been so good to me.

Actually, he hacked me into that college. Sure, I paid the fees and everything, and it's even out-of-state tuition because I haven't lived in Colorado for a year yet. But still, he cheated to get me in because I was supposed to take a test to see which classes I was eligible for, and I never did that. He faked my test scores because he's a super hacker genius or something. I'm not really one hundred percent sure what Ford is, I just know he can do that shit like Jon. Only better, because we won and Jon lost. And it was all because of Ford.

And Spencer is so nice. I've spent a lot of time with Spencer, very close and intimate time, and he was never anything but nice. I love the hell out of Spencer.

Of course, he does have guns stashed everywhere. Like *everywhere*. In the kitchen drawers, in the couch cushions, in the fucking towel cabinet in the upstairs bathroom. I found that one looking for washcloths last summer when I stayed up here on the weekends.

He's obsessed with guns. When he told me he stashes them everywhere and forgets them, he was not kidding. And he's got a huge safe down here on the other side of the basement where he says he keeps the 'good ones', whatever that means.

My phone buzzes inside my purse and I jump up to get it.

Ronin.

Sorry for being so busy this week, Gidge. I'll make it up to you tomorrow. Night, baby.

He's not a bad guy. He's not. I'd know. I mean, I was very discerning when we first met. I looked for signs and signals at every turn. I found them even when they weren't there. But still. Ronin has secrets. They all do. And I know nothing about them, really.

But what I do know is good.

This is a useless battle. I get up and run the water for a shower, then strip and get inside. I let the hot water beat the day off me and when I'm done, I feel warm and tired.

I'm gonna ignore it. I'm not gonna say anything because I have no idea if they're guilty but I do know there's no way I'm gonna ask them about it.

I do *not* want to know.

I don't. Period.

I'm ready to play dumb for a while and just let life move forward. These guys are not killers, they've done nothing but give me opportunities and love. So as long as I don't see anything weird, I'm gonna let it go.

I text Ronin back after I turn the lights out and climb into bed.

Miss you. See you tomorrow night! xxoo Rook

CHAPTER TWENTY

Ronin

The test shoots this week have been a nightmare. Total nightmare. These girls are so snooty and high-maintenance, I just want to drop-kick them.

I sigh as yet another one pouts and huffs over in the make-up salon. Elise is on hiatus with Antoine. Both of them hang around the periphery once in a while, but for the most part, Josie is in charge of the salon right now. And Josie is about to smack this girl, I can tell.

"Look," Josie snaps at the blonde with aquamarine eyes. "I might not *speak* French, you stupid bitch. But I certainly do understand it. So shut your—"

"Josie!" I call out to her just before she loses her temper. "Come here a sec, will ya?"

The model sneers as Josie walks over to me, straightening her black jacket a little. "Sorry, Ronin. But that girl—"

"I heard. Let me handle her, just start on the next one, OK? Send her over to Roger with no make-up or hair, let's see how much she enjoys that."

Josie peeks up at me through her dark bangs and smiles. "OK."

She walks away laughing and I watch the model's horrified face as she directs her hate over to me. I give the bitch a little wave of my hand and then point to a group of girls sitting at some tables near the kitchen, waiting their turns.

French blondie gets up with a breathy blow of air and makes her way towards me. *"Comment osez-vous?"*

I point to myself. "How dare I? Are you fucking kidding me? You're pretty, you're experienced, and you're here—that's about all you have going for you right now. If you want this job you'll be nice to my family. That woman over there"—I point to Josie who is already busy with another girl—"is like a sister to me. Do not piss her off."

Aqua Eyes looks me up and down for a few seconds, then turns away.

"Oh," I say, stopping her. "And no more French. Unless your last name is Chaput, it's fucking rude. Speak English when you're dealing with us or hit the road."

I forgot what bitches these outside girls are. The regular Chaput models are all pretty nice. At the very least, they all know the rules and one of them is that I don't put up with that catty princess bullshit. I've been spoiled working with Rook, she never pulls any of that crap. She's almost always polite, except with Ford, and she's not high maintenance at all.

She's perfect.

I wish she was my Gidget instead of all these girls.

I look back over to Barbie Bitch and she's pointing at me as she spouts off to Clare in French. I shake my head as Clare looks over at me.

Clare has certainly had her moments as far as temper tantrums go, but she's been a completely different person since she came home from the treatment facility. I watch carefully to see how she handles this.

She stays perfectly still as the model complains and

points to me and Josie in the salon. Clare replies in a soft voice and points to the front door.

Frenchy shoots me hate and I let out a small chuckle as I walk over to them, covering the distance in just a few paces, that's how long my pissed-off strides are. "That's it, I warned—" I stop talking just as my gaze finds the man standing at the front door. Tall, black suit, looks like the government.

I turn back to Clare. "Get rid of Aqua Bitch, OK? I've got a visitor."

Her gaze travels to the guy at the door and she looks back to me and swallows hard. "OK. Sorry, Océane, you're no longer needed. Thank you for—"

And I walk away as the bitch starts screaming in French and make my way over to the man at the door. "Can I help you?"

"Like racehorses, I guess, huh?"

"What?"

"High-strung, these girls."

We step aside as Clare pushes the girl past us and then follows her out into the stairwell and closes the door behind her. The screaming is still loud, but better than it was. "I'm sorry, let's start again. Can I help you?"

He smiles at me and I know immediately what this is.

"I'm looking for Ronin Flynn. That you?"

"And who might you be?"

"Agent Abelli, FBI." He flashes a badge, which I study quickly, then thrusts a little white card towards me, but I don't take it or even look at it.

"How can I help you, Agent Abelli?" My sincere con man voice takes over because I just punched the time clock. "I'm sort of in the middle of a model melt-down." I gesture to the door with my head then turn slightly and start walking towards Antoine's office. He follows like a good little chicken. What choice does he have? I'm walking away, he wants to talk to me, he has to follow. "So sorry about the theatrics. It's tough working with all these young women every day, right?" I give him a slimeball wink but his expression remains stoic.

I turn before the real grin pops through my facade and motion to a chair on the opposite side of Antoine's excessive desk and then I take the boss position behind the monstrosity, leaning back in my chair and kicking my feet up.

Abelli eyes the chair I pointed to and prefers to stand. "Mr. Flynn, I'd like to ask you some questions—"

"Oh, sure. I figured you guys would be around sooner or later." I stop to watch his confusion for a beat. "But I figured it'd be a lot sooner than this, to be honest. No matter, you're here now. What can I do you for, friend?"

Abelli narrows his eyes at me. I smile back at him. "Well, Mr. Flynn, I'm here on another matter, so—"

"Oh, Rook? Yeah, I've been telling her to get ready for this, ya know? She's so fragile. Testifying against Jon will be traumatic, I think. She might not make the best witness, but we gotta use what we have, am I right? Make sure that scumbag never hurts anyone else again." I stop to shake my head and look down for a moment. "What he did was so, so... so animalistic." I look up. "Ya know?"

Abelli clears his throat and tries again. "Actually, Mr. Flynn, we're here—"

"Ronin?" Clare says in a sweet voice as she belatedly knocks on the open door. "Sorry to interrupt, sir," she says, looking at Abelli. "But I need you, Ronin. Océane is gone, but there's another girl. I tried to screen them, but I think—" She stops to look at the agent.

"Go ahead, Clare, he's cool. You can say it."

"She's high, Ronin. We need to fire her, I think, and I don't want to be the one to—"

"No, I got it. One sec, sweetie." Clare leaves and I get back on my feet and walk over to the door, pause. "Well, sorry about being cut short, Agent… what was your name again? Maybe I should take a card?"

He takes a step towards me and I turn and walk back over to the front door, shaking my head at the screaming coming from the dressing room, look over my shoulder to see if Abelli is following—he is—and then pull the front door open and wait for him to catch up. He's got the little white card in his hand and I take that and put a hand on his back. "Sorry, I'm sorry you had to see this. We typically run a tight ship here, but…" I huff out a long exasperated breath. "You know, new blood always causes friction."

The screaming in the dressing room takes on a whole new level of crazy and I wince in that direction, then turn back to Abelli. "I gotta go, man, OK? Let me know if you need any help, any help at all. We gotta put that sick fuck behind bars for a long, long time, right?"

I clap him on the back of the shoulder and walk off towards the dressing room. I turn the corner, out of Abelli's sight and then start yelling in French as Clare slips past me to go make sure Abelli is gone. Inside the dressing room Josie is throwing a fit by herself. Screaming about drugs, and dieting, and the scale, and the clothes, and fuck all else. Pretty much everything she can think of. I try to calm her loudly until Clare comes back in and closes the dressing room doors.

"He's gone."

Josie skips past me, planting a kiss on my cheek as she goes, and then calls out, "You owe me a fat bonus for that performance, *brother*."

"Is it serious?" Clare asks as soon as Josie's gone.

I let out a long slow breath. "Maybe. He never got past hello, but he'll be back."

Clare and I go back out into the studio. She does her job herding the girls for their test shoots, me hassling Roger and generally being an asshole, like they expect me to. No one mentions my visitor, no one mentions the fact that Josie threw a fit and then came back to work like nothing happened. The day just moves on.

I'm not really avoiding the FBI, just laying a foundation on which I can build. I don't call Spencer or Ford because this has absolutely nothing to do with them. If Ford were to get pulled in for hacking he'd never tell me about it. So maybe he's already been questioned, I have no idea. And Spencer really has no tangible role in this latest job, not like the others. Rook filled in for him in this case, and she's clearly the victim, so I doubt they're hassling her.

But me, I'm the face. The front man. Which means they come to me first because I'm the one who's acting all in the know, right? I'm the talker, the amicable participant, the one who answers every question without fail.

That's the only job I have. To clean the shit up after the fan throws it all over the fucking place.

I'm not one hundred percent sure why Abelli was here, but I can take a good guess.

I suddenly want a cigarette very badly. I don't really smoke, but there are times when I want to. This is one of those times.

But I don't smoke. Because that's an indicator that I'm nervous about something. And I *cannot*—can-fucking-*not*—afford to deviate from normal now.

CHAPTER TWENTY-ONE

Rook

I smile the whole way down to Ronin's. Even though I absolutely did fail that math test last night and that fucker Gage did tell me my boyfriend and two of my besties all got away with murder, it doesn't touch me today because I know in my heart that these guys would never do that. Sure, they did some illegal things, but they did those things for *me*. Not to hurt people. They stole Jon's money because he tried to steal mine. They set him up with kiddie porn because he took advantage of me as a young adult.

And even though I am ultimately responsible for my own decisions and actions, there really *was* a point in my relationship with Jon when things stopped being my fault. I need to stop feeling responsible for what happened and Jon needs to accept the fact of what he did, what he made me do, and what I became.

Because there really *was* a point where I was stripped of all my choices.

And I think that it's OK to put all the blame on Jon for those parts.

So fuck it. I love Ronin. Ford and Spencer are my friends. And that's how it's gonna stay unless I get information that requires a one-eighty.

I ease the Shrike Bikes truck off the freeway and take Park down to the stadium, then turn onto Blake and pull into our garage. Ronin is kicking back on one of his motorcycles, talking on the phone as he waits for me. He's wearing old jeans, a black t-shirt, and his favorite black biker jacket. He waves as I pull in a few spaces down and then walks over to me as he ends the call. My eyes linger on his body as he approaches and I let out a sigh. God. This man is like my smile button. He appears and I smile.

I'm smiling right now.

I giggle a little at that and throw my arms around him, taking in his scent. He smells like Sexy Man. I'm not sure what that exactly is, but if sexy man smell has a dictionary entry, the picture next to it is Ronin Flynn. "Oh, my God—I missed you so much!"

He hugs me back and hums against the tender skin on my neck. "I think we should stay in the entire weekend."

I pull back with a serious expression on my face. "And do what?"

He grabs my backpack and purse from the seat, then closes the truck door and takes my hand. "Ah, my schoolgirl needs to learn some patience, I think." We take the elevator up and then he lets go of my hand and points to the dressing room. "There's a hanger with your name on it. Meet you upstairs."

I stand there as the heat creeps up my face, just watching his ass in the moonlight as he goes up the steps. "Chop, chop, Gidget. You'll be spanked if you're late."

My chuckle comes out automatically as I make my way into the dressing room. There's just one hanger on the rack and yup, sure enough, it's got my name on it.

I peek inside and smile. Boys and their Catholic

schoolgirl fantasies. He *went* to Catholic school, surely he must've gotten his fill?

I unzip the garment bag all the way and start pulling stuff out. There's a crisp white button-up blouse, a little red tie, a red-and-black tartan skirt, and some very naughty black lingerie that probably came from the GIDGET contract. The whole ensemble is completed with a pair of six-inch stilettos.

I'm already feelin' the heat down below.

I take it all over to the armless couches in the middle of the room and take off my clothes, tucking them back inside the garment bag. I line up each piece of lingerie and look it over real good. I'm not all that up on what does what, so this takes me a few minutes to figure out. I slide the black lace demi bra on and then the matching panties, garter, and stockings. I hook it all up, slip on the shoes, and check myself out in the mirror.

Not bad.

The schoolgirl stuff goes on next and by the time I'm all dressed, I'm a little sweaty and out of breath from all the anticipation.

Ronin and I do some roleplaying. Mostly that stupid cop stuff because I said I was checking to see if he was drunk when I got caught sniffing him back when we first met. It kinda stuck, and it's fun, but we both end up laughing too much to continue the fantasy. Maybe I'll try a little harder tonight.

I bite my lip as I exit the dressing room and climb the stairs to our apartment. I feel like I've been gone forever instead of just a week and my stomach gets a little flutter as I make my way down the hallway. I strain to listen for noise, but even Antoine and Elise's apartment is quiet. When I get to the door I take a deep breath and straighten my blouse a little, pulling it down a bit to reveal some of my goods.

I decide to start the roleplay with a knock. I hold my breath as the click of fancy shoes sounds behind the door and then it opens. Ronin is wearing a gray suit coat, some gray slacks, a long black tie, and no shirt.

"My, my, Mr. Flynn. You certainly look handsome tonight. I feel underdressed."

He waves me in. "If anything, Miss Corvus, you're overdressed."

I smile up at him and walk into the living room. We have no formal dining area, just a nook that connects the kitchen and the terrace sliders. But we do have a nice dark mahogany table and right now it's filled with flickering white candles. No other lights are on in the entire apartment, so the glow is soft and golden.

"Well," I say, turning to face Ronin, "there's no room on the table for food, so we must not be eating dinner."

He slides his hands around my waist and pulls my lower body tight against his, allowing my upper body to sway backwards slightly and pull the white shirt apart just the slightest bit. He peeks down and then finds my eyes. "Are you hungry for food?"

"No," I whisper as I lean forward and lay my head on his shoulder. "I'm hungry for you."

"How about dessert, then?"

"Mmmmm, maybe," I purr into his neck. "What do you have in mind?"

He leans down and kisses me softly on the lips. It's just a feather of a touch, just the slightest bare flutter of his lips against mine, just enough to create a spark of heat and then leave the cool emptiness as he pulls back. "I made a promise to you a while back and I figured it was time to make good."

"What promise?" I ask with a stupid grin, frantically racking my brain for what he might have in mind. Ronin is not an easy guy to predict, that's for sure. Whenever I think I know what he's doing, especially when it comes to the erotic photoshoots or sex, I'm almost always wrong.

I love this about him because it means he thinks about me. A lot.

Even over the summer when he was hesitant to get more adventurous with our lovemaking he always kept me on my toes with small things. A command to come before we climaxed together. A kiss in a totally unexpected place, like that dent behind my knee. Or hoisting me up against the wall of the shower, my legs wrapped tight around his middle—and then *not* fucking me, but instead talking me into an orgasm with the most amazing combination of words ever strung together in the French language.

Of course I didn't understand a single thing he said, he could've been reciting our grocery list for all I knew, but it totally got me off.

"Want me to show you?"

A shiver runs up my back as his fingertips slip around across my jawline and caress the nape of my neck.

"Please, yes."

He grins. "I love it when you say please." His fingers leave my neck, trace down my shoulder, then my ribs, and finally grab my hand. He laces us together and pulls me with him down the hallway towards the bedroom.

"Dessert is in the bedroom?" I giggle a little.

He looks back at me with half-hooded lids and simply nods.

Our bedroom is also lit up with candles, only in here they are all on tall candelabras. Some are placed on the dressers and tables so they reach halfway up the wall, the shadow of flames caressing the ceiling. Others are on the floor and light the dark hardwood below my feet.

On the nightstand is a bowl of cherries and a bottle of champagne in an ice bucket. Two flutes are already filled with golden bubbles.

"Yes, Mr. Flynn, this is definitely dessert." I look up at him and his blue eyes are sparkling in the candlelight. "Would you like to hear how I did on my math test?"

"No, I'm not at all interested in your grades tonight, Miss Corvus."

I cock an eyebrow at him. "You're not?" I look down at my schoolgirl outfit and then back up at him. He's not smiling. "Then what's with the outfit? I thought you had something to teach me?"

"I do," he says softly, pulling me towards him. "I'm going to teach you what it means to be loved by me."

And then his mouth takes over. Both hands cup my face, pulling me into him, then one slides behind my neck while the other slides over my throat, pauses to palm it and then falls to my breast and palms that as well. My hands slip to the front of his pants and his cock comes to life as soon as I glide my fingertips over it. He groans and then his hand removes mine. "Not yet," he breathes into my mouth.

I push him, making him take a few steps back, and he ends up against the wall, but he takes a step forward before I can do anything about it. "Maybe I'd like to call the shots tonight. Did you ever think of that?"

His eyebrows shoot up. "You can try."

I almost laugh, in fact, I huff out some air before I can stop it. When I look up at him he's grinning like the devil. I push him again and this time he lets himself settle against the wall, ready to see what I'll do. I slip my hands inside his suit coat and drag my fingers across the hills and valleys of his perfect abs, then up across his chest, stopping to rub his nipple. When I look up he's got his eyes closed and his head tilted back against the wall. He likes this. I slip the suit coat down over one shoulder with one hand and drag my other hand up and around his neck, pulling on him so he will lean down enough for me to kiss him.

He refuses, simply keeps his head pressed up against the wall. "You want to be in control, right?" He opens one eye and smiles. "Control me, then."

Oh fuck. The wetness slips out between my legs and suddenly everything is throbbing. "I *can*, you know."

This time he doesn't even open his eyes. "Tell me how."

I bite my bottom lip a little and think this through in the few seconds I have before I ruin the mood. "Well," I say, a little breathless. "I could do all the predictable things." I kneel down, my hands sliding down his chest and settling on his hips as I sit back on my butt. I watch his face the entire time. He doesn't open his eyes or make any detectable shift in position. "Like bury your cock in my mouth."

This makes him let out a breath and grin, but his eyes remain closed.

"But I'm not gonna do that."

He chuckles. "Tease."

I stand back up but my hands stay between his legs. I grab him and squeeze until he moans. I leave one hand there and then take his hand and place it over the buttons on my blouse. "Undress me, but keep your eyes closed."

His other hand comes up and he works the topmost

button free, but instead of unbuttoning the next one, he tugs the shirt out from my skirt and starts on the bottom ones. He releases each one until there is just a single button holding the two sides of my shirt together, the one right between my breasts.

"Do that one too," I command in a whisper.

Ronin ignores me and instead slides his hands around my hips and settles on the zipper running up my ass. His fingers linger there for a second, his eyes still closed, his breathing a little more labored now. His hands flip up my skirt and slip around the cheeks of my ass. He squeezes, slips his finger between my legs, finds the wetness, and smirks.

His eyes still closed, he says, "I think you're doing my job for me, Gidget. Stop turning yourself on." He plunges a finger inside and I gasp and my head falls back a little. Except for his hands, he remains motionless against the wall. "Are you still in control?"

"Absolutely," I say.

He laughs. "Is that right?" Before I know what's happening my skirt is unzipped and falling to the floor. I'm just coming to terms with that fact when the button of my blouse goes shooting across the room and my shirt joins my skirt. This time when I look up at his face his eyes are open.

I'm standing in my sexy lingerie while he's still got all his clothes on.

He laughs. "Good try, Gidget."

"I'm not done!"

He spins around and suddenly we've changed positions. I'm face first against the wall, my hands spread out above my head and his thigh between my legs, asking me to open for him. He presses his full erection against my ass, one hand caressing my thigh while the other plunges back into the crease between my legs. "Oh, I think you're about to come *un*done, Miss Corvus. I'm about to make sure of it." His breath is hot against my neck as the words come out and then his tongue is teasing my earlobe. The hand on my thigh presses against my skin, travels upward with the same firm pressure, and then rests on my breast. He squeezes hard now and I moan and pull away.

"Hold still now, Rook," he commands in a harsh voice as his fingers continue to probe me between my legs. His thumb finds my sweet spot and caresses tiny circles around it.

I exhale and push back against his chest because I'm having trouble getting enough air back inside my body, that's how ragged my breathing is. "Please," I whimper.

He pushes himself into me, forcing me against the wall. "Please what, babe?"

"Give me what I want."

"What do you want?" he whispers into my ear. "Tell me what you want."

"Make me come."

He pulls back, like all the way back, until he's no longer touching me. I look over my shoulder to see what he's doing.

"You're one crazy chick if you think you're gonna get off that easy."

"What do you mean?"

"'Make me come'—pfft. Gidget, I can make you come anytime I want. Tonight you're not gonna just come, babe. I'm gonna blow your fucking mind."

CHAPTER TWENTY-TWO

Ronin

I swear to God, her whole body blushes pink with my words and it takes all my self-control to keep from smiling.

This fucking girl. I just want to scoop her up and devour her.

I lace our fingers together and pull her away from the wall. She's suddenly very shy, her eyes avoiding my direct gaze, her head a little bowed. I lift her chin with a fingertip and then kiss her gently on the mouth. "I love it when you watch me."

She smiles, almost tips her chin back down in embarrassment, but corrects that action before she commits. She stares back at me. "What will you do now?"

I lead her to the center of the room, drop her hand, then sit down on the bed and lean back. "Take your clothes off, Rook." I unbutton my suit trousers and slip my hand in my pants. My gaze never leaves Rook's face. She watches everything I do and when I grab myself she takes in a short quick breath, then looks me in the eyes and slides her hand down her hip until her fingertips reach the first clasp on the garter. In seconds, all those straps are hanging loose and she wiggles the thin band of lacy fabric over her curvy hips and it drops to the floor.

She steps out of the little circle and sticks one leg out in front and bends the other so she can lean over and roll her stocking down. When she gets it to the ankle she steps forward and places her foot on my thigh.

I accept her invitation and slide the stocking off with her stiletto. They join the garter on the floor, a small pile beginning to form.

She repeats this and then my heart starts to beat wildly as she slides the straps of the sheer black teddy down her shoulders. Her nipples are bunched up and hard and her breasts push against the fabric as she wiggles it free from her body.

And then she takes my hand and places it on the string of her panties.

But I take her hand and place it between her legs. "You love it when I watch you, too."

Her fingertips start a slow circle over her slit and then push against the fabric of her panties. And I swear, I swear to fucking God, I have to reach out and make her stop or I'll lose it.

Her eyes rest on mine and she smiles.

She wins this one.

"Take them off, please," she says sweetly as she pulls the string against her hip, then releases it, making it snap against her skin.

A guttural growl escapes from my throat as I tug her panties down and let them drop to the floor. She stands naked before me. "Now what?"

I stand up and undress myself slowly. Her eyes never leave my hands. Her gaze follows my suit coat as I drape it over a chair then returns to me in time to catch me removing the tie from around my neck.

Her little Gidget tongue darts out, wets her lips, and

then she takes a deep breath that makes her chest expand and lift up her breasts. My dick is so hard it's holding up the damn trousers and it takes me a second to free myself from the pants.

"Now, the shower," I finally answer her.

She tilts her head and smiles. "I thought shower sex was boring?"

"Who said anything about sex?"

She cocks an eyebrow at me. "I'm listening…"

"Follow me, Gidget." I take her across the hall to the bathroom and flick my fingers across the control panel to bring up the steam and a light drizzle. This is my favorite setting, the setting I always use when we're about to get busy in the shower. When I look back at her she's biting her lip. "What?" I ask.

"Looks pretty boring so far."

I laugh. "Is that right?" I take her inside the shower and gently push her until the backs of her knees hit the tiled bench at the far end of the stall. "Have a seat," I say in a whisper. She smirks at me, like she knows what's going on. But her expression falters when I look over my shoulder as I walk out of the shower and open a small built-in cupboard on the other side of the bathroom. I pull out a brand-new lady razor, the kind with all that soapy shit attached directly to the blade, and snap it on the handle.

"What are you doing?" Rook asks as I kneel down in front of her.

"What's it look like I'm doing?" I press against her inner thighs and open her legs up and then palm the light covering of hair between her legs and tickle her until she squirms.

She chews on her lips, trying to chase her blushing

smile away. "But you told me to let it grow out after the body painting."

"I did."

"Why?"

"So I could shave it off." I grab her hair conditioner off the shelf and squirt some on the tips of my fingers and gently cover the little strip between her legs. I don't check her expression again, but I know exactly what it looks like based on her breathing. I start at the top of her hairline and use long strokes to shave her smooth. I want to rub my whole hand over the skin there, but I'm trying to keep her from coming as long as I can, and that would definitely work against me.

When I finish with the easy parts I grab her ankles and lift them up next to her hips so her feet are flat on the bench and I have access to the hidden parts. I take a lot more time in this area and I have to stop periodically to allow her to calm down from my touches. It's inevitable that my fingers will drive her crazy. I mean, they are *my* fingers, right? I wink at her after I finish this thought. She's too busy squirming to notice.

When I'm finished she's a panting mess, her back slightly arched, her head tilting back a bit, and small whimpers escaping her mouth. I spray her gently with the shower head and then sit back and enjoy my handiwork.

She opens her eyes. "Now what?" she asks softly.

"You can come now, babe."

"Touch me, Ronin," she begs.

I shake my head. "Sorry, no can do, Gidget. But I'll let you watch as I touch myself and let's just see if that's enough to get you started." I reach down and grab my dick and start pumping. Slow and long strokes.

Her mouth falls open, then closes a little as her eyes

lower to watch my hand. She bites her lip again, but this time it's not to try to maintain control. I pump a little faster and that makes her breathe out a seductively long moan and close her eyes.

"Watch me, Rook," I command. She opens her eyes but she only manages half-mast.

My plan was to make her come without touching her. I've done it before, but my tongue is far too eager to taste her newly smooth skin. She knows I'm about to cave and she wiggles a little, one foot dropping down to rest on my thigh, the other propped up on my shoulder like an invitation that I am powerless to refuse. I slide a finger inside her and pump with the same rhythm I'm using on myself. Her whole body tenses up, her back in a severe arch and her head pressing back against the tiled wall. I sink my tongue into her folds, flick against her clit, and we explode together—our moans echoing off the tiled bathroom walls.

We sit still for a few moments to enjoy the aftershocks, but then I get to my feet and pull her up with me. "OK, I think we're ready to get started."

She laughs as I lead her out into the bathroom, shut off the shower, and then grab a fluffy white towel and pat her down. I towel myself down a little as well, and then lead her back into the bedroom. "Lie down for me."

She obeys, taking herself over to the king-size bed we share. Everything in this room is white except for the furniture and the floors. Those are both a dark mahogany wood. The soft flicker of candlelight makes her look like a goddess as she lies there, complacent and happy, wet and pink with the heat of the shower and her desire. I stand next to the bed and grab a cherry, then straddle her legs and lean down to touch the cherry to her lips. "Bite, please," I ask softly.

These cherries came straight from the fruit basket on Antoine's desk this morning. And even though it's a little late in the year for cherries, they are soft and plump because all the fruit that comes in a basket to Chaput Studios is succulent and sweet and perfect. Just like my Rook. Her teeth sink into the flesh and she pulls back, chewing.

I take the other half and bite out the pit, whoof it into the waste basket near the nightstand, and then paint the juice around her mouth. "I told you, back when we did that first photoshoot, that if I had you naked with cherries, I'd drip it all down your belly and lick it off."

Her seductive smile lets me know she's remembering our first erotic shoot together.

"But before I do that…" I eat this cherry, then grab another one and put it up to her mouth. She bites, again leaving the pit for me. I whoof it and drag the fruit around the rosy areola in the center of her breast, making her nipple bunch up tight from the cold. The cherry turns her pale skin a deep red and I almost want to explode, that's how hard this makes me. "I'm gonna do this." My mouth covers her nipple and I lick the juice, then squeeze more, and lick it again. I do it all again on her other breast and when I'm finally ready to start on her belly, she's all stained up with red juice.

I move down her abdomen, kissing her gently as I go, dragging my scratchy face along her sensitive skin, and then grab a whole handful of cherries and place them on the pristine white sheets next to me. It's gonna stain the fuck out of them, but that's the price you pay when you wanna have fun with fruit.

I bite and drip, bite and drip, then do it several more

times until the little concave dip of her stomach is holding a pool of sweet nectar and her adorable belly button is overflowing. I push a fingertip into the liquid and drag it down towards her slit, stopping to let the juice collect in her folds. I repeat this until the red is diluted pink with her own wetness.

And then my tongue takes over. I eat her out like I'm starving for her sweetness, like I didn't just take her in the bathroom twenty minutes ago, like this is my last chance to ever pleasure a woman between her legs with my mouth.

She moans, she whines, she whimpers. Her whole back buckles up, cherry juice drips down her body, dirty words are coming out of her mouth, and she starts fighting to get her chance to show me what *her* mouth can do to pleasure me back.

But I don't let her up. I keep her there, at my mercy, holding her down and begging for more.

I blow her fucking mind with my tongue and fingers. I make her whimper and moan, squeal and fight when it gets too intense.

And then I fuck the shit out of her until we are exhausted and the hazy light of predawn is seeping through the blinds.

CHAPTER TWENTY-THREE

Ronin

I wish I could say we enjoyed all the hundreds of things there are to do in Colorado on Saturday. Like went up to the mountains and marveled at the fluttering golden wave created by the thousands upon thousands of aspen trees that line the cliffs. Or took advantage of an early mountain snowstorm and went skiing up at A-Basin. Or hell, stayed in town and caught an Aves game.

But we did none of those things. Because we never got out of bed.

She's still fucking trying to sleep right now and it's almost eleven on Sunday. "Gidget," I whisper into her ear. She swats me away with her hand, slapping my arm pretty good. "Gidge, we're putting clothes on today, babe. Like it or not, we're leaving the house."

"To go where?" she moans.

"The mall. Elise wants us to go baby shopping with her."

Rook grunts. "She does not. That's dumb, why would she want us to tag along?"

Damn, she's sorta cynical. And she's totally on to me because Antoine begged me to come with him so he and I can nurse some beers and watch the Broncos annihilate the Eagles while the girls shop. But I'm pretty good at faking shit, so I try it out on Rook now. "Serious, she says she wants my opinion, she knows I'm all into this baby shit. And you need some girl time, you have no girlfriends."

She turns this time, her mouth all screwed up. "Is *Clare* gonna be there?"

"Uh, well, yeah. She's really not allowed to go anywhere alone these days. She's gotta be with one of us at all times."

"You look guilty, are you lying to me?"

"Gidget, I am nothing if not honest with you, babe. Seriously. Elise wants you to come, I swear." That's not a lie. Elise does want Rook to come. She has fully accepted the fact that I plan on marrying this girl as soon as she's ready to commit.

It takes me another hour to get Rook up and ready and by that time Clare, Elise, and Antoine are already heading out to the restaurant where we're gonna have lunch. "You look great, let's go." I jingle my truck keys at her from the front hallway, but she ignores me and just sits calmly on the couch and laces up some black work boots. Combined with her faded and ripped jeans, white t-shirt, and Shrike Bikes leather jacket, they make her look like a hot punk chick.

If we don't get out of this fucking apartment soon I might have to jump her bones.

She catches my daydream and says, "I'm sore as shit, so stop with the *I wanna fuck you* looks."

She walks over to me as she straightens out her jacket and I take her hand and lead her out the door and down the hallway. There's some commotion downstairs in the studio and when we turn the corner at the stairs, Roger is messing with a large flat package. "What's that?" I call down to him as we descend.

"That rush job for the GIDGET campaign."

It takes me a second to figure out what he's talking about and by that time it's too late. He's already ripped the brown paper off the frame and his head is tilting to the side a little as he critiques the image.

Busted.

"What the hell is *that*?" Rook asks in a huff.

She can clearly see what it is, a fucking life-sized picture of me sticking my tongue down Clare's throat, but I usher her past in a hurry. "It's an old photo the GIDGET people wanted to use for promo. We had it blown up so we can use it for the shoots this week."

Even though she's walking away from it, her eyes never leave the image. I whisk her into the stairwell and pull her out of range. "Hmmm…" is all she says.

I change the subject. "Hungry?"

"Yeah, actually I'm starving."

She chats about lunch after that. Maybe the image is still on her mind and maybe it's not, but she's dropped it for now and that's about as much as I can ask for.

The ride down to Cherry Creek Mall is uneventful beyond getting stuck in construction traffic, and by the time we make it to the sports bar at the mall, I'm starving as well. Antoine already got us a table and Elise is chowing down on fried cheese. Rook looks happy though, so maybe she's gonna let the picture drop.

It's not my fault, really. The image had to be used. I never told Rook this, but Clare was always my first pick for this contract. And we did a lot of promo stuff together to show them that I had a vision and could handle something this big on my own. That was almost a year ago now, and honestly, it never occurred to me that they'd want me to model for them. I'm the marketing manager for the campaign, I never signed anything saying I'd model. And they are certainly not paying me enough to fuck things up with Rook over some pictures. But this one was already a done deal. I had very little room since it was submitted with the project bid.

Luckily Antoine got us a table near the flat screen on the wall that's blaring the game, so he and I concentrate on that while the girls chat. I look over at Rook a few times to see how she's doing with Clare, but it doesn't seem to be an issue.

Maybe I'll get away with this fuck-up after all?

CHAPTER TWENTY-FOUR

Rook

"Adorable!" I squeal as Elise holds up a tiny blue onesie with light green sea turtles swimming across the front. It is cute but honestly, how many freaking onesies can you look at in one day and still get excited? She throws it into the waiting hands of the Gymboree sales person and continues sorting through racks of clothes. Clare is much better at this shopping stuff than I am. I'm not against shopping, I just prefer to do it online. Or have a set plan in mind when I go in. For me, shopping is more like a military exercise—get in, complete the mission, get out. Bam. Now you have the whole rest of your day to kiss your boyfriend, or eat, or watch movies.

"Hey, since we're out, you guys wanna catch that new SF flick over at the Metroplex?"

Clare sneers at me.

I hate that bitch, I swear. I'm not really a hater, I mean I can typically find the good in just about anyone. And I'm definitely not a fighter. I prefer the whole cheek-turning thing over fists any day. But I tell you what, I'd like to slap the shit out of Clare. She is the biggest fucking kiss-ass on the planet. And she blatantly flirted with Ronin all through lunch and then had the nerve to insult my choice in food.

She called me a boring date because I always get the

hamburger. So I like burgers? Just because she likes weird stuff like mushroom pecan fajitas doesn't mean she's not boring. Seriously, she can't even go anywhere alone because the heroin might jump her ass and turn her back into a junkie...

OK, I went a little overboard on that one. But shit.

I huff out a long breath and busy myself shaking a baby rattle. "Hey, Elise? I'm gonna just pop over to the..." I squint out at the store across the way from Gymboree and read the sign. "Brookstone." Yeah, that's a much better store. They have cool shit in there. "I need some overpriced gadgets."

"Rook, if you're not going to help, just go back to the restaurant and watch football with the men, OK? This is a big deal for Elise."

"Rook," Elise counters, "I'm almost done, OK? Then we'll go upstairs and do grownup shopping. The guys said they'll meet us over at the baby crib store at five, so we have plenty of time."

I smile and nod. Great, crib shopping. I'm not into thinking about this baby stuff, let alone shopping for one, and it just reminds me of how different Ronin and I really are when it comes to long-term plans. I might like a kid someday, and that's a big maybe. But right now I'm all about *not* having a kid. I'm not ready for crib shopping, even if it isn't for me.

We spend the next fifteen minutes checking out and then make our way upstairs to the cool level of the mall. At least there are stores here I recognize, if only because I have clothes in my closets with these names on them. Clare heads to Lucky Jeans and I follow her in while Elise rests her feet outside the store and pokes through her bags of baby clothes.

"What size are you, Rook? I'll help you choose."

"Noneya, Clare. I'm not an infant, I can pick out my own jeans." Fuck, she is such a bitch. How can Ronin even like her as a person? And I can only imagine how unlikeable she was as an addict. I flip through some jeans laid out on a table and then decide this is stupid. "I don't need any clothes, I'm going to sit with Elise."

I walk out before she can answer and plop down next to Elise on her bench. "I'm sorry, Elise. I'm just not a shopper."

She pats my hand like a mother. "I don't care, Rook. And don't let Clare get to you. She's just high-maintenance all the time. Isn't there anything you need while we're here? You might as well pick up something."

"I could use some lotion, now that I think of it."

"Oh!" Elise squeals. "Let's hit the Crabtree & Evelyn store, it's just right over there."

Lotions I can handle. Just pick out some that smell good and pay. No need to try things on or make it match your socks—just good old-fashioned plunk-it-in-the-basket-and-pay-up-front shopping. Elise calls out to Clare as we walk past, telling her where we'll be.

"So, Rook, how are things up with Spencer and Ford? I haven't had a chance to talk to you in weeks, it seems."

"Pretty good. The job is painfully boring, you know, compared to what I was doing. But it's OK. I'm good with slipping back into regular life."

"And school?"

"Well, I don't know. I like it, and I really like the idea of going to film school. But it's a lot of work, ya know?"

She laughs. "I never went to college, so actually, I'm not a good one to ask."

"No? How'd that happened? I mean, Ronin got an

excellent education, so I just figured you did as well."

"I was already grown up when I met Antoine. I did go to beauty school eventually. At first I was just Antoine's personal make-up person and he showed me what to do. But when we finally settled down in the States I had to get a license. Antoine and I wanted Ronin to have all the opportunities I never did, so we always made education a big deal."

"Maybe not everyone is cut out for a college degree?"

Elise stares hard at me as we enter the store. "Are you having doubts?"

I shrug and pick up a bottle of lotion and sniff it. "Some, maybe. It's hard. I'm not very good at it, Elise. I'm terrible at math and the science is interesting, but I have to memorize a bunch of stuff. It's just... hard."

"Everything worth getting is hard, Rook. You gotta want it real bad, right? Like Antoine, for instance. He actually comes from a pretty wealthy family in France and they had a lot of preconceived expectations for his life. Things Antoine was not remotely interested in doing. They have a big construction business over there, major contracts all over Europe. But my Antoine decided to come to America. He had money for school but not much else, and he came here to study photography and now look at him." Elise stops to smile as she thinks about her incredible baby daddy. "He fought for his dream, Rook. My dream was to make sure Ronin turned into a good guy so that's what I fought for. And Ronin *is* a good guy, so I'm happy that I made that dream come true. Now I want my own family so I'm gonna fight for that. And if you want to get your college degree, then that's your fight."

I think about this for a few seconds as we continue to browse the lotions. "But—what if I'm fighting for the wrong thing? What if I just like the *idea* of film school and I'm not dedicated to putting in the years of hard work to make it real? What's that mean?"

"Not everyone who loves taking pictures wants to be Antoine. Not everyone who wants to putter around with a video camera needs to make blockbusters. Maybe movies are a hobby? I'm not sure, so don't take what I'm saying as gospel, OK? Because only you can figure out if it's worth it."

"Ronin wants to fight for a family too, Elise. He's so, so serious about that and I'm not sure if I feel the same way."

She sighs up at me, silent for a moment. "Not all families are bad, Rook. I did my best to make sure Ronin understood this as he grew up, but I think you need to hear it more than he ever did. Not all families are bad. Some people get stuck with bad parents, or they have a failed marriage because they ended up with the wrong partner. That's just how things shake out sometimes. But not everyone's life is like that. It took me twelve years of unconditional love from Antoine to understand this myself. So you know, if I can save you from wasting all that time doubting yourself and what you and Ronin have together, then that's a huge win for all of us. He's moving too fast for you, I get that. But he'll wait, Rook. And if you love him and can see a future for the two of you, then let him have his dream while he waits. Because Ronin just wants to put down some roots. Even though we've called Antoine's place home for more than a decade, we've always been pretty transient. He just wants to plant himself somewhere and let out a long breath of relief that this life is permanent now."

Wow, I should've talked to Elise a long time ago

about this stuff. She's like a walking reality check. "Thanks," I say as I hug her.

"Hey!" Clare calls from outside the store. "Look! It's Ronin and me!"

Elise and I are both confused for a moment, but as soon as we walk outside and direct our eyeballs across the mall where Clare is pointing, we both get it.

Because right there in the front window of the lingerie shop is a giant poster of Clare and Ronin and he has his hands all over her body and his tongue down her throat.

And this is definitely *not* the picture I saw back at the studio.

"When did you take that?" I ask.

"Oh, this one…" She stops to think.

"Last fall," Elise offers. "That was taken last fall. When Ronin was getting ready to bid on this GIDGET contract. He put together a whole fake campaign with Clare."

"Yeah, that one was a while ago, but those GIDGET people liked it so much, they had us do another shoot this week. I think the proof was getting delivered from the printer today. Did you see it when you left, Rook?"

She bats her eyelashes at me. Clearly she knows I did. "No," I answer, shaking my head. "Never saw anything." She scowls at me, not sure if I'm lying or not, not willing to push things in front of Elise. I smile back at her, playing it off.

But inside, I'm seething. That fucker. Mr. I'm-nothing-if-not-honest fucking lied to me!

CHAPTER TWENTY-FIVE

Ronin

I tug Rook into my chest and wrap my arms round her. "How about this one?" I point to the white crib with a sleigh bed shape to it. "It's sorta classic, right?" She glances over her shoulder and gives me a dirty look. I know she hates this but I can't help myself. "What? What's that face for?"

"Nothing," she replies with an annoyed growl.

Something's up but I'm just not sure what it is yet. Something happened when she went shopping with the girls but she's not acting mad. Just not happy either. I'd ask Elise, but she's way too into this crib-buying stuff. Hell, even Antoine is into it. He's all for the white cribs too, but Elise wants something dark. Apparently she has a vision of what her little boy's room should look like and nothing will deter her.

And there's no way I'm bringing Clare in because that would just make everything worse. In fact, I'm pretty fucking sure whatever did happen at the mall, Clare is the reason. I pull Rook over to the crib bedding and point down to a baseball-themed set inside the crib. "I'd pick that one."

"Yeah, that's nice."

Well, at least she didn't growl. "You wanna get out of

here?"

Suddenly she's interested. "Really? But what about Elise?"

"She's got it under control. Hey, Ellie! We're taking off, see you guys later, OK?"

And that's that. I lead Rook out of the store and swing her hand as we walk to the truck.

The drive home only takes about ten minutes, but it's ten minutes of silent hell. I know we have to talk about it, but since she's in no hurry to bring it up, well, then neither am I. I turn the truck off in the garage and then look over at her. She's fucking with her phone—doing what, I'm not sure, because the only people she really texts are me, Spencer, or Ford and I'm pretty sure she's not having some deep convo with Ford or Spencer while she sits in my truck. "OK, what's up, Rook? Obviously something is wrong and it's got my name written all over it. So let's just get it out in the open."

She flips the handle on her door and jumps out, leaving me no choice but to follow her over to the elevator. The ride up is slow and silent and never in my life have I wished for an instrumental version of *Hey Jude* to be playing in an elevator more than I do right now. Anything to break the uncomfortable silence. When the door finally opens she walks out, but instead of taking a left to head towards the stairs, she walks out into the center of the studio and stands in front of that big promo picture of Clare and me.

"OK, this is the problem?" I ask as I wave my hand towards the poster.

Rook holds up her phone and there's another picture of Clare and me on the screen. "Do you know where I took this pic, Ronin?"

I take the phone from her and look a little closer. "Shit."

"Yeah, shit. You lied to me. This picture," she says, snatching the phone back, "was the one you guys took last year and it's on display at the fucking mall. This one," she says, jacking her thumb behind her to the poster, "was a rush job shot last week. At least, that's what *Clare* tells me. So would you like to explain why you lied?"

"Well, I'm busted, what do you want me to say?"

She gasps. "Uh, how about 'sorry?' Jesus fucking Christ, Ronin. I mean, look, I'm not gonna throw a fit or some shit like that, but fuck, I hate liars. Seriously cannot fucking stand liars. OK? I like the truth, thank you. I enjoy knowing what the fuck is going on, and I thought I could trust you."

"I didn't do anything more with Clare than you did with Spencer or Billy, Rook. It was one fucking shoot. They wanted an updated image now that Clare is back to being healthy, that's all there is to it."

She walks away. Just heads to the stairs and starts hoofing it up to the apartment. I catch up with her at the top, just as she's about to turn the corner, and grab her arm. She pulls away so hard she stumbles backwards. "You're walking away again, Gidget. I'm not gonna let you do that."

She pushes past me and stops at our apartment door. "Like you can stop me?"

"So you're walking out over this lie? This one stupid, meaningless lie?"

"First of all, it's not meaningless. Maybe it's not Earth-shattering, but it's not meaningless. Because relationships are all about trust and now I'm having doubts."

"Welcome to my world."

She snorts. "Welcome to *your world*? So you're having doubts about *me*? Then just break it off if I'm not the girl you want. I'm clearly not what you're into, Ronin. I mean what the fuck was all this baby shit today?"

"This was about Elise, not us."

"No? You know I'm not ready to think about this shit and you don't even care! You have no idea how fucking confusing it is to be around Elise right now. To watch all you guys get excited over this baby and have to feel... *nothing*. I can't feel anything, OK? And all you guys are gushing about cribs and stupid outfits and baby bedding, for fuck's sake!"

Well, that's not what I was expecting. "So this isn't about the photoshoot I did with Clare last week?"

She sighs. "Yes, of course it is!"

"I'm officially confused."

"Forget it, OK? I'm not gonna throw a temper tantrum and start a huge fight over it, so just forget it. You just do your thing and don't worry about me and I'll do the same. How's that?"

She reaches over to punch the code in the door and I grab her wrist and pull it away. "Hold on," I say calmly and wait for her to look me in the eye. "I'm not even worth an argument? Really? You just want to get as far away from me as you can right now so you can avoid... what? *Dealing*?"

She laughs. "Oh, I'm not dramatic enough? Is that it? You want me to fight with you?"

"No," I say gently as I lower her hand and bring it to my waist, forcing her to touch me. "I want you to fight for *us*, Rook. You never want to fight for *us*, you just want to walk away whenever it gets hard. And dammit, this is not hard, Rook. This life we're living right now is fucking paradise. So how will you act when the shit gets out of control? Will you just leave me when I need you most? Because I'd never leave you. I hope you know that, Rook. I'd *never* walk out. I'd fight for you every single time. You'd never even have to wonder if I'd be there because I'd show the fuck up before that thought could ever cross your mind. I want you, I'd risk everything for you. I already told you I'd wait. Whatever it takes, however long it takes. I'm still gonna be here. I do want babies, I do want you as my wife, but I can live with a promise."

She swallows and looks down. I take her other hand and press it against my waist so she has to turn and face me.

"What I can't live with is you sabotaging our relationship every time you feel uncomfortable. Eventually, you're gonna have to fucking figure this shit out. Because the thought of you walking out on me just tears me up."

And then I take her purse off her shoulder and drop it on the floor so I can slip my arms around her and pull her close. "I'm sorry about the Clare shit. I'm sorry that I lied earlier. I just didn't want to talk about it right then, that's all. I was stalling for time. Of course I was gonna tell you, but it's sort of a long story and I didn't want to tell it right then."

She leans her head into me and I play with her hair a little as I talk. "Stop with the Clare jealousy, OK? I know she's irritating, I realize she's probably baiting you to piss you off, but I'm not interested in her. At all. She's living in a fantasy and I'll set her straight tonight and let you watch if you want. Because I have no problem fighting for us. None."

Rook stays silent for a few seconds and relaxes against me a little more. I sigh as she begins to speak softly. "I was pissed about the Clare thing because she knew I didn't know and it makes me feel so stupid. I felt so foolish that she knew you were keeping a secret from me. And I'm not a very confrontational person so my first reaction is always to run away. I know that. I get it. I'm just not sure how much I can do about it. When I get scared, I run. And so much about you—about us—scares me. It makes me want to just give up so I don't have to deal with it."

I tilt her chin up gently so she looks me in the eye. She fights it for a second, then relents when she realizes I'm not gonna let her get away with it. "I really don't need much, babe. Just make me feel that I'm worth something. That you'll take a risk on us, like you said on the phone the night I dropped you off at Spencer's. I just want to know that when things start to look hopeless you'll still be willing to show up and give it your best, ya know? At the very least, be willing to put in an appearance. I mean, I'd love it if you just stuck to me no matter what for everything, but seriously, I'd settle for a half-hearted try right now."

She pushes her head into my chest. "So you want me to be your Shrek?"

I can't help it, I bellow out a laugh. "What?"

"You know? When Shrek is rescuing Fiona—"

"Does it always come back to a movie with you?"

"—and he chains up that bitchy dragon named *Clare*—"

"You are too much…"

"—and breaks Fiona out of the tower. You want me to be Shrek and fight for you, get you out of that stupid tower, fine. I'll work on it."

"I'm pretty sure I'm Shrek and you're Fiona, Rook. I let you make me be Larue, but I draw the line at Fiona."

"Whatever."

I cup her face in my hands and plant a little kiss on her lips. "I love the fuck out of you, ya know that, right?"

"Now all we need is a donkey to get Clare pregnant so she'll stop braying at us. I vote for Billy."

Oh, God. I just want to squeeze her, that's how cute she is. Just squeeze her until she admits she'll never leave me. Because even if she doubts herself, I have total faith in this girl. I know she loves me. I know she'll stick. Ford was wrong, she's not gonna check out, she's in—I can feel the truth just as well as I can tell a lie. She loves me, regardless of the nightmare past that still seems to be haunting her. I lean in and kiss her again, whispering into her little Gidget mouth. "I'm sorry I lied to you and did a shoot with Clare without telling you first."

She looks up at me now, pausing to smile. "I'm sorry I threatened to run away and I'll make an effort to fight with you more."

I chuckle again. She's adorable. Everything about her squeals *perfect*. "I would like to marry you, stick you in a kitchen and get you all barefoot and pregnant. But I'll wait. I'm not in a hurry, I'm enjoying every second we spend together. I'm really not trying to pressure you with the baby talk."

Her sigh is actually a long low moan that comes off mournful. "I think you are, but it's OK. I'll learn to deal."

"Hey," I say softly as I tip her chin up. "You don't need to learn to deal with me, Rook. You got something inside that head of yours you need to get out? What's going on with the baby stuff?"

She pulls back and turns away. Not a good sign.

"I just..." She looks at me over her shoulder and then lifts her eyes to meet mine. "I'm not ready yet, OK? I told you some of what happened that last time Jon went off on me, how he found the birth control and why I felt I needed it. But there's more to it." She takes a long breath, holds it, and then lets it out slowly. "But I'm not ready to think about it yet."

Her chest expands suddenly and I know she's about to cry. I reach out and turn her around as I pull her into me. "Hey, it's OK. You don't have to talk about it." She shakes a little as she sobs and all I can do is hold her tight. "Shhh," I murmur next to her ear as she tries to stop. And then I stop trying to quiet her because there's something I've noticed about Rook over the past few months. She hardly ever cries over her past. She cries when she's frustrated about things between us and she cried pretty hard that day she found out about the missing person's report, but really, she should maybe cry a little more. She holds things in until it boils over.

So I just hug her tight and kiss her head and try to say something soft and soothing. "Don't panic, Gidget. Be still and stay calm. We'll be OK, I promise. Just keep calm and it will all work out."

And she spends the next few minutes with her face buried in my jacket letting it out in her own way.

Ford said she's got more secrets, but I figured that was about her relationship with Jon. I think this is something else, because this baby stuff is sorta coming out of nowhere and she's not making much sense. Just the few things she's told me about what that sick fuck did to her are enough, but I'm getting the feeling that as horrific as those incidents were, it's nothing compared to the secrets she's got buried inside her.

CHAPTER TWENTY-SIX

Rook

Ronin wanted to drive me back up to Fort Collins but I told him no. I need the alone time to be honest. I found out Elise was pregnant almost two months ago, so why now? I don't get it. The miscarriage is ancient history and still, I can barely even think about it without wanting to break down and cry.

I never had any counseling for that. Not even when I was living in the homeless shelter before I met Ronin. I gave the shelter people a fake name every night I stayed there, but I had to tell them about Jon just in case he came looking for me so they sorta forced that 'talking it out' shit on me. I was really paranoid for the first few weeks but Jon never showed up. And I figured if he did go looking for me he probably went to Vegas first because on paper, that's where I went. My bus ticket said Vegas. In the movies people get on a bus to Hollywood so they can make all their dreams come true, but it would've cost me another two hundred bucks to take that bus to LA and Vegas was on special when I bought my ticket.

So that's the ride I bought.

Jon went to Vegas a lot when we first started going out, but he never took me. I always wanted to go back then, but by the time I was eighteen I'd lost all interest in doing anything with Jon. He took one of the other girls instead.

And if I had answered Ford's question of how I got here more completely, that's what I would've told him— that I was heading to Vegas on a dream of being someone special. But Ford was more concerned with the dream that landed me in Denver than the Vegas one I let drift away. After a few days on my own in Colorado I came to my senses and figured I'd just move forward here and try my best to slip back into a normal life. Denver was screaming normal, boring almost. Slow and safe. That's how I saw it back then. The complete opposite of Vegas.

And most of that stuff was pretty easy to let go. I just packed it up and put it away. Blocked it out.

But not all of it.

The baby was the only thing that still tore me up inside because you can't just grow a life inside you, allowing yourself to get used to the idea, and then turn it all off like a faucet when it's ripped away.

Every time I think of children I think of the one I lost. And even though I know it was for the best, that my life would be so much worse if I was trapped back in Illinois with this baby, and it's even possible that the baby would be in a lot of danger and we'd have very little chance of escaping together... a part of me still wishes that things would've turned out differently.

And that part of me feels so... *sick*. It makes me feel sick to want that because Jon was included in that life. And the worst part is that I can't let it go. All because of that baby. It probably means I'm really fucked up in the head. I should not want those things. But I just can't separate the two. If I love the baby then it feels like I have to love Jon, too.

I'm so fucked in the head.

It's true that I never wanted to start a family with Jon, and believe me, he threw that little fact back in my face for months after the miscarriage. He totally blamed me for the 'accident'. But once the whole pregnancy thing became real to me it changed things. I got on board, I was in, I took the vitamins, and watched what I ate, and made sure I never missed a check-up.

But in the end none of that mattered. And I can't help but feel helpless. I always feel like it's just me against the world. How do I win that fight?

I can't.

Me against the world is not a good plan of attack in the war that is life.

I blow out a long breath of air and try to think about something else. Because it's not fair for me to take out my unresolved past on Elise, Antoine, and Ronin. They are baby people. Totally. And they are so excited. It's not fair that I disrupt their good vibes with my bad ones.

I pull into Spencer's driveway and park the truck and then grab my backpack and get out before Spence feels the need to come check on me. He's a good guy, even if he does have an unhealthy obsession with guns. I glance over at the shop and it's all dark. So that probably means Ford isn't home because it's way too early to be in bed. I go inside and drop my backpack on the floor next to the basement stairs, then go into the kitchen and look for Spencer.

"Spence?"

"Back here," he calls out from the living room.

"Whatcha doin?" I ask him as I take in the images spread out on the coffee table.

"Putting together a portfolio for you, Blackbird. So

you can have a record of what we did last summer."

I plop down next to him on the couch and pick up a few of the images. "They turned out pretty good, huh?"

"Pretty good doesn't even cover it, Rook. I've sold more bikes in the last month than my old man did the entire year before I took the company over."

Spencer continues what he's doing, sorting through the images and choosing some to put into the clear pages inside the black book. "Thank you for this," I say as I watch him choose. "Which one's your favorite?"

He flips through the book to the first page. "This one," he laughs. "That's why it's first."

I take the book from his outstretched hands and look over his choice. It's Spence and me. I'm painted up with all his tattoos on my top half, and my bottom half is a painted-on version of his ripped and faded jeans. "You know what's funny? That was my favorite outfit as well. I'm not sure why, it's just too cool that you and I had the same artwork on our bodies at the same time, ya know?"

Spencer smiles. "Yeah, that one's called *The Team*." He leans back on the couch and looks over at me. "That's what the four of us are now, you know that, right? We're a team."

And my thoughts flood back to me. The day I met Ford and we all went to dinner to celebrate our partnership at that French restaurant. That's what I thought about Ronin and me that day. That we were a team. "I'm a lucky girl, Spencer Shrike. Because this is one special team and I'm honored to be on it. I just hope I can live up to your greatness and not disappoint you."

He chuckles. "Shit, Rook, we're still floored that you put up with us at all. And Ford? You seriously deserve a fat cash bonus for mellowing that asshole out." We sit in silence as I flip the page of the book. The second picture is of cyborg sex-kitten Rook and Terminator Ronin. "That's Ronin's favorite," Spence says softly.

"I love this one too. I was so sad that day and Ford read to me and then Ronin and I had a very serious conversation about my past in the shower." I look up at Spencer to see if he knows about this, but if he does, he holds it in.

I flip the page again. This time I'm the catwoman. "That's Antoine's favorite," Spencer adds as he flips to the next page. "And this one is Ford's." The fourth image is me in the white bikini. "Because he said you started growing a backbone that day."

A laugh busts out of me unexpectedly. "Fucking Ford."

Spencer leans in and puts his arm around me, then kisses me on the head. "You know I'm here for you, whatever you need. Whenever you need it. OK?"

I look up and the tears are starting again. "Ronin called you?"

Spence nods. "Yeah, and it's gonna be OK, Rook. I'm not sure what's going on with you or whatever. But it's gonna work out."

All the tears spill out now and I shake my head. "I'm not so sure, Spencer," I whisper. "I'm really not so sure. There's so much more about my past than I've told you guys. I have so much locked away inside."

He just lets me cry and holds me close as he continues to turn the pages of the book, commenting on each outfit until I'm calm again.

Spencer Shrike is a good guy. I feel it in my heart. He's so calm and understanding. Nothing much fazes him. Spencer Shrike screams strength.

And we're a team, he said. It doesn't have to be me against the world.

Because I'm part of the team.

CHAPTER TWENTY-SEVEN

Ronin

I pull Clare aside as Roger dismisses today's models for lunch. "I need to talk to you, Clare. Wanna have lunch with me upstairs?"

She winds her arm around mine and smiles brightly. "Absolutely!"

We walk up to my apartment together and I usher her in after I open the door. "Rook made some pasta yesterday. Want some of that? Or I have cheese and stuff."

"Rook doesn't look like the domestic type. I'm surprised she even knows how to cook pasta."

I close the fridge and turn around. "See, that's pretty much what I have to talk about. This animosity you have for Rook has to stop. I love this girl, Clare. I'm not breaking up with her, she's not breaking up with me, we're gonna get married and live out all that happily-ever-after bullshit. Because she's the one. You need to stop talking shit about her."

I expect a total capitulation, but she hands me a shrug. "I don't believe you, Ronin."

I laugh, seriously let out a total guffaw. "Which part is giving you trouble then? I'll try to be clearer."

"The part where you think Rook is sticking around. Everyone talks about her, ya know. All the Chaput models have filled me in on how things went when she got there. Even some of the photographers think she's got one foot out the door."

I can only shake my head at her brazen audacity. "Clare, listen to me very carefully, OK? Shut the fuck up about Rook. I do not give one shit what you think about my relationship with her. It's none of your goddamned business. And if I fucking even get a whiff that you're being nasty to her, or telling her shit about photoshoots, present ones or otherwise, I'll fire you from this contract so fucking fast your head will spin."

She laughs. "You couldn't fire me, Ronin. The GIDGET people want me. They'd be pissed."

"You must be under the impression that I give a fuck what those people want. I don't. I bid on this contract because it was a challenge, not because I need the fucking money. And I'll tell you something right now. I'll throw it all away, pay off every fucking model, every fucking photographer, and every fucking crew member and walk away in a second. This job is a commitment I chose to fulfill because it looked fun, and nothing else."

The shock on her face starts somewhere in the middle of my speech and by the time I'm done she looks ready to cry. "Why are you being so mean to me?"

"Mean? Fuck, girl. I've done nothing but help your ass for months. The least you can do is be fucking cordial to the woman I love."

"Ronin! I've always had your back, you know that. We've always been tight."

"We've always been friends, nothing more. So what's with all this new relationship shit?"

"I just think she's unpredictable and she's gonna end up hurting you, I can feel it."

"Well, look, Clare. I'm a big fucking boy, OK? If she does take off, you can rest assured that I can handle it. She's not gonna, by the way. She won't." My phone buzzes and I take it out of my pocket and check the message. "Someone's here to see me, so is this all clear, then?" Her look is defiant but she keeps silent as she nods her head. "Good, then let's go."

We walk back downstairs and as soon I spot my visitor near the front door I know what's up.

FBI is back.

Fuck.

I don't look at Clare but I know she knows what's up too. I just hope our little moment doesn't come back to haunt me in the form of her talking to the fucker in the black suit when I'm not looking. I straighten up my back and head over to him. "Mr…" I trail off like I forgot his name.

"Abelli," he adds to my silence. "Agent Abelli."

"Right, I knew that." I smile at him. "What can I do for you?"

"Well, Mr. Flynn, we've been noticing some discrepancies in your statement to the Denver police and we'd like you to come down to the station and take a polygraph. Do you think you could oblige us with that?"

Aaaaannnd… game starts now.

I widen my smile. "Oh, absolutely. I'd be more than happy to." I grab my leather jacket from a hook near the door and wave him out of the studio. "I'll meet you down there."

"Actually, my partner dropped me off, so if I could catch a ride with you, that'd be great."

"No problem. What'd he do, go grab some donuts?"

Abelli laughs but the tension lines on his face tell me

it's forced. "No, he just needed to get back to the station and set up the machine."

"Just messing with ya, dude. I know you're not really donut eaters."

He shuts up after that and I just unlock the doors to my truck and we both slide in. The drive down to the station only takes a few minutes since it's mid-morning and traffic is light, but it feels like an eternity as we sit and listen to the radio. What the fuck could this be about? It can't be Jon. I had nothing to do with any of the hacking. And Rook would've called me if they had Ford in custody, even if Spencer wouldn't. No, it's not about Jon. I didn't even really have to lie when I gave my statement. The only thing not true was the text message. And even so, it was present and legit by the time the cops checked the phone.

No, this isn't about that asshole, but beyond that I have no other info. But I will. Because they're fishing for answers with this polygraph, which means they have to tip their hand with the questions they ask.

Well, bring it on. Because as Spencer said last summer when he was painting Rook, everyone has one God-given gift.

And mine is lying.

Actually, it's acting, but what's the difference, really? My time in India was not wasted with trips to the Taj Mahal with the tourists because there was another American artist in the hotel with us and this guy was filming a documentary about poor kids. Kinda like *Slumdog Millionaire* except it was supposed to be real. But no one wanted to talk to this guy or let their kids be manipulated into revealing how horrible their lives were, so he hired me to be his star poor kid even though I was an American living in a five-star hotel.

Turns out the guy was quite the liar himself and he set the whole thing up to be believable.

Let's just say it was an elaborate plot with parents being robbed and killed on vacation and me running for my life from the Mumbai underworld after witnessing it. He did get caught faking the documentary but he played it off like it was sort of a *Blair Witch* thing, right? And this is when I discovered I was a fucking natural liar. *Actor.* Same thing.

I saw the movie a few years later—he won some independent film award for it, even. I would cry and look desperate and beg people for money on the streets, and I told a story that had Elise uncontrollably sobbing, that's how fucking sad I made it.

But that guy never did out me. That was one of the terms in the contract Elise signed. No one would know it was me and I got a stage name. I got five thousand dollars for lying while we were in India. Which was a lot of fucking money to Elise and me at the time.

Then the modeling gigs started coming in and they wanted me to act but not speak. So I learned to talk with my body and facial expressions.

And this is how my gift works in a nutshell. You wrap your mind around a scenario, you believe that scenario with all your heart, and then you just react—body and mind together. It's not hard at all, not really.

I never did any acting in the States because by the time we settled back down and I was in an actual school full time I was too cool for that theater shit. There is no record of Ronin Flynn ever being an actor. And if there's no record of it, it never happened.

So polygraphs? No problem. This asshole has no idea what's coming.

CHAPTER TWENTY-EIGHT

Rook

"Done yet?"

"You just fucking asked me that twenty minutes ago, Ford. No, I'm not done. I'm not quick at this shit like you are, OK? Just let me think it over." I drum my fingertips on the coffee table and try and come up with three reasons.

"Rook, the application must be in by Friday or you'll have to wait another semester to get into Boulder."

Maybe I don't want to go to Boulder, did that ever occur to him?

But I don't say that out loud because he's just trying to help me. Instead I chew on my thumbnail as I try and think of how to start. It's an application essay. I'm just a few weeks into community college writing, so yeah, I'm not that good at this shit yet. I've barely mastered the topic sentence. Ford eyeballs me as he drinks a beer in the kitchen. "It's a little early to start drinking, don't you think?"

"You *drive* me to drink, Rook. What's the hold-up? They want to know why you want to go to school. Surely you can handle *that*?"

I sneer at him and take my attention back to my laptop. The problem is I might be lazy. Now that I have all this money I don't have the same drive to push myself in this area. Would I be a waste of space at this school? I'm pretty sure there are people a lot more deserving than me who could use a shot at this education that I'm not fully appreciating.

The cushion sinks as Ford sits next to me. "What's going on?" he asks softly. "You're not interested?"

I lean back and sigh. "I'm just not sure, Ford. This school stuff is not easy."

"I'm not following. You thought it would be easier or it's harder than you expected?"

"Both, I guess. I'm not super smart like you guys, but I'm not stupid, right?" He puts an arm around me and I almost have a heart attack. "What are you doing?"

His eyebrows go up. "Comforting you. Am I doing it wrong?"

A laugh bursts out and I just shake my head. "No, this is correct, I guess."

"Do you want to quit school, Rook?"

"Am I a failure if I do?"

"Yes," he says with zero emotion.

I laugh again. "Fuck, Ford. What the hell? I thought you were comforting me!"

"Do you want me to tell you the truth or lie?"

"Lie!"

"I'm sorry, I'm the honest one, remember? You *are* smart but you have almost no education. You should be embarrassed by that."

"What the fuck? That's enough comforting, thanks." I finagle my way out from his embrace and try to get up but he grabs me and pushes me back on the couch. "I'll do it in my room. Let me go."

"No, we're writing this essay and you're turning in the

application. You have brains, you have money, you have people supporting you. A few weeks ago your dream was to go to film school so I've pointed you in that direction and you're staying on that trajectory and seeing it through until you have a damn good reason why the dream has changed. If you get in, *then* you can decide if you want to go or not. But you don't get to give up before you try just because it's *hard*. That's unacceptable. You have thirty minutes to write this essay or I'll ground you." And then he winks. "And if I was Ronin I'd spank the shit out of you and make it hurt for being such a brat."

I scoot over to the other side of the couch and kick him with my socked foot. "You're dumb."

"You're juvenile. Now give me the three main reasons you wanted to go to school."

"If it was that easy—"

"Just the top three, Rook. It's not brain surgery. Off the top of your head, right now."

"Money."

"OK, you don't really need that anymore. What else?"

"A cool job."

"You have that as well. Or you could if you wanted, but you decided to take a boring one. You have options, should you ever want a cool job again, though, right?"

"Yeah, I guess."

"So give me an internal reason. Something you can't have, something you will *feel*. Like pride. Will education make you feel proud?"

"Sure."

"What other internal things?"

"Well, respect, I guess."

"Respect from whom?"

"I'm not sure. Me? I think I am capable of more than

I've been doing with my life, so getting a college degree would make me feel like I'm fulfilling my potential. Does that make sense?"

He smiles and puts his arm around me and this time I lean in. "Yes, that's a great reason. You should write that down and tell the admissions people all the reasons why you believe you have potential and what it means for you to live up to it."

"You're sneaky."

"I've been known to sneak a time or two."

I turn to my computer as Ford gets back up to grab another beer and heads out to the shop. I still, *still*, have no idea what Ford does here as far as work goes. It's like he's only here to be my friend or something.

Hmmmm...

Those sneaky fucks.

I stay and finish up the stupid college admissions application while Ford covers for me on the phones, and picturing this is so freaking funny to me that I have to get out there and actually witness it myself before I go to tutoring. I pull the door open and immediately Ford puts a hand up, like he's shushing me. Whatever. I stand patiently while he chats on the phone about this person's custom order and upcoming meeting with Spencer.

Then I sigh.

Then yawn.

"Can I help you?" Ford asks as he hangs up the phone.

"I think you're trying to replace me, actually. Since when are you polite?"

"Rook, I am nothing if not professional."

"Yeah, you're about as professional as Ronin is honest."

Ford's whole face turns white. "What did you say?"

"It was a joke, I caught him in a lie last weekend right after he fed me that same line, only it was about him being honest." Ford just stares at me for a second, then relief washes over his face. "What. The. Fuck?"

"How's your tutor? Is it time to go?"

"Oh, yeah," I say, glancing up at the clock. "I do have to go or I'll be late." I think avoiding talking to Ford about anything to do with that tutor is a good idea right about now, so I give him a wave and skip out.

I think about what Gage will say to me tonight all the way over to the college and when I finally get there and park, he's waiting for me outside again. "Wanna go to the student lounge and study instead of the math center?"

"OK." I could care less where he checks my work, as long as it gets checked and I can turn it in before midnight, because that's the deadline for this set of problems. We walk across campus to the building that contains the bookstore and the only café-type place on the small campus, order our drinks, and then find a table near the back where there are only a few other students studying. I hand my paper over to Gage and busy myself watching people as I wait.

He works on it for a little bit, then hands it back with all the wrong answers circled in red and a short note about where I went wrong.

I'm not stupid at math, I just get mixed up at what I'm supposed to do at each step. I forget how, but once

Gage points it out to me, it makes sense again. So I guess if I just tried a little harder to memorize the steps I might do better. Gage busies himself grabbing some paperwork from his backpack while I work and then I hand it back.

He checks it again. "Yeah, that's good. Now just enter it into the computer and you're all set."

I do and then tick the little box that says *I promise I didn't cheat*, and press enter.

"Done! And we're early, it's only seven forty-five." I reach down to get my backpack so I can shove my shit inside and leave, but Gage slides some papers across the table at me. "What's this?"

"Printouts of your friends, Rook. I hope you thought about what I said last week. They're dangerous."

I roll my eyes at him. "Gage, I think I know them better than you. They are the farthest thing from dangerous I've ever seen in my life. Maybe you've just been really sheltered or something?" I flutter my eyelashes a little to play it down and make him back off.

"Uh-huh." He pushes the papers towards me with one finger. "Just read them, OK? Read them and then I'll never say another thing about it. Deal?"

"Whatever. I already saw them, though. I looked it all up online."

"This stuff isn't online, Rook. So just read it."

I pick up the stack of papers and read the first headline. It's not a newspaper. It's an FBI report. "What the fuck is this?"

"Just read it."

It looks like your basic FBI wanted poster you'd see on TV, except it doesn't say 'wanted,' it says 'person of interest.' And that phrase conjures up only one image since the 9/11 attacks. Terrorists. I look up at Gage and raise an eyebrow.

He pans his hands out in an innocent shrug. "Just read it."

I continue. It's all about Ronin. Height—so very, very tall. I snicker to myself. Weight—buffed the fuck out. Eye color—electrifying. Age—young. He's only nineteen in this dossier. "Well, these are his general stats which I am already very familiar with. And his picture just makes me want to kiss the photo." I look up with a smirk.

"You're laughing now, but wait."

I glare over at Gage and toss the paper back to him. "I'm just not interested. I don't care what he did in the past or why the FBI thinks he's important. It's over. He's a good guy. I love him. I'm thinking having his blue-eyed babies might be a good idea in about ten years."

"Ronin Sean Flynn, age nineteen—"

"I said I'm not interested. Besides, that was years ago if he was just nineteen."

"—picked up for human trafficking, cocaine distribution, grand larceny—"

My heart about beats out of my chest at the first charge. *Human trafficking?* "No! That's not him. He didn't do that stuff." This is some kind of joke, for the show or something? I look around wildly.

"Rook, I swear to God, OK? The fucking FBI handed me these papers not two hours ago, they wanted me to tell you so you don't get caught up in this, they would like you to talk to them—"

I grab my bag and bolt out the door, leaving Gage there with his stack of bullshit papers that might be ripping apart my whole world right now. I look around. Are they watching me? I stop in front of my truck, scanning the dark parking lot.

Nothing. No one out here at all.

I get in and take a few deep breaths. This is not my Ronin. Whatever those papers said, it's a lie. He's not involved in that kind of stuff, I know it. No man as gentle as him could possibly be involved in that stuff. I pull out of the parking lot, trying my best not to speed so I don't get pulled over, and head east towards College Ave.

Shit. Who the fuck can I ask about this?

Why don't I have any friends?

I chew on my cheek as I think. I have Elise, Spencer, Ford, Antoine, Ronin. That's it. My whole fucking circle of friends could possibly be involved.

Except one, maybe.

Veronica.

I know for a fact that Spencer is a commitment-phobe, so even if some of this stuff with them is true—and I'm not even thinking it is yet, but even if it was—I don't think Veronica would be involved. Spencer refuses to even call her his girlfriend.

I turn left on College and head up towards downtown to her tattoo shop. It's Monday night so the place might not even be open. But it's all I have right now.

Veronica, the girl who endured the agonizing pain of a bullet-induced scrape across her hip, called my ex an ass-faced bastard, and probably saved me from being dragged back to my own personal hell in Chicago, is as good as I've got as far as second opinions go.

CHAPTER TWENTY-NINE

Ronin

So this is how it works.
Listen to the question, breathe. Stop. Blink. Breathe. Recite the question back to myself so that I understand every word. Answer yes or no.

That's it.

Of course, they're trying to make you fuck up. They ask the question a few different ways. They give you throwaway questions—which, depending on the question, may be a good time to just outright lie. Like if they ask *Is your name Ronin Flynn?* And you're me? I say yes, of course, because everyone knows that's my name. But if they ask *Have you ever stolen anything?* That's a dummy question because it's an absolute—everyone has stolen something at one time or another, even if it was by accident or whatever. It's throwaway. So to that one I lie immediately and say no, but the needle stays calm, indicating I'm being truthful.

And then I sit back and smile.

Because I just did two things. I set up their machine to record that kind of response as truth and I lied to their faces but it didn't record and they know it.

A good operator will know what to do with that. They'll set me up in a pattern of repeated questions, phrased with slight variations, so that I will unconsciously lie. But I'm telling you, this is my God-given gift. Spencer paints naked girls, Ford is some evil version of Einstein, sans the bad hair and *with* the slight insanity issues, and I'm the sweet-talking bullshit liar.

That's just how it is.

I can be whatever people want me to be. You want me to be guilty? I can play that part just as well as innocent. In fact, sometimes I do play guilty when I'm being questioned. That really fucking throws them off.

And none of what I'm doing is special, not really. I'm just observant, calculating, and I spent just as much time learning to turn off my emotions as I did turning them on.

"Is your name Ronin Flynn?"

I'm all hooked up to the computer now, sitting in this slightly over-warm room that will at some point in the middle of questioning turn slightly too cold, and I'm ready.

"Yes."

"Do you live at the Chaput Studios Building in LoDo?"

"Yes." That's a lie, but I say it with confidence and the machine agrees with me. Our building is technically in Five Points, not Lower Downtown, but like I said, dummy questions.

The suits bob their heads together on that one, then regroup. "Do you live at Chaput Studios in Five Points?"

"Yes."

"Do you live in LoDo?"

"Yes." I blink and breathe to give them something to think about besides my lie. I can do this all day long.

"OK, Mr. Flynn," the older man running the machine says. "Let's get down to business. Are you aware of any human trafficking in Denver?"

"No."

"Have you ever had a conversation about human trafficking?"

"No." I blink and breathe again. What the fuck is this about?

"Do you know Rook Walsh's real name?"

Blink, breathe. "Yes."

"Is it Rook Walsh?"

"Yes." Another lie. This is a good one because they don't know if I know it or not.

"Has Mrs. Walsh ever mentioned her husband Jon Walsh?"

Ah, here we go. "Yes."

"Has Mrs. Walsh ever mentioned a safe deposit box in Las Vegas?"

I blink, breathe, and lie. "Yes." Because this is getting weird and these assholes actually get a little excited about that answer.

"Did she tell you what was in the box?" Abelli asks hurriedly.

A break in protocol from Agent Abelli is not a good sign. "Yes," I lie.

"What was it?"

I just stare at Abelli and then ask calmly, "What?"

"What's in the fucking box?"

"That's not a yes or no question. Take the straps off and we can talk normally, but I'm not answering any more questions that deviate from the standard test format."

Machine guy cuts in. "We're done here. You're free to go."

And then I'm being unstrapped and ushered out of the room and over to the elevator where I'm handed off to some bald-headed goon in the FBI uniform.

The next thing I know I'm fucking driving down Speer Boulevard towards home. I cut over on Market and then swing around the building and park the truck. "What. The. Fuck. Just. Happened?"

Human trafficking? That's what this is about?

It's bizarre, but I've been gone almost three hours so I gotta get back upstairs and check shit out with the girls and Roger. I might have to get in touch with Ford tonight and set up a meeting. Vegas. Safe deposit boxes and human trafficking. Yeah, this is not right. This is just not right. Because typically when I'm called in for a polygraph, you know, I'm being questioned about a crime I'm actually *connected* to. And I don't know anything about human trafficking or a box in Vegas that may or may not have something to do with Rook.

But I have a very bad feeling that Rook does.

I take out my phone and almost press Ford's contact, but then I come back to my senses and clear the screen.

That's what they want me to do. Call my partners and give the Feds another clue.

Fuck.

I get out of the truck and hop the stairs three at a time. Everyone is busy inside the studio. Clare is doing a shoot with Billy, the other girls are milling about in lingerie or getting fixed up in the salon, and even Elise and Antoine are hanging out in the kitchen eating fruit.

"Antoine," I say in French. "I need a minute." He follows me out onto the terrace where the roar of afternoon traffic down on 21st Street is enough to layer over our conversation if someone is getting nosy. "I just got back from the police station," I continue in French. His eyes dart back and forth, a slight panic becoming detectable by the pulsing of his carotid artery in his neck.

"Don't worry, it really wasn't about me. I think it was about Rook. I think I need to go up North tonight and ask her some questions. Should I go?"

"Do you think it's safe to involve Spencer and Ford?"

I shrug. "Not sure, really. I'm not sure this is really about us, Antoine. I think it's about Rook."

He stares down at the traffic for several minutes and ponders the question. Antoine would never make a good partner in our little private business because he can't make hasty decisions. He likes to think for a while before committing to things. Most of the time this drives me up a wall but not this time. Rook might be in trouble and I only get one chance to make a move. It's worth the extra time.

"I think it's too risky, Ronin. You don't have enough information yet. Give it one more day, then one of us will go up to the shop tomorrow and see if they've heard anything. OK?" He puts a hand on my shoulder and squeezes.

"Yeah, all right."

"Just go back to work and we'll talk more later."

We go back inside and I take my place near Roger, pretending to have an opinion on the shoot Clare is doing or what the fuck ever. But really, all I can think about is Rook.

What if she's in danger again?

And what if this time I'm not around to help her?

CHAPTER THIRTY

Rook

Downtown Fort Collins is at the north end of town and even though the main drag is still College Avenue, it's not wide and busy like it is down south by the Best Buy and PetSmart. It's one of those old historic Western towns and has cute shops and lots of restaurants and bars. There's even a trolley that runs down Mountain Avenue from Old Town to City Park. And Spencer has told me numerous times that it's seriously been voted Best Place to Live in the World or some shit like that. I can see it, actually. It's got a big university smack in the center complete with veterinary hospital and research buildings, but it's still old-timey in many ways. Like parking in the middle of the street to shop in downtown. Literally. You pull into the center of the street and park between the north and southbound lanes of College Avenue.

I've passed by Veronica's downtown tattoo shop dozens of times, so I know where it is, I've just never been inside. I pull the truck into a spot a few businesses down and turn the engine off. My stomach is doing all kinds of flips.

Why? Why does everything have to be so dramatic? I know the guys have secrets, but I just assumed that the secrets were about the hacking stuff they do. Did. Do. I'm not sure if they still do that shit or not. Obviously they did it for me, but whether or not they're doing it for someone else right now, I have no idea.

But stealing from deadbeats and selling human slaves are two very different things.

It doesn't add up.

I am kicking myself for not taking those papers from Gage right now. At least then I could read the whole thing. Because last time Gage said they were accused of murdering someone and got away with it. So when you combine all the shit Ronin is being accused of human trafficking, murder, grand larceny, and selling blow.

I have no idea what this means, but I'm not buying it one bit. It's total bullshit.

I get out of the truck, wait for a few cars to pass by, then jog across the street and head up towards the tattoo place. I stop outside and look up at the sign. It says *Sick Boys Inc.* According to Spencer, Veronica Vaughn is the youngest non-Y chromosome member of the Sick Boys gang and she, her father, and all four of her brothers work at this shop. Apparently she is just one of the Boys around here, because from the sign you'd never know there was a girl inside doing ink.

It's dark out now and the lights are on, but I can't see anything because the front windows are frosted up like they belong in a bathroom. So all I can make out is a large blurry shadow and the faint buzzing of a tattoo machine.

I pull the door open and walk in, get slightly disoriented by the massive wall of tattoo photos that practically slams me in the face, and then startle at the voice to my right.

"Shrike Fucking Bikes? Roonnnnnnn-eeeeeee," the guy bellows out in a deep voice. "Spencer's Blackbird is here!"

I turn around to see someone who is probably one of the Sick Boys and look him up and down. He's huge, for one. Massive. Like over six foot two. And his tatted-up biceps are bulging out from a t-shirt that hugs every spectacular muscle on his upper body. His light hair is cropped close, military-style, and his dark eyes convey a roughness that matches the scruff on his chin. "Who the hell are you? And how do you know who I am?"

"Vic Vaughn, and your name's on the sleeve of your jacket and the backside says Shrike Fucking Bikes. Not Shrike insert-expletive-here-because-we-are-so-cool, but actual Shrike Fucking Bikes. Like that's the name of his business. And only Spencer Shrike would put 'fuck' in the name of his business on the back of a jacket. You don't need to be Cujo to figure that one out."

I squint up at him because that just makes no sense, then look down at my jacket sleeves. One is painted up to say Blackbird and the other says Gidget. I automatically get a little protective of Spence and retaliate appropriately. "Cujo is a nasty-ass, rabies-ridden dog. You're thinking of *Columbo*. And this is a pretty hot fucking jacket if you ask me."

Vic Vaughn winks at me. "So's the girl inside, even if you didn't ask me. And I was just testing you on that Cujo thing. I heard you're a film freak. You should come by the FoCo Cinema sometime, me and the boys wouldn't mind gettin' ya in the dark for a movie."

"Shut up, Victor," Veronica says as she comes around a corner dressed like she's doing a root canal back there. She's wearing pink scrubs, a white lab coat, a pink visor with a clear plastic face shield that she flips up as she approaches, and a blue mask over her mouth. "Hey, Rook, come by for your free tat?" she says through the mask, making it puff out a little with each word.

"Uh, no." I stammer for a moment because her get-up is pretty distracting. "Actually, I was wondering if you had a minute to talk. About..." I look over at Vic, and then cover my mouth and whisper, "Spencer, Ronin, and Ford."

"Hey, Blackbird? You're like two feet away, I can still hear you. Well, Ronnie, I win this bet. I said a week and it's been"—he looks over at the calendar—"nine days."

We both ignore that remark and I change the subject and point to her clothes. "What's with the outfit, Veronica?"

She absently looks down at herself. "Blood-borne pathogens. Did you know that an ink machine can spray minute particles of blood into the air and you breathe it in if you don't protect yourself?" Veronica grabs my arm and pulls me to the back of the shop. We pass a few more rooms, each with tattoo machines buzzing—but all of the male Sick Boys look like regular ink artists with their t-shirts, jeans, and tatted-up arms.

"Come on back, Rook. I've got a guy in the chair, but he's such a pussy, he can use the distraction." She drags me into a small room that looks like a cross between a hospital surgery room with the different doctor office-type stuff lined up neatly on a long counter, and Fran the Nanny's mother's living room—because just about every single surface is covered in plastic.

You could kill someone in here, *Murder by Numbers* style, and just roll it all up in plastic and toss it in the dumpster when you were done.

I shiver.

A very large biker who has half his arm bubbling up

dots of blood from the partially finished tattoo shifts in his chair and makes the plastic crinkle. "You get used to it," he says matter-of-factly, panning a hand up at the sheeting that covers the flat screen on the wall. I spy Milla Jovovich with orange hair so I'm pretty sure it's *The Fifth Element* playing, but it's hard to see through the wrinkles. "She's got a germ issue and a blood phobia."

I almost snicker as I picture her back in the Chaput parking lot freaking out about her bullet scrape. It makes more sense now.

Veronica ignores the dude and absently waves a hand at him. "Rook, this is Tiny. Tiny, Rook. Rook here needs to girl-talk with me. You don't mind, do ya, Tiny?"

The big biker smiles at me through his full beard and I force one back as well to be polite. "Nah, you girls just go right ahead."

Veronica offers me an extra face mask and visor shield, but I hold up my hand and refuse. "OK, Rook, spill it. What's up?" She slips her gloves off, washes her hands, and then snaps on a new pair, grabs her inkwell, flips down her clear plastic face shield like she's getting ready to do some welding, and the buzzing starts up again.

She is one strange chick.

"Well, it's sorta private, ya know? Like, I'm not sure I should—"

"Rook," she puffs through her mask, "we've got a pool running on how long it would take you to come by asking questions about your new roommates. It's no secret that Spence, Ford, and Ronin are knee-deep in controversy and shit. So just tell me what's on your mind."

I sigh and then try for vagueness so I don't involuntarily let out any *new* secrets. "OK, let's start with the murder charges. True or not?"

"True," Veronica says. "At least the charges part is. I have no idea if they actually did it, but everyone knows the state dropped the charges because of a procedural technicality."

OK, that I figured. Obviously, since it was in the paper and all. "How about drug-dealing?"

Veronica snorts at this one. "That's a first for me. Who says they deal drugs?"

"My math tutor had a print-out of a file the FBI is keeping on Ronin, and it said something about dealing coke, grand larceny, and..." I look around, then down at Tiny, who is all ears, just soaking up my girl gossip. "And something else that I won't repeat."

"Do you think Ronin's dealing coke? I mean, you've lived with him for a few months, right?"

"I can't see it, Veronica. I can't see any of it to be honest. He seems like a really good guy. You saw that party he gave me. And yeah, Spencer throws that danger vibe at times, but he's pretty normal as far as I can tell."

"How about Ford?"

She stops the tattoo machine and then all four of the Vaughn brothers appear in her doorway and the place is suddenly very quiet, like everyone wants to hear my answer. I shake my head nervously. "I'm not talking to an audience, guys."

Vic steps forward. He appears to be the oldest and he's definitely the biggest, so maybe he's like the family ringleader. "Hey, you came here to talk to *us*. Not the other way around."

"I came to talk to Veronica."

"Veronica is a package deal. You talk to her, you talk to us. Besides, she's been dating that fuck Spencer for years now, and I'm curious about these guys. So tell us what you think of Ford."

I guess that's fair. At any rate, I don't have a lot of room to negotiate. Either I give him what he wants so I can get their opinion on things, or I walk out. And I really need a second opinion on things, even if it is over a tattoo machine instead of coffee. "Ford's good to me and we spend a lot of time together. I like him a lot. But there's just some weird shit going down and I'm trying to figure out who to trust. I don't need to know the specifics, Veronica. I just want to know if you think they're OK."

"Well, aside from Ford, I'd say yeah. Ronin and Spencer are good guys. But Ford..." She shakes her head at me. "I'm sorry, Rook. You saw that display at your party. He keeps those girls as his pleasure slaves."

I swallow hard as Ford's words come back from the exit interview for the pilot show. *I'm not a good guy, Rook. I'm not even close to a good guy.*

This cannot be happening. Seriously cannot be happening. "Against their will? Does he keep them against their will? Or is it mutual? He took her to the party, surely it must be mutual?"

Veronica shrugs. "How should I know? You're his friend, do you think he keeps them against their will?"

I'm not sure. In fact, I have no idea whatsoever. I've never seen Ford outside our little friendship sphere. I only found out his last name because Gage blurted it out last week. "Well, that's all I needed, I guess I'll go." I get up to walk out but all four of the Vaughn brothers are still standing in the doorway. Blocking it. "Excuse me," I say nervously. The hard bodies part and I slip through. I walk quickly down the hallway, round the corner to the front reception area, and I'm just about to break through the door when a hand grabs me from behind.

"Hold on, Rook," Vic says softly as his grip loosens. "I'd like to give you my opinion."

I shake my head. "No, I've heard enough, Vic. I'm not interested."

"Well, you're gonna get it anyway. So, for what it's worth, I like Spencer. Just don't tell him that because we have this whole 'I'll kill you if you fuck over my sister' thing going." And then Vic smiles down at me and my heart slows a little at his unexpected quiet voice and gentle touch. "You know, he plays tough guy. And he's got the shit to back it up. And maybe that reputation he has is even halfway true. Maybe he did kill that guy? I have no idea. But I let him take my sister out, so you know, I think he's OK."

Vic releases my arm and I push through the door, mumbling out a 'thank you' as I slip into the darkness.

Maybe Spencer *killed* that guy? That's even a possibility?

Holy fucking shit. I'm sure Vic thought his words would make me feel better, but they don't. Because I never, not for one moment, really believed these guys actually *murdered* someone.

Until now.

Just when I think my day could not get any worse it starts to rain.

I walk hastily down the sidewalk, look both ways, wait for a car to pass, and then head towards my truck. I fish my keys out of my pocket, look up, and then stop dead in the middle of the southbound lane of College Avenue.

Wade fucking Minix is standing six feet away.

CHAPTER THIRTY-ONE

Rook

A set of headlights flash, then a horn honks but I can't drag my eyes away from the man standing before me. *Where the hell did he come from?*

Then Wade has me by the waist and he throws me down on the wet ground near the back tire of my truck. My breath comes out with a loud oomph with the impact and then my head slams back onto the concrete, temporarily stunning me. "Jesus fucking Christ, Rook! You almost got flattened by a goddamn van!"

He lies there on top of me, breathing heavy, staring into my eyes, and I'm paralyzed. He comes back to his senses before I do and stands up, extending his hand.

I process what he's doing but nothing moves. I'm just frozen. "What the hell are you doing here?"

He reaches down, grabs my arm, and hoists me to my feet. I lean back against the truck and realize he never answered me. "I said—"

"I heard you, Rook," he says so softly I can barely make out his words over the constant stream of traffic flowing through the little downtown. "Let's sit in your truck. Can we sit and talk in your truck?"

I'm too stunned to even answer. I haven't talked to this guy in five years. The last time we had a conversation

I was a kid, about to be thrown back into the foster care system because his mom wanted to keep us apart. Wade takes the keys from my hand, unlocks the door, and pushes me to get in the driver's seat. I watch him walk around the front of the truck, then get in next to me, setting a backpack down on the floor in front of him.

"Rook—" he starts. But I put up a hand.

"Don't. I don't even know why I let you in this truck. Give me the keys." I hold my hand out and he drops them into my palm. I shove the key in the ignition and start the truck. "Leave. I have nothing to say to you, Wade. If I wanted to talk to you I would've done it up in Sturgis."

He shakes his head at me and I take him in. Like, really take him in for the first time since that horrible day that changed my life forever. His blond hair is wet and plastered against his face and even though I know he's got gorgeous green eyes, I can't really make out the color in the dark. He's a lot bigger than I remember him, maybe because we were just kids back then. Five years can mean a lot of changes to a teen boy's body.

"Rook, listen to me, OK? I just want to talk to you, that's it. I just want a chance to talk to you."

"Why? What could you possibly have to say to me that hasn't already been said?"

"I'm sorry." His eyes search my face, almost as if they're pleading.

"Sorry?" I shake my head. Un-fucking-believable. "You're sorry? You're sorry for what, Wade?"

"For what happened." I just stare at him. "What happened after... you know, after my mom kicked you out and you ended up with that Jon guy."

"*What?*" I ask, stunned.

"I know what happened, Rook."

"You don't know shit. Get the fuck out of my truck."

"I know everything, Rook." And then he reaches down into the backpack and removes a folder and thrusts it at me.

I just stare at it. And I'm not sure how I know, but I know—"I do not want that."

"I don't care," he says in a low voice. "You're taking it. They've been trying to reach you through your math tutor but you just won't listen."

I look around wildly. They *are* following me! "Who sent you with this?"

"The FBI, Rook. You're in so damn deep, baby, they just—"

"Do not fucking call me baby, OK? I'm not your fucking baby."

"Sorry," he says, raising his hands in an *I surrender* motion. "Sorry, I just need to talk to you and then I'll leave if you want."

"I'm not talking about Ronin, Wade. I'm not sure what's going on, but that paper Gage showed me was utter bullshit. He's not any of those things they say he is and I don't care what kind of so-called proof those guys have, I'm not buying it."

"This isn't about Ronin, Rook. It's about Jon, and those things he was doing back in Illinois. The things he made you participate in, the things—"

"What the fuck are you talking about?" My heart is racing so fast I might pass out, that's how rattled I am right now. "Who sent you?"

"I told you—"

"No, who specifically. I want a name, right fucking now, or I'm calling the police and reporting you for stalking."

He hesitates for a second and then gives it up. "Agent Abelli, he's out of the Chicago FBI field office. He's been hunting Jon down for years and they were very close to busting him when you took off to Vegas last spring. Jon disappeared after that and then, of course, he resurfaced here."

I've never heard that name. Who the fuck? "So? Why do they want to talk to *me*?"

"They think you have something of Jon's. Something you got in Vegas. Did you get something of Jon's in Vegas, Rook?"

My entire body is buzzing with anxiety right now. What the hell is all this about? I want to say I never went to Vegas and I have nothing of Jon's, not a damn thing. But I'm just not sure I should play that card so soon. "What if I did?"

Wade breathes out a sigh of relief. "Oh, fuck, thank God. You need to hand that over, Rook. These people are not fucking around, OK? They want that information and if you saw any of it, you better pretend you didn't." He stops and grabs my shoulders with both hands. "Did you read any of it?"

I shake my head, far too frightened to actually form words right now.

"Where is it?" His eyes race around my face like he's too amped up to concentrate on one point for more than a millisecond.

"I never saw it," I say, backpedaling. I know Jon went to Vegas on business sometimes, but I have no idea what he did there. "I lied, I never saw it. I never went to Vegas, Wade, I came straight here, to Denver. You can check, I was in a homeless shelter, then I had a house-cleaning job—"

"So you never went to Vegas? Do you know if he had a security box there?"

I nod my head, because he is freaking me the fuck out and I need to give up something. "But I don't know anything else about it. Not where it is or how to get into it, nothing."

"Well, they checked the box, Rook. And it's empty." He sorta laughs here, but it's one of those I'm-about-to-go-insane laughs and my heart rate jacks up about a thousand notches. "So that means someone has the stuff." He shakes his head. It's a jerky motion that definitely tells me he's about to lose it and then he turns, his head down a little so his eyes are peeking up at me though a curtain of wet hair and dark lashes. He whispers, "Do you have the stuff?"

I swallow down the fear and say calmly, "I have no stuff, Wade. I don't have anything of Jon's."

"Rook, listen to me, OK? You and those guys you're with are the only ones who've had access to Jon, OK? So one of you has the shit they're looking for. And let me just tell you, these people are not fucking around, OK?"

Each time he says 'OK,' the pitch of his voice raises, making him sound even more crazy, and my whole body begins to tremble, because I might not get out of this. Wade is not acting right.

"If you have it, Rook, you gotta tell me. Because they've got my mom, Rook. They've got my mom locked up on some fake-ass charges and they'll send her to prison if I don't figure out where this shit is. Do you understand?"

This snaps me back from the edge of fear and puts me on the offense immediately. "Am I supposed to give a shit about your *mother*?" I laugh. "Really? Let them lock her up! After what she did to me!"

"I'm sorry about that. I tried to stop her, you know that. I tried to stop her from sending you back to the State. She just wouldn't listen and she threatened to cut me off. I needed her help to race."

"You were a grown-ass man, Wade. You were eighteen years old. You could've helped me if you cared one shit about what was happening."

"Yeah, and you were underage, Rook. It's called statutory rape, sexual predator-type stuff—it was a huge risk."

He's serious. This asshole thinks that saving me from living on the streets, from those crack-houses the fucking foster care people sent me to... *saving* me was a *risk*? "You're pathetic. You have no idea what it means to take a risk for someone you love. To put it all on the line for them. None. You're nothing but one pathetic, selfish, fucking asshole."

"What was I supposed to do, go to jail for you? That would've helped how? How would throwing my life away help you?"

"Oh, you poor, poor baby. And for your information, Jon was twenty-one when he found me. And he sure the fuck found a way to keep me."

"Yeah, and look what that sick fuck was doing!"

"And you know who I blame for all those years, Wade? Just take one educated guess." I stop to glare at him, the full depth of my hatred for everyone who ever met me as a child coming out, seeping through my pores like some hot sticky mess left over from all that sex I had with Jon as a teenager. All that filthy fucking sex that was not anything close to love. That entire relationship made me feel dirty, and unwanted, and useless, and... and... and *insignificant.*

"You, that's who," I say in a whisper. "I blame you for all the terrible, horrific things that happened to me back in that house. All of it. It's one hundred percent *your* fault. Because I was just a girl, you were a man. I asked you for help. You said you loved me, for fuck's sake. And then you just walked out. You are nothing but a selfish fucking piece-of-shit coward! You left me to live on the streets, to be picked up by that predator, to be held under his thumb for years."

"That wasn't me, Rook. I had nothing to do with that. That wasn't—"

"You are the darkness, Wade. You are nothing but my dark, disgusting past trying to suck me back in to a life of shame."

"I just want to say I'm sorry, Rook. And please, just listen to me about this FBI stuff, OK? I need you to—"

"Get out!"

My scream is echoing though my head when someone knocks on my window and scares the fuck out of me. I take a deep breath and realize it's Vic Vaughn. I roll it down and look up at him.

"Everything OK in here, Blackbird?"

I shake my head. "No, he's bothering me. I want him to leave."

Vic reaches into the truck and presses the unlock button. The other three Vaughn brothers appear, open the passenger side door and pull Wade out.

"Rook, listen to what I said, OK? Read those papers. They took my mom and they'll take someone from you too. They will, Rook, you'll see!"

Vic and I watch as the Vaughn brothers drag Wade across the street and throw him on the ground in front of a candle shop that's closed for the night. "You want some help, Rook? Want me to drive you home? My brothers can follow us, make sure everything's cool."

My first instinct is to say, 'no, thank you.' But I stop the words and nod up at Vic. "I would really appreciate that, thank you."

"Scoot over, Gidget," he says with a smile as he pushes me into the passenger seat. "And I swear, you'd think one odd name was enough, but woman, you seem to have a collection of them. Hey, Vinn!" he calls out the window. "I'm driving Rook over to Spencer's, you guys follow to keep an eye out for any more psychos." And then he gets in the truck and I breathe out a huge sigh of relief.

Until I pick up the papers and see exactly what they say. I scan the stack quickly. All bad stuff. All the same stuff Gage was trying to tell me.

All stuff that can't be true.

But maybe it is?

And then the fear comes back and it takes all my willpower not to collapse right there in the front seat.

CHAPTER THIRTY-TWO

Rook

I stuff the papers into my backpack and listen as Vic calls Spencer, telling him we're on our way. He gives a few curt responses to whatever Spencer's saying, then holds the phone out towards me.

I turn my head and stare out the window, ignoring the phone, and Vic tells Spencer we'll see him in thirty minutes. I have no idea what to think right now. I just need time to process all this information, make sense of it. Vic talks to me constantly as we drive down the dark and deserted road. I hate this road at night. It's curvy and when it's wet, like it is now, you can't see the lines painted on the road. One side is the damn river and the other side is just forest. It creeps me the fuck out.

I catch Vic eyeballing the rear-view the entire way there, but the only other headlights behind us are his brothers. When we pull into the driveway Spencer and Ford are already outside waiting in the carport to stay out of the rain. Ford opens my door and pulls me out as Spencer talks to Vic.

"What happened?" Ford asks.

I'm not sure I should reveal all the FBI stuff, so I just say, "Wade."

"Oh." That's all Ford says.

"Did you know who he is?"

"I know, Rook. I saw him hanging around up in Sturgis and Spencer filled me in on the missing pieces. Did you talk to him?"

I nod. "Yes, but I never want to talk to him again. *Ever.*" I push Ford away and go inside, wanting very badly to hide away in my room, but there's no chance of that until I talk to them, so I just grab a beer from the fridge and sit on the couch. They come in a few minutes later and I catch the crunch of gravel as the Vaughn brothers leave. They must think I'm crazy. And they probably told Spencer I was just at their shop asking questions about him and Ford.

Great.

Ford sits down next to me and Spencer flips off the TV, taking the chair across from the couch. "So what's up, Rook? You got something to tell us?"

I shake my head. "Nope, nothing. Wade showed up, I sorta lost it, end of story. I don't want to see him again." I stop to look up at Spencer. "Ever. I'm going to call the police if he comes near me again."

"I thought this guy was your old flame or something?" Spencer asks in a low voice. "You sorta sounded like you'd like to see him again when we talked about it."

"I was just depressed that day, reliving the past. Thinking about the good things when the only ones that count are the bad. I'm over it. I want the past to go away and stop fucking up my new life."

"Rook, I'm not sure you're telling us the whole story. Let's start from the beginning, OK?"

"Fuck the beginning, Ford. The beginning starts with my life back in Illinois, and I'm not reliving that shit with you, no matter what. I'm done talking about it, I'm done thinking about it, I'm done answering questions, I'm done with secrets, and fucking Jon, and everything else." I stand up. "I'm done." I step over Ford's legs to get past when Spencer's phone rings.

"Antoine. Hmmm, wonder what the fuck this is about? Yeah," Spence barks into the phone.

I stop in the middle of the living room and listen to the frantic French that is almost fully audible even though the phone's not on speaker, that's how loud Antoine is talking. "What? What is it?" Spencer ignores me, just listens and shakes his head. When I look down at Ford he's wincing. "What happened?"

Spence ends the call and looks over at me. "Ronin just got arrested. They're booking him into Denver County right now on felony obstruction charges."

I collapse back into another chair near the hallway. "Why?" But as soon as the word leaves my mouth I know why. Wade. And that FBI shit. And Gage. They did just what Wade said. They took someone I love. I lean over and prop my head in my hands and then Ford and Spencer each have me by an arm and they're dragging me outside. "What the fuck?"

Ford leans down into my ear and says, "Shut it, Rook. Just shut up for once and do as you're told." He jerks on my arm a little to make his point and I'm powerless to fight.

Spencer leads us across the backyard and towards the woods and then I really start to freak out. "Why are we going in the woods?" I struggle but they hold tighter, say nothing, and by the time we make the tree line they're dragging me through the mud. I start kicking and screaming, but Ford's hand clamps over my mouth and I have to use all my energy just to breathe. They drag me down towards the river and I swear, I am so fucking stupid for trusting these guys. They're gonna kill me and throw my body in the river.

"Rook," Spencer says this time. "Just calm the fuck down. We need to get away from the house to have this conversation, OK? Just relax." We stop next to the river and he pushes me to sit on a rock.

"Are you gonna be quiet and listen?" Ford asks in his most businesslike voice. "Because I'm not in the mood to baby you tonight, got it? We need to talk."

I nod, but my body is trembling badly, the adrenaline still rushing through my bloodstream. Ford removes his hand. "I've tried to tell you this several times but…" He stops and runs his fingers through his hair and looks away. "But you never wanted to hear it, so I let it go. But you need to know now, because this shit with Ronin is big time, got it? We're playing in the majors right now, Rook. This is real fucking shit, serious shit, and you have to follow the rules now because you're on the team. Do you understand this?"

I look over at Spencer. "The team?"

Spence nods. "It's got a lot of perks, Blackbird. But it's got a lot of rules too. So you need to know the rules. Because it's gonna get ugly and the only way we all stay out of jail is by following the rules."

Ford kneels down next to me and Spencer sits on the rock, squishing his body into mine. "First of all, you know what I do on the team, right?"

"Computer stuff," I say in a small voice.

"Yes. And Spencer here is our logistics guy, OK? But he's also the muscle. So if we need someone roughed up, that's Spencer's job."

I look up at Spence and he shrugs. "Can't help it, Blackbird. I'm the biggest guy here, I got the job by default."

"Did you guys murder that businessman, like all the papers say?"

"Rook." Ford pulls my attention back to him before Spencer can answer. "Look, we don't go looking for trouble and we're not violent. You shot Jon, not us. We had no intention of physically hurting him. But as you saw firsthand, things don't always go as planned. Veronica showed up and as good as that was for you, it almost got her killed, right? Even though we never intended for her to be involved, let alone get hurt, or God fucking forbid, killed. Sometimes shit happens and the plans just disintegrate."

"Did you guys murder that businessman?" I ask again.

"Well," Spencer says. "Look, it wasn't meant to happen. It was not meant for him to die, all right? I did what I had to do to prevent him from involving another innocent party."

"I need to hear this whole story. Like now. I never signed up for this, Ford. I never wanted to be a part of this shit."

Ford opens his mouth to speak, but Spencer's words are the ones that come out.

"I killed him, Rook. We were stealing his money, money he used to fund too many dirty things to even list off the top of my head. Shit like drugs, embezzlement from non-profits, porn. Just filthy shit. And we needed to get inside the house for some codes and it just all went down wrong."

"How did you find that out? The bad stuff he was

doing?"

"His daughter told us," Ford says. "Told Ronin, actually. She never knew we were involved until after and the papers got a hold of the story. But this isn't what you need to know. We're telling you about that because you're already in and we need you to trust us, to cooperate, and to understand what it means that Ronin is in jail."

I have a very bad feeling about this.

"You see, what I do has risk. I hack into very secure databases and networks. Some of them very high-level. I'm risking a lot of prison time, possibly even a treason charge when I do some of this. Do you understand?"

"OK."

"And Spencer's job has risk. He killed that man. He's guilty as fuck, Rook. He's got a murder charge all over him. Do you understand this? Spencer's job has risk."

I nod but I'm not liking how often he's repeating the word *risk* one bit.

"Ronin's job also has a risk. Ronin's job is to be the front man, the face of the operation, to clean up the mess. Lie to the police, take the heat, and get the rest of us off. Ronin's job is to lie, Rook. He's a very, *very* gifted liar when he's working."

"Oh, God," I moan. My boyfriend is a professional liar!

"Ronin is the only one of us allowed to talk to the police. He's the only one allowed to give a statement. If Spencer and I are brought in or questioned for any reason—for *anything*—we are to exercise our right to remain silent. And if we ever get to court, we are to plead the Fifth and not testify. We are not allowed to be involved, Rook. We cannot in any way make a statement in favor of or against ourselves or each other. Only Ronin is allowed to talk. Do you understand this?"

"No. I don't get it."

"Oh, I think you do," Ford says in a cold voice. "You get it, because you're not stupid. But I'll spell it out for you anyway. Ronin is the *fall guy*, Rook. If Ronin gets picked up and we don't, we do not help him. His job is to get himself off. And we won't be getting involved in this mess right now, either. I've got no idea what he's in for—it reeks of that Boulder job, but it's got Jon written all over it as well. So we can't take any chances. We will stay up here, shut our faces, and sit tight. Do you understand?"

I nod, because what choice do I have? I've got a psycho hacker on one side and an admitted murderer on the other. I'm out-gangstered on both ends. But as we walk back to the house, the guys still holding on to my arms—I'd like to think to prevent me from falling in the moonless dark, but that's wishful thinking—the only thought running through my head is that I need to grab my shit and go.

CHAPTER THIRTY-THREE

Rook

"Sit." Ford's words come out as a command. My training kicks in and I sit the fuck down in the nearest chair and keep my mouth shut. Spencer takes the couch and Ford stands in front of the TV. "Who's hungry?"

Who's hungry? I roll my eyes at him but I ask permission before I get up. "May I go downstairs and take a shower? You guys dragged me though the fucking mud."

Spence mumbles out a, "Sure, go ahead."

"I'll go with you, Rook. Spencer, you sweep the place and lock us up." Ford grabs my arm and pulls on me until I stand. "Come on. I don't like the basement, I don't want you down there. There's no escape except for the window well in the bedroom."

"You know what I don't like?" He doesn't answer, just walks me through the kitchen and waves a hand at the stairs. "Well, I'll tell you anyway, since you've suddenly found your mute button. I hate being treated like I'm weak and stupid. If you'd told me to follow you outside I would've gone, you didn't need to try and suffocate me as I was being pulled through the mud."

"Well, Rook," he says as we enter my little apartment. "You are pretty weak and you do a lot of very stupid things. So"—he stops to look me in the eyes—"you can expect to be treated like a liability until we know what part you'll play and where your loyalties lie."

"Ha! Where my loyalties lie?" Oh, I am so angry. "That really pisses me off, you know that? I trusted you, I—"

The hand clamps over my mouth again. "No talking. Just get in the shower and I'll wait here." His hand is still firmly pressed against my mouth as he stares at me. "I expect an answer, Rook. So nod, or give me the sign language version of a *yes, sir*."

I nod, but what I really want to do is bite his hand.

He releases me, huffs out a long breath of air, plops down on my couch and turns on a hockey game.

I go into my room and throw open my closet door, grab a clean pair of jeans, a long-sleeve white thermal, and a Shrike Rook t-shirt.

The backpack is calling my name before I even get the shirt off the hanger. I peek out my bedroom door and listen. Ford is still watching hockey and the announcer is screaming "Goal!" so I figure he's pretty wrapped up in it. I turn the shower on and then go back to my closet.

This backpack is the only thing besides my Converse shoes that I have left from my other life.

I can't help it, I fall to my knees and slide the drawstring cord to open it up, then check the little side pocket for the key. I took it from Jon's office before I left. The other stuff inside is everything I need to make a quick escape. I packed it up the day I shot Jon in the knee because I figured even if I wasn't arrested, I might still get in trouble. Maybe not from the cops, but eventually *someone* would come looking for me. It was a given.

And I was right. All those someones are breathing down my neck right fucking now.

Inside the bag I have twenty thousand in cash. I take the money out and flip the bills like you see people do in the movies. Twenty grand doesn't look like much when they're all hundreds. You'd be surprised how small it actually is when they are wrapped up in two little bundles. I've also got one change of clothes and some basic toiletries and the fake ID Jon made me use when we went places before I turned eighteen.

I stuff the backpack under the hanging t-shirts and go take my shower. When I get out I put clothes on and when I walk out in the living room Ford gives me a dirty look.

"What are you wearing?"

I roll my eyes. "Clearly you can see what I'm wearing."

"Are you going somewhere?"

"No, Ford. I just like being fully clothed when I think something bad might happen. There's nothing worse than running for your life through the woods wearing a nightie with a crazed boyfriend on your tail. Believe me, I know from experience. I'm wearing clothes, so shut the fuck up about it."

"Whatever. Let's go upstairs."

He gets up and I follow. I guess my sympathy card with Ford has been played, because that last remark didn't even get an eyebrow raise. I might as well settle in and be nice, that'll make my night go a little easier.

"Find anything, Spence?" Ford asks.

"No, I swept the downstairs at least. We'll just stay in here. But"—Spencer looks over at me—"no talking," he says, putting a finger to his lips. "We need to go outside if you feel the need to *talk*, and to be honest, we should just wait and see what happens tomorrow at Ronin's arraignment. So it's no use anyway."

Ronin is in jail.

It hits me hard and I sink down onto the couch and scrub my face with my hands, trying to stave off a headache. I'm pretty pissed that I didn't figure out these guys had a past. *I mean, fuck, Rook. How stupid can you be? How gullible? How naive?* And now I'm right back where I was when I showed up at Antoine's.

Confused.

Is Ronin a good guy?

Fucking Ford admits *he's* not a good guy. That shit came right out of his own mouth at my birthday party. In fact, he brought that woman on purpose, to show me specifically that he's got serious issues. The kind of issues I am very familiar with.

And Spencer admitted to killing a guy.

And they're all responsible for at least two illegal jobs that I know of. How many more are there?

"Rook," Spencer says as he takes a seat next to me. "I'm the same guy I was last night when you cried on my shoulder. I'm the same guy who painted your body all summer, remember?"

I sigh. "I know, Spencer." He does know *me* awful well, doesn't he? Practically reads my mind now.

"And even though Ford is an asshole when he's working, he's still the same guy he was this morning when he took you running. Right?"

I look over at Ford and he's glaring at me. "What's with that look?"

"Blackbird," Spence says, pulling my attention back to him. "He's still the same guy. You've just never met the asshole version we all know and hate. And right now we *all* have to morph into that other version of ourselves. Because we gotta get out of this, Rook. No one's coming to help us. So please, we just all need to do our jobs."

"But what's my job, Spencer?"

"Be quiet and do what you're told. Just let us handle this one, OK? Just let us take care of it."

"But you said you're not gonna help Ronin, right?"

"Ronin will help himself. He's good at what he does, he's smart, he's devious and sneaky and all those things you hate about men and certainly don't want to hear are your boyfriend's God-given gifts. But he'll figure something out. It just might take some time, that's all."

I avoid Ford's penetrating stare as I mull all this over. Because I don't want to know these versions of my friends.

I want Ford to stay the guy I trust to point me in the right direction and force me to do things that are good for me even though I hate it.

I want Spencer to stay the guy who makes me laugh, paints me pretty biker jackets, and makes scrapbooks of our body art so I'll be happy.

And I want Ronin to be the guy I spend forever with. I want to sleep next to him, and go on long vacations with him, and take beastly sexy showers with him.

But as long as this shit is hanging over us, nothing will ever be like that again.

So I just curl up on the end of the couch and close my eyes. I'm tired and I'm gonna grab some shuteye while I can. Because I will be one busy girl in a few hours.

CHAPTER THIRTY-FOUR

Ronin

This is how I get through jail. Because this isn't the first time I've been under suspicion, nor will it probably be the last, considering the wake of crime spraying out behind me from all our previous jobs. But this is what I do.

One. Embrace the orange jumpsuit. You cannot fight it. It's dirty, it smells like that cheap-ass soap they use, and it's had more hands on it than you want to think about. But unless you want to go naked—and you don't, trust me, the mattresses are revolting enough to make you want to sleep on the floor, even with the sheets and orange jumpsuit—just learn to love it.

Two. Do not eat more than once a day. No matter what. They really are trying to poison you.

Three. Do not think about what you might be guilty of. That just makes you vulnerable to questioning.

Four. Embrace your alone time. No people to talk to means fewer ways to screw yourself over.

Five. Try your hardest not to think about the girl on the outside and what she may be thinking of you right now.

Rook has got to be out of her mind. And the really fucked-up part about all this is that I have no idea what

I'm being held for. They said felony obstruction, but that could pertain to just about anything I've done over the past five years. I've had a long career of justice obstruction.

But I'm not supposed to think about that shit, or Rook, or Spencer, or Ford, or Elise.

Elise is gonna kill me.

I am so fucking dead when I get out of jail. She's gonna want answers, she's gonna want promises, she's gonna want all kinds of shit I might not be able to tell her.

Damn, this jumpsuit is itchy. And I could really go for some fresh fruit.

A loud buzzer sounds and my door clicks open. A guard appears with his hand on his weapon. "Flynn, you've got a visitor."

"Awesome, finally someone to talk to in this shithole."

Did I mention rule six? Don't fool yourself into thinking you can stick to these rules. Because jail, and especially county jail, sucks ass. And you will have no choice but to wish for company, think about the shitty clothes, the poisonous food, your crime—real or imaginary—and your girl, who probably left your ass as soon as she heard you were incarcerated.

I pass by the guard and then follow the hallway until I get to a door. This visitor can only be one of two people. Elise—and I'm so hoping not, because she's gonna cry and shit and that's just not good for the baby—or Rook. Because our partnership rules state that Spencer and Ford are not allowed to come visit.

They buzz me into the visiting area where a few guys are already talking to their friends or family, and then the guard barks out, "Last stall."

I can't see my visitor as I walk down the aisle because they have cinder block walls between each visiting station. Thick Plexiglas separates the prisoner and the visitor, so there is no hope of any contact at all. And a phone hangs on a holder affixed to the wall. I try not to notice a dude crying his eyes out to his pregnant significant other, another guy pressing his hand up against the plastic as his little girl presses back on the other side, and some kid who doesn't even look like he's old enough to be in the county lockup as he tries to comfort a woman who might be his mother.

I am fully expecting Rook to be my visitor, but it's not Rook.

It's Clare.

I stop and do not approach the bench where I'm supposed to sit and talk. I look her in the eye and mouth the words, *What the fuck are you doing?*

She picks up her phone, then taps it on the Plexiglas, indicating I should sit down.

I do. I pick up the phone and all I hear is her breathing.

"What the fuck are you doing, Clare?"

"She ran, Ronin."

"Who?" I ask, even though I know who.

"Rook, she's missing. She left sometime in the middle of the night, she—"

I don't catch the rest because I hang up the phone and walk away.

So much for rule number five. I go to the door, wait for the buzzer, and then exit back into the hallway. There's no guard this time. That fuck Abelli is waiting for me.

"Mr. Flynn, we'd like to speak to you, if you don't mind."

"I do mind actually, I'm still waiting on my lawyer."

A guard grabs my arm and escorts me the opposite direction from where I came from, then Abelli opens a door and waves me inside. "No need for lawyers, Flynn. Just an informal chat about your missing girlfriend."

I take a deep breath. *Games, Ronin. Keep cool, they're baiting you,* Spencer's voice says in my head. *Just games, dude.*

Right. *Shut the hell up, Spencer.*

This is what a little bit of alone time in a cell does to you, so yeah, rule number four creates condition number one. Two-way conversations with people who are not, in fact, present.

"Sit," Abelli commands.

I sit, because I might as well play a little, pass the time, right? I'm in no hurry to get back to my cell, that's for sure.

"We know where your girlfriend is. Would you like to know?"

"OK, sure," I answer. "Tell me."

"Well, see, we were hoping you'd do a little information exchange with us if we give you that info."

And this, little grasshoppers, is what I like to call the no-lose situation. Pay close attention, because here's how it goes down.

"OK, you go first, tell me what you know. Where's Rook?"

"Bahahaha, Mr. Flynn, not so fast. We deserve an answer to one of our questions first, don't you think? Since we're the ones with the information you need?"

Just agree at this point. The correct answer would be, 'uh, fuck no,' but you want to keep them rolling. "Sure. Shoot, how can I help you folks?"

"What do you know about the contents of the security box in Las Vegas?"

Ah, Vegas box again. So this *is* about Rook. See, grasshoppers, this is all I needed. I am free to move about the cabin because I already got what I want from Abelli. He's got nothing on Rook's whereabouts because obviously she would know more about said Vegas box than I would. So, Clare's right. Rook left. Which means Rook's *doing* something. Which means this guy wants to know *what* she's doing. As do I, but I'm not gonna get that info from Abelli.

In addition, I also found out this is not about my illustrious obstruction of justice career, but about this guy and his obsession with this stupid box in Vegas. And this, in combination with the slip-up during my polygraph, means this is personal for him.

His ass is on the line. Somehow, some way, Abelli is in deep.

"I'm done here."

He eyes me cautiously. "You didn't answer my question."

"No, but you just answered *all* of mine. So I'm done here." I fold my hands over my chest and wait him out.

He talks, he screams into my face, flinging his spit all over my cheek, he stomps around like a baby, he sends in the good-cop partner and that guys flips out when I start humming a pretty dead-on balls accurate rendition of *Bohemian Rhapsody*—the *Wayne's World* version complete with head bang and air drums—and then finally, some fat higher-up comes in and says they need the room back.

I am escorted to my cell to wait it out alone, ready to put all the rules back into practice.

CHAPTER THIRTY-FIVE

Rook

Spencer drifts off some time after two AM. I know because I wake up around midnight, hoping they'll be asleep already, but no such luck. Ford, on the other hand, lasts until almost four. And say what you will about Ford, but he takes his sentry duty very seriously. He sits in a chair in the pitch dark, no lights on in the house, no lights on outside the house, staring out the window for hours.

When he finally does drift off I creep downstairs, grab my backpack, and slip out the bedroom window. I only own one mode of transportation, my Shrike Rook. So I push it down the road so I can start it up without being heard and take off.

Because this whole thing is bullshit. And I'm tired of it.

Once I get back into FoCo I head east on the highway until I hit Sterling, then catch the 76 up to Julesburg and get on I-80.

And this road will take me straight to Illinois where I will stop running for good.

I'm so tired of waiting for things to go bad, for things to fall apart, for that stupid fucking rug to be pulled out from under me. I mean, they're doing a pretty good job right now, right? Ronin's in jail, the FBI has Wade tracking me down, and I just learned that my best friends are killers and maybe even traitors. I'm not sure what that remark was from Ford—I'm hoping a generic *I hack into secret databases* type of treason—because one needs to draw the line somewhere and betraying my country is pretty much where the Crayola comes out.

And a motorcycle is definitely not the best way to travel a thousand miles, but I've got no choice. I have the money to charter a jet—wouldn't that've been awesome? But there's the whole TSA thing and I can't risk them knowing where I'm going until I get what I need.

Lincoln, Nebraska is about halfway to Chicago, so I pull into a Holiday Inn Express. I know from commercials that they have a free breakfast in the morning with one of those do-it-yourself waffle makers. Why this makes a difference to me when I have twenty thousand dollars in my backpack, I have no idea. It just does. I park the bike in the check-in carport, then duck into the restroom so I can shuffle out a few hundred-dollar bills. My gaze catches my reflection in the mirror and I wince.

Damn, I look tore up. There are dark circles under my eyes from riding the last eight hours, my hair is a rat's nest even though I braided it before I left, and my face is pale white. I splash some cold water on my cheeks and then rub them with a scratchy paper towel to force some color back.

It almost works.

I get my money out and then go to the front desk.

"Can ah help ya?" the girl behind the desk says in a friendly Midwest accent.

"I just need a single room, no reservation."

"OK, I can do tha-at." Her drawl makes her words slower than normal and it's almost comforting. "But check-in isn't until three, so I'll set it up and you can come back in then, will that be okaaaay?"

"Sure," I mumble. Like I have a choice. "Is there an electronics store around here?"

"Ye-as, just down on Superior. Would you like me to print you out directions?"

"Yes, please. That'd be great." And ten minutes later I've got my room reserved, a key card that will activate at three PM, and I'm on my way to the Super Wal-Mart. When I get there I wait around for a near front parking space because I suddenly have a bout of paranoia that someone will steal my bike. It is a custom Shrike, and those can't be common around here.

I head right to the electronics section and pick up a pre-paid iPhone and some minutes, pay cash at the counter, then go get some cheap clothes and snacks to hold me over until I get back home.

Home. I shake my head at that internal slip. That place is not my home anymore and it repulses me to think of it like that.

I pay up front for the rest of my stuff, then sit in the attached Subway drinking a soda while I deal with my phone activation and by the time that's taken care of, it's almost three. I shove my purchases into my backpack and head over to the hotel and find my room.

It's a room. King-sized bed, ugly-ass comforter that I remove immediately, a nightstand, a desk, microwave, and a table. I take a shower and watch TV from bed.

How long has it been since I was really alone somewhere? When I got to Denver I was pretty lost, but I found the homeless shelter. God, I don't know how I did all that by myself. I was such a mess. I'd never been in a homeless shelter before so I had no idea that you had to get in line for a bed. I spent the first night at the bus station because there were no beds available. And that was so fucking scary and cold. It was late March and it snowed that night and even though the bus station had heat, the doors were constantly opening and closing, so it was never warm.

I learned my lesson. I got to the shelter early the next day, got a number for a bed, and was once again on the streets that night because I didn't know you had to get there right at six PM to line up with your number or they'd give your bed away to someone else.

I think I cried the whole night. And one night in the bus station is forgiven by the Denver PD, but not two.

Two is a habit, the cop told me. But he let me stay because I was so upset. In fact, he almost called social services thinking I was a runaway. But I showed him my ID and told him a little bit of my story, so he never ran my name. He even bought me a cup of coffee from the vending machine.

By day three I had learned the ropes. I got my bed number, I got in line early, and I finally got the pleasure of sleeping on a cot in a smelly room filled with drunks, addicts, and criminals. And a couple weeks later I was still there, being robbed of all my clothes and trying my best not to get raped.

Just after I got robbed of my clothes, I met Ronin wearing my thrift store equivalent replacements and my whole life changed.

What if I had never met him? What if I hadn't spent that last ten dollars on a ridiculous coffee at Starbucks? What if those models hadn't sat next to me and what if I hadn't been so upset and desperate that taking a chance on a test shoot with Antoine Chaput seemed reasonable?

It makes me so sick to think about that. How horrible my life would be if Ronin wasn't in it. And not because of the money and the jobs, but because of *him*. I've never known love until him. He's everything to me now. Everything. I do not care what he did in the past, and I know that's probably wrong in all kinds of ways, but I can't even muster up some righteous indignation to feel bad about it. Because life is not some cakewalk through the land of the straight and narrow. Life is a crazy, crooked, fucked-up road that sometimes requires a bit of cheating.

Sure, you gotta do your best to prepare for your luck to arrive, and you have to be ready for the opportunities, but in the end it always takes more than luck. And sometimes, skill isn't enough either.

So if something is important—I'm not talking pre-algebra important, OK? I'm talking real life-or-death important shit—well, then you do what you gotta do.

When you want to win no matter what, you just get the job done and say fuck the straight-and-narrow. Karma can kiss my ass for this one, I earned it.

Life is not always fair, but it does present you with choices. I could've taken my ten bucks and bought food. I could've ignored that card and called myself delusional for even thinking I could be worthy of that kind of job. I could've walked out when I heard what the TRAGIC contract really was and I could've told Spencer Shrike no when he asked to paint my body.

Fate is fragile. Deviate from it just a tiny fraction and you end up somewhere else. And as scary as that sounds, what it really means is that I'm the one in control. I've always been the one in control, I just never saw it clearly before. *I* control my reactions to the things life throws at me, so *I* control my fate.

Ronin might not be perfect, but he's close enough for me.

I want him, I love him, and he's mine.

That's why I'm on the road right now. I know Ford and Spencer are probably going crazy—and if I turned my phone on I'd have dozens of messages telling me how pissed off they are—but I do not care.

Ronin might be required to take the fall for them, but he will *not* take a fall for me.

No way.

I'd rather go down fighting than give up and slink away like a coward. I can fix this, I know what that FBI guy wants, and I'm gonna go chase it down and get Ronin out of that jail cell if it's the last thing I do.

CHAPTER THIRTY-SIX

Rook

The drive to the village where my life with Jon made my dark childhood look like a bright Easter morning sunrise is long, filled with dread, and scary as fuck. I have all that time to just replay all the terrible things that happened inside that house.

Wayne, Illinois is not the kind of place where horrors happen. Wayne is the type of place where little girls join the Pony Club, boys get Porsches for their eighteenth birthdays, and parents stay together because there's too much money at stake to split up. At least that's how it is now. But a hundred years ago it was just another farm town known for breeding draft horses.

Our property butts up against a pretty forest preserve and I pull into a parking lot about half a mile from the house. The park is deserted this time of year unless there's a classroom of little kids on a field trip, and today there isn't. So no one notices when I ride the bike into the woods, weaving my way between trees, until I get far enough away from the lot to hide it behind a thicket of shrubbery. This way I can walk up to the house from the back and make sure no one's waiting for me. It also gives me a nice hidden getaway route and all that fucking running with Ford is gonna pay off big if I have to make a break for it.

The house Jon and I lived in is at least a hundred years old and when it comes into view through the heavily wooded trees, I get the same creepy feeling I did that first day we came to look at it after his uncle died.

Picture the house in *Night of the Living Dead*. Not that pussy remake where the house is some beautiful, sprawling Victorian-ish thing. But the original *Night of the Living Dead*, the black and white one from the Sixties that has that two-story farmhouse sitting off in the distance in a large field, white siding, half-ass porch, and those tall, skinny windows that just scream horror movie.

That's my house in Wayne, Illinois.

The first time Jon and I came to look at it I refused to get out of the car. I was so creeped out he didn't even push the issue, simply left me there in the passenger seat while he went inside and looked around. He only stayed about fifteen minutes and when he came back all he said was, *I'll clean it up and remodel the kitchen*. I just stared at him. Because it was so out of character for him to give a shit about what I thought that I couldn't even process it. I have no idea what he saw that day but I can take a good guess. Because his uncle was psycho. Psycho as in *I keep my quadruple amputee mother under the bed on wheels, X-Files style*.

I'm not exaggerating. Uncle Pete was caught with body parts in his basement and died while on trial.

I almost forget to breathe as little by little the house comes into view. It looks small on the outside but inside it's one of those old places with huge rooms. It's dumpy because the outside never got any attention. The siding is still a dingy grayish white, the tall hedges that line the far side of the property are all overgrown and bushy, the unattached garage roof is slightly sagging, and the yard grass is knee-high. But if you include the third-floor attic and the basement, it's almost three thousand square feet of dump.

I never once set foot upstairs. Not even the second floor. It was off limits to me and even though it was kinda cramped only living in that little bit of space, I had absolutely no problem with that. I gladly made do.

Money did not make a shit of difference in my life once I got with Jon. When I was out on the streets, hungry, cold, and desperate, I thought for sure money was the answer. That's the whole reason I went home with Jon in the first place. He had it all. He was cute, he had the job, the college degree, the Lincoln Park condo, the car, the clothes. He had everything I thought I wanted.

Just like Ronin, right? Ronin had all that too. And he wonders why it took me so long to get on board with him. It was a *fool me twice* kinda thing.

And seriously, if you were me back then and you suddenly had an established, nice-looking guy interested in taking care of you, you'd go for it too. What girl on the streets would say no to that? Who?

No one, that's who. But I know better now.

Yeah, everything I did with Antoine and Spencer was for money, but it was *my* money. Not someone else's. There's a big, big difference. After I left Jon I wasn't looking for the things money could buy, I was looking for the freedom to walk away any time I wanted.

That's what money really gives you. Walking privileges.

I hesitate at the edge of the woods. I don't see anyone but I stay hidden and stalk around the perimeter as best I can before setting foot out on what's left of the lawn. Both of our cars are still there. He must've picked mine up from where I left it the day I ran. I peek in the window as I walk past and catch sight of the crystal glass hanging from the rear-view. I open the door impulsively and snatch it until the nylon string breaks, and then close the door gently.

It glitters in the sun and makes my stomach turn. Jon gave me this early in our relationship. I huck it out into the grass because it needs to be forgotten, just like all the rest of the stuff in this place. I continue on to Jon's car and peek in his windows too. Mine's an old Toyota Camry, but Jon drove a late-model Mustang. There's nothing in there, not even a scrap of paper from a straw wrapper.

Jon is a neat freak.

I suppose he left his car here because it would be stupid to disappear in your own car. I don't open his door, just continue walking up to the back stoop. No railing, just five concrete steps leading up to a door. I stop and lift up the roof of an empty birdfeeder off to the side and take out the spare key taped to the top. The back door doesn't function. Nailed shut courtesy of Psycho Uncle Pete. Too close to the basement, I always figured. So I creep around to the front of the house and listen for signs that someone might be inside.

I wait a few minutes and then hop up the identical stoop in front, push the key in the lock, and twist the door knob.

It swings open with a creak and I hesitate for a second, but I'm more afraid of someone pulling into the driveway and catching me here than I am of crossing the threshold.

So I step inside, close the door, and remind myself it's just a place. It's not alive, it's not evil, it's just a *place*.

But it's a place that has been tossed from ceiling to floor. The leather couch is standing on end, the lining underneath split open. Every cushion as well. Stuffing coats the floor and it looks like it snowed in here. The end table drawers are upside down on the coffee table, their meager contents—Jon never did tolerate a junk drawer—spilled out. All the pictures are strewn about, their canvases split open, like we were hiding secret documents under the paintings.

When I look to the right the kitchen is in the same state. I walk in there. Jon did live up to his promise. My kitchen has granite countertops, maple cabinets, travertine tiles on the floor, and stainless steel appliances. All of which are dented now with what looks to be booted footprints. The French doors of the fridge are open, as is the lower freezer drawer, the contents inside long past spoiled. All the cupboards are open and the remains of the dishes are scattered around on the floor, my boots crunching in the debris as I back out and wind my way through the strewn-about furniture, towards the first floor bedrooms.

I want to stop myself. I want to scream at myself, tell the inner Rook not to go there. Nothing good can come of it. Just turn back and get what you came for.

But I can't.

I can't leave here without looking at it one more time.

All the doors are open as I pass. Our bedroom is ransacked, the guest room is ransacked, the hall bathroom is ransacked, and the office is also ransacked.

But one door remains closed and this alone makes me want to cry. I walk slowly to the last door on the left at the end of the hallway and open it.

My baby's room is not a mess. In fact, it's almost neat and tidy—the bedding in the crib is in a heap, the mattress ripped down the side, but it's all there. When I pull open a drawer all the tiny clothes are messed up, but they are all still there. Proof that whoever the searcher was, they must've either taken their time to look through things properly or they fixed everything after they were done.

I wonder what kind of thug does that?

The crib is white and the bedding is blue. All the bottles are lined up near the bottle warmer on the changing table. The Diaper Genie is still standing at attention in the corner, its askew top the only clue that it was searched by the thugs who trashed my house.

I suck in a breath as my eyes wash over the picture frame on the dresser.

It's me. Eight months pregnant.

I'm wearing a fluffy peach dress, I'm barefoot, I'm huge, and I'm standing outside in front of the blooming purple lilac bush on the east side of the house.

I'm also smiling. Because even though my world would fall apart very soon after this picture was taken, I was happy that day. I was hopeful that Jon was changing, that this baby was a good idea after all, that he'd be better, happier, satisfied—if he just had a son.

I didn't miscarry at six weeks like most girls. I carried that baby to term.

I went to all those check-ups, heard the heartbeat, saw the ultrasound, had a name picked out, had a room, a car seat, a crib, breast pump, baby swing, the cute bedding, the adorable onesies, the rocking chair by the window, and a baby bag packed and ready for the hospital—I had *everything*.

I slip the photo out of the frame real fast and stuff it inside my jacket. I didn't want it when I left because I thought I could just forget it ever happened. Just put it behind me and move on.

But I can't move on. I never had the chance to properly grieve because as soon as I came home from the hospital, Jon was even worse than ever. He blamed me. And I never had a chance to feel the sadness. I had to push it away so I could survive.

I don't have time to feel anything right now either, but some day. Someday soon, I will look good and hard at that picture and figure it out. Let it all out and really say goodbye like I should've when it happened.

I take one last look at what I almost had and then I back out of the room and pull the door closed behind me.

Let that one room remain sweet and hidden away from the ugliness out here.

I walk briskly down the hallway, picking my way through the various pieces of broken things, and go through the kitchen to the back of the house. The basement is where I need to be. That's where everything is. All the horror, all the tears, all the beatings, all the death, all the sickness, all the filth, all the bad, bad things that happened in this house took place in this basement.

When I get to the top of the stairs I stop and replay it all in my mind.

His hand on my shoulder.

The smack across the back of my head that turned into a push.

The fall.

The blood.

The hours it took for Jon to decide that I really did need to go to the hospital.

The look on the doctor's face when he told me it was too late.

The screaming as they strapped me to a gurney and rolled me down the hallway so they could medically induce me into giving birth to a dead baby.

And then waking up in a hospital bed to the man who caused it all, handing me balloons.

Balloons.

And a card.

The anger and hate I felt that day washes over me again. But I let it flow like wind and then it dissipates. Because I came here for a reason and this memory lane shit needs to be over now.

I walk slowly down the steps and let the baby go so the other horrors can fill in the space. The basement is tossed too, and while it does make me a little sad to see all my things trashed upstairs, down here nothing belonged to me. Down here I was a piece of property. Down here I was *his* piece of property and I spent most of the months after the baby down here being punished for some reason or another.

Jon likes the kinky stuff. And I'm not talking the fun kinky stuff. I'm not talking about cute pink cheeks from an erotic spanking, or teasing a girl so she wants to come, but can't. Or any of that play stuff.

I'm talking painful, 'I never signed up for this, there is no word that will keep me safe, I don't want this, it does not feel good, please, for fuck's sake, stop' kind of kinky stuff.

Ford likes the kinky stuff too, so he hints. And Ronin *thinks* he likes the kinky stuff.

But I'm doubting either of them have ever hog-tied a teenager and hung her up from the ceiling with a ball gag in her mouth and then proceeded to sexually torture her and called it fun.

I eye the ceiling hook as I step onto the cobblestones that line the basement floor and let out an uncontrollable shiver before taking my attention to the room around me. Most of the walls are made of some sort of gray rock. The floors are these old-ass bricks in some places, and crumbling concrete in others.

I head to the laundry room where the floor is crumbling concrete and try not to look at the shattered pieces of the St. Andrew's cross as I pick my way past. This is a long room, but it's pretty much bare of anything except the laundry stuff. Washer, drier, ironing board, folding table.

And one secret.

There is only single small basement window on the far side near the utility sink. The late afternoon light seeps in and blasts about six feet of air with illuminated floating dust particles. Across from that is the massive coal-powered furnace left over from when the house was first built. I used to hide behind it sometimes, but Jon always found me. He *always* found me.

I bend down and pick up the crowbar that's mostly hidden underneath the washer, then insert it into the large drain grate in the crumbling floor. It lifts up so I set it aside and I lie down so I can peek in, straining to see if what I'm looking for is still there.

It is and the tips of my fingers just barely graze across the metal safe when a car door slams outside.

Fuck!

I get up and run to the little window which looks out to the front walkway.

Men's voices.

And one of those voices belongs to Jon.

CHAPTER THIRTY-SEVEN

Rook

How? How is this even possible? He's supposed to be in jail!

I'm so stunned I stand there gazing up at three sets of feet as they walk up the front steps. I waste any time I might've had to get out of this basement. The front door slams closed and I panic. What the fuck?

I look around frantically for a hiding place. The coal furnace calls to me, I could crawl behind that, but what if Jon knows I'm here somehow? He'll definitely look there first because that's where I always went. Hard footsteps thud over my head as the men walk across the living room floor. My gaze travels past the coal chute and I rush over, swing the door up, and I'm just about ready to climb in and crawl up to the side yard when I realize the footsteps are crossing into the kitchen.

They're coming down here.

I give up on the coal chute—I'll be caught for sure—and I refocus on the drain where we hide the secret shit. I'm not as skinny as I was when Jon made me climb in here, dig out a hole around the sewer pipes, and shove that fire-proof box in a little nook down there. But I wiggle as the first thuds on the basement stairs pound in my head, then slip through and pull the grate over the top.

Fuck, I left the crowbar. The footsteps are louder now, but not down yet. I slide the grate, grab the crowbar, slip back inside the hole, and slide the grate again.

"We're tired of playing, Jon," a voice says. "We know it's here and the only way you're getting out of here alive is if you give it to us. So let's make this easy."

I scoot away from the light filtering through the grate and push my back against the dirt wall as the men continue to talk near the stairs. I fish out my new iPhone and start the video camera and set it on a pipe on the other side of the hole, pointing up at the grate.

"Where is it?" another man says.

I'm so busted if he tells them because I'm sitting right next to the very thing they're looking for.

"I told you," Jon says. "I gave it to friends to hold for me. You kill me, they release it to the public. We walk out of here together or we don't. But if I go down, so do you."

A loud crack and a thud as someone falls to the ground almost makes me gasp. "You want to threaten me?"

There's more shuffling and then the men are headed my way. I hold my breath.

"It's in this basement, we know it is. One of your buddies gave you up."

"That right?" Jon says, then spits on the floor, swallows hard, like he's swallowing blood, and then coughs. "Then why don't you tell me where it is, since you seem to know so much."

They hit him again and this time he falls to the floor and his cheek lands right on the grate above me.

I suck in a long breath.

His eyes shift downward.

At first I think he can't see me. And then his

expression morphs though several different phases. Shock. Grimace. Anger.

And then nothing.

We open our mouths at the same time, but only he speaks. "I'll never tell," he says, looking me straight in the eye.

What? Is he talking to me?

One of the guys kicks him in the ribs and he spits out more blood. This time it clings to the rusty grate and drips down.

Please, God, I pray. *Please don't let me be caught here with these men.*

"I won't tell," he says in a low voice. "I won't tell."

"You'll tell, asshole. Because we're gonna beat the living shit out of you if you don't," one of the other guys says.

"They ransacked the baby's room, but I cleaned it up as best I could," he chokes out. And then he whispers so softly I almost miss it. "I swear it was an accident. I swear to God, *it was an accident.*"

He *is* talking to me. I sink back against the wall and try to hold my tears in.

"Yeah, yeah, your dead baby's room. We've already heard about it. Now you either tell us where the shit is, Jon, or we'll go get that little raven of yours next. And if she thinks what you did to her was bad, she's in for a surprise. I have a guy in Columbia who'll pay a half a million for a girl like her. I can pick her up and have her sold before anyone knows she's gone. We've got her boyfriend in jail, and she's on the run from the other two, just like we planned. Hell, they might not even miss her. Might just figure she moved on and found a new place to hide."

Jon coughs again and more blood comes up. "I'm so sorry," he breathes, again so low it almost doesn't exist. He stops for a moment, his eyes still looking down at me. "I'm sorry. You'll just have to kill me, boys." And then his gaze finds the iPhone in a hazy beam of light that slips past his body and hits it in just such a way as to create a glint. He smiles for a moment, the blood spilling out of his mouth, and I quickly reach out and move the phone slightly just as Jon rolls himself over.

"It's not here, Agent Abelli," he says loudly. Plenty loud for the phone camera to pick up the name. "I gave it to the media, so just do what you want, I've got nothing to give you. Nothing at all."

I close my eyes and put my fingers in my ears after that. They beat him, they kick him, they lift up his head and crack it against the grate so hard pieces of blood and bone from his cheek spray down on me.

His screams fill the basement and then, gradually, they turn to moans.

And even though I spent years wishing I could make him writhe in pain like that, it brings me no comfort.

I hate this. I hate everything about this. It makes me sick.

But I'm forced to listen for what seems like an eternity as they pummel him, knock him unconscious, bring him back, and then do it again. Until finally, he's unable to be brought back and there is a moment of heavy silence when everyone realizes it's over.

"Shoot him to make sure he's dead then burn this place down. I'll be in the car," the Abelli voice says as he walks away. "If he's hidden anything here, it'll all go up in flames."

That Abelli guy doesn't even make it to the basement

stairs before the gunshot rings out and pieces of Jon splatter down into the hole.

I clamp my hand over my mouth and close my eyes tight as the smell of gasoline fills the basement.

I wait for the whoosh of flame and then the heavy footsteps of the other man going back upstairs. I frantically push against the grate so I can climb out, but Jon's body is in the way.

My breath starts coming in ragged gasps as the smoke fills the basement and I start to panic, my chest hitching as I try to take in air and push against Jon's body. I'm ready to give up when I think of Ronin's words the last time I saw him. *Don't panic, Gidget.*

Calm down, Rook, and push for fuck's sake!

I get to my feet, still crouched down, and push my shoulder up against the grate.

It moves, barely, but it moves. So I do it again and Jon's body rolls a little. I do it again and again and again.

And finally the grate flips on its side.

I reach up, push the grate across the floor, and then shove Jon's body until he's clear of the hole in the floor. I'm so filled with adrenaline and fear trying to make my escape, I almost forget the phone and everything I came for. I grab the key from my pocket and try my best to steady my shaking hand as I insert it into the lock. For a second it refuses to engage and I swear to God, I almost have a panic attack. My whole plan flashes before my eyes and I feel the crush of defeat.

Keep calm, Gidget. Don't panic. Ronin's voice in my head soothes me and I take a deep breath, push the key in farther and feel it click into place. I turn it and swing the metal door of the safe open.

I scan the contents then stuff all of it inside my jacket

pocket and pull myself back up into the basement. The smoke is so thick I can't even see the stairs and the flames are too high that way to even consider escaping. I panic again.

No, be still.

"How will I get out?" I ask Ronin's voice in my head. I look over at the window, already coughing and gasping as the thick smoke penetrates into my lungs. But it's just one of those small basement windows. And this house is too old to have a window well as a fire escape. My eyes dart around, panic starting to consume me again, when I spy the coal chute. And then I'm lifting up the metal door and shoving myself inside.

The negative pressure from outside sucks the fire in my direction and the flames are nipping at my boots before I'm even halfway up.

I scream from the heat and then the outside chute opens, forcing the flames to lick up against my legs even higher. Two hands reach down to grab my wrists. It never even occurred to me that those bad guys might still be around, but it's too late now.

The hands pull me up with force and then the fresh air rushes into my lungs and the heat on my legs is replaced with cool autumn air.

I land in a heap at the feet of some biker boots.

And when I look up Spencer Shrike is shaking his head at me. "I'm gonna tell Ronin what you did and he's gonna spank the shit out of you for this."

I pat my jacket as he lifts me up and pulls me back towards the woods. "I have so much proof," I cough out as I half-limp, half-run from the burning pain in my lower legs as Spence and I make our way through the nature preserve.

And when I look back at the burning house I realize something...

All my old demons are going up in flames with that piece-of-shit place.

I'm finally free to fight another battle.

And I've got a team to help me.

CHAPTER THIRTY-EIGHT

Rook

Spencer and I trek all the way back through the woods, me coughing so hard I keep looking around to make sure no one is gonna come kill us because I can't be quiet.

"Don't worry, Rook, Ford's just up ahead with the van. He's got your bike loaded and I saw those assholes back there leave, we're cool."

"How'd you know where I was?"

He chuckles and grabs my arm hard, saving me from a nasty fall that could've made the pain in my burned legs unbearable after I trip over a tree root. "I put a tracker on your bike and your jacket. You're not gonna get away from us that easy, chick. We're a team, remember?"

"But you're not allowed to help."

He glares down at me for a moment and then the hard expression in his eyes softens a little. "We have rules for a reason, Rook. You could've really fucked things up. You could've been killed, you could've—"

"OK, I get it. But Spencer—" I stop and pull on his leather jacket to make him stop with me. "If you knew what I got out of that house you wouldn't be angry with me."

"You're wrong. If they knew you were there they

would've killed you, you almost got burned alive. You got lucky, Rook. And we're all pretty attached to you. Ronin will get himself out of this eventually. And when he does, the last thing he wants to hear is that the girl he's gonna marry died doing something stupid."

I stay quiet and just limp along after that. We exit the forest a few hundred yards down from where I went in and there's a large white van waiting for us. Ford gets out of the driver's seat with a gun in his hand, not even trying to hide it. Spencer and I are walking casually across the parking lot when Ford's expression rests on me.

I stop dead in my tracks, making Spence stumble. "He's mad at me."

"Damn right he's mad at you. And you deserve it." Spencer pulls on me hard and hands me off to Ford, then walks over to the driver's side and gets in.

I look up at Ford and try a pouty frown.

"Save that shit for Ronin. It won't work on me. I am not talking to you. You scared the fuck out of us, you made me drive a thousand miles in a van alone with *Spencer*. You missed your university application deadline, and most of all, you didn't trust me enough to help you."

Ford takes my arm and pushes me over to the van, opens the door, and barks, "Get in. Sit on the floor between Spencer and me, there's only room for two up front and I don't even trust you enough to stay out of trouble locked in back with the bike right now."

I do what I'm told. They did come get me after all. And my skin might be falling off from the burns instead of screaming at me from the pain if Spence hadn't pulled me up out of the coal chute. There's a small space behind the two front seats and a few sleeping bags lying longways on the floor, so I just lie down, stretch out, and let out a long breath. "I might need to go to the hospital. My legs really hurt."

Spencer has already started rolling and Ford is just getting settled when this comes out. The van stops short and they both look down at me. "What do you mean?" Spencer asks, so I scoot around so I can prop my leg up on Ford's thigh.

"I'm burned from the fire." They both look down at my jeans, charred and with a few holes in them, and then Ford lifts up my pant leg and winces.

"Shit, Rook."

"Is it bad?" I ask. "It hurts."

"Drive, Spencer. I'll check it out." Ford lifts up my pant leg and unties my boot and slips it off, then asks for the other leg. "Take off your pants, Rook. Spencer, we need to find a drug store."

"Is it bad?" I ask again as I wiggle out of my jeans, trying my best not to cry out as the rough fabric rubs against my red skin. Ford doesn't even glance down at my goods, just lifts my foot back up. And why should he look? He's seen me naked so often it hardly matters.

"No, I don't think so," he says, patting the skin on my calf gently, but not gentle enough to keep me from wincing. "It's like a really bad sunburn, but if we find a drug store I know what will make it feel better." And then he smiles and I lie back and relax.

I'm forgiven. His worry about me outweighs his anger.

I reach into my jacket pocket and pull out the contents of the basement box and my new iPhone and hand it up to him. "Here, Ford. I think this will help us get Ronin out."

One eyebrow raises. "Is that why you ran?"

"I didn't *run*, I just… left. To go get this stuff. And I did trust you, Ford. I trusted that you guys were telling the truth when you said you weren't gonna help Ronin. So I'm sorry. But I know what these people want. Jon was into some really bad shit and he made me help him hide a whole bunch of evidence in case his partners ever turned on him. It implicates a lot of very important people in the buying and selling of girls to rich clients all over the world. That FBI guy in the house with Jon was involved—"

"What?" they both say together.

"Jon?" Ford asks.

"FBI guy?" Spencer adds.

I gulp some air and swallow, not quite ready to talk about what just happened but knowing I have to anyway. "Some guy named Abelli was the one in charge here and somehow he got Jon out of jail so he could make him give up the evidence. I was hiding in the floor grate, that's where Jon and I made a safe place a couple years ago and put that stuff." I nod at the flash drives in Ford's hand. "Jon's dead now though. They beat him until he was unconscious because he wouldn't tell them where it was hidden. And then they shot him and set the house on fire to cover it up." I leave out the part about Jon apologizing and saving my life. I'm not sure how to process that just yet.

Ford looks down at the drives I handed him and then grabs a bag on the floor near his feet and fishes out his laptop. He looks at me for a second as he pushes the flash drive in a USB port and waits for the files to appear. He studies it as Spence and I wait in silence. I'm not sure I want to know what's on that drive and Spencer is navigating his way through a nearby town looking for a drugstore, so we sit quietly.

"What's on the iPhone?" Ford asks after Spencer parks and gets out to go buy me some aloe vera sunburn spray.

"A video of that Abelli guy admitting he was gonna kidnap me and sell me to a guy in Columbia for half a million dollars."

Ford's eyes squint down into killer asshole mode.

"And Jon getting the life beat out of him and getting shot in the head."

His eyes soften at this. "Did you see it?"

I nod.

"I'm sorry," he whispers. "No one should have to see that." He watches me struggle with the tears and then leans down a little. "It's OK to feel bad about it, Rook. Even if he was evil. It's still OK to feel bad."

"Jon saved me at the end. He saw me hiding down in the grate hole. He pretended like he was talking to those guys, but he was really talking to me. He apologized."

Ford stares at me for several silent seconds and then shakes his head and lets out a long breath. "Is it over? Can you let go now?"

I nod. "Even though he's not here to witness it, I've decided to accept his apology." I shrug my shoulders and start to cry. "I don't want to hang on to that stuff anymore, Ford."

Ford scoots around to the edge of the seat and pulls my head into his lap. "You're allowed to do that, you know. It's OK to forgive him and let it go."

Spencer opens the door and jumps in the van, handing Ford the bag of spray. "You OK, Blackbird?"

"No, not yet," I say as I sniffle my nose back under control. "But I will be if we can use that stuff to get Ronin out."

"Lie back, Rook," Ford says quietly as he opens the bag.

"I got you some shorts, too, Rook. Just cheap drugstore leftovers from summer, but it's better than sitting in your panties." He winks down at me. "Not that we mind, you know, but I'm sure Ronin would not appreciate us driving you all over the Midwest in your panties."

Ford hands me the shorts as Spencer takes us back on the road. I wiggle into them, which is not easy considering I'm sitting on the floor of a van behind some seats and my legs are burning like hell, but I manage after several embarrassing seconds of Ford watching.

"Put your foot up here," he says, pointing to his lap.

I do.

He shakes the can of aloe vera and I wince as the fine mist hits my skin and then the cold spray settles and relief washes over me. "Ohhhhhhh," I moan. 'That feels so much better I can't even tell you."

Ford smiles and lifts my leg up to spray the underside. "Give me the other foot, Rook."

We repeat the whole procedure and I moan again. "Thank you, Ford. You're a genius."

He shrugs and then he and Spencer exchange a conspiratorial look.

I've seen that look before. Back when they started thinking about taking Jon out.

"What are you guys doing? You have a plan I need to know about or something?"

"Rook—" Spencer talks this time. Which means this is a delicate subject. I know them all pretty well by now. And whenever they need to give or get information to or from me, they take turns based on what kind of conversation it needs to be. When bluntness is needed, Ford takes the lead. When the talk involves personal things it's supposed to be Ronin. And when someone needs to keep things light because I might freak out, that's Spencer's cue to do the talking.

But Ronin's not here, so I guess Spencer is the personal guy now too.

"—we really need to know the whole story before we can do anything with this information, OK?"

I just lie down on the puffy sleeping bags, enjoying the relief from the spray and the coolness of the synthetic fabric. "What exactly do you need to know?"

"Everything," he says. "We need for you to start at the beginning. Like Rook's story, day one. And we especially need to know why your ex-husband had this shit in his possession, what his role was..." He hesitates and lets out a long breath. "What *your* role was. And how all these people are connected. *If* we get Ronin out, you have to understand, we're missing a pretty important part of the team, OK? He's the cleanup, he's the whole reason we get away with this stuff. Yeah, I make good plans, and yeah, Ford's good at covering his tracks. But this is the FBI, Rook. They do not take kindly to being fucked with and they ask a shitload of fucking questions, no matter how good the plan is. A shitload of questions. And our front man is incarcerated. You understand this?"

I swallow hard. "I do, Spencer."

"So, here's what we're gonna do." He stops to look at Ford and Ford nods at him to continue. I guess Spencer really is the logistics guy. "We're gonna go to Ogallala, Nebraska, lie low and get your story from beginning to end, and then figure it out. Sound good?"

"What's in Nebraska?" I ask.

"The safe house. And we definitely need it because these guys will pick us up as soon as we go home. We talked to Clare before we left and she said the guy who came to talk to Ronin twice before he was arrested was named Abelli. This Abelli guy is our main problem, because it looks like he was involved in this trafficking stuff and this means he's desperate to keep his name out of things. Desperate men are very dangerous."

I wait for him to finish it, but the seconds tick off and he keeps silent, so I have to ask. "What do you mean by that?"

He lets out another long breath. "We could all end up in prison or dead, Rook. Those are the facts we're dealing with now."

I stretch my legs out on the sleeping bags and close my eyes. "I'm not gonna think about that, Spencer. Ronin's in jail because of me and I told him I'd fight for us. So that's what I'm gonna do. I'm done running, these people are all guilty, there are dozens of women I know of personally who are wrapped up in this trafficking stuff. And I talked myself into leaving without them the first time. I rationalized it. I'm just one single tragic girl, what can I do? And that was probably the right decision back then because I was all alone."

I stop for a moment and Ford turns to look at me.

"But now I'm on the team, so I'm out of excuses."

CHAPTER THIRTY-NINE

Rook

Ford and Spence take turns driving through the night and by mid-morning the next day we're at Lake McConaughy in Nebraska pulling into a campground.

"The safe house is in a campground?" I ask Spencer as I strain to see out the window. It's pretty boring sitting in the makeshift back of a van on the floor, not even able to gaze out at the passing countryside.

"Not just any campground, Rook. My campground." He swings the van around a circular driveway that allows him to pull up next to the main office and parks the van. "Wait here."

I jump up into Spencer's seat so I can at least sit in a real chair for a few minutes. "Spencer sure does own a lot of businesses."

"Yeah," Ford replies. "He's not into holding onto money. He spends it as fast as he makes it." And then he stops to look up at me. "He likes to own property and businesses. Some grand scheme of his." Then he absently looks out at the campground. "He tried to get me to come deer-hunting with him out here a few years back." I try to picture Ford deer-hunting and then we both burst out laughing. "It's like he had a mental breakdown that day. I dunno." And then he looks at me again and gets serious.

"I do not *hunt*."

"I figured. Me either. I won't be joining that party."

Spencer returns and pushes me out of his seat. "We got the Eagle's Nest cabin. Sleeps ten, but at least it has a bathroom."

We stop off at the campground market to pick up provisions, then head out to our new digs. It's a pretty place—very Daniel Boone.

Inside the cabin is just like a three-bedroom house, complete with wi-fi and satellite TV. Spencer starts the grill to make burgers, Ford is still messing around on his computer, and I just sit and watch them from the dining room table, thinking about home. "Maybe we should call Elise or Antoine and see if there's any news of Ronin."

"Negative," Spencer says. "Those FBI assholes are just waiting for us to show ourselves."

When lunch is ready we all grab some food and eat in silence and then when we're done, Spencer hands everyone a beer and brings a bottle of Jack and three shot glasses out to the living room, beckoning us to take a seat. I take a large overstuffed chair, Ford sits opposite me in a wingback, and Spencer stretches out on the couch. "OK, Rook. Spill it. Start from the beginning and end with climbing up a coal chute yesterday."

So I do.

And it feels good to finally get it all out. I tell them about my mom overdosing when I was just a kid, all my various foster homes, and how I ended up with Wade. Spencer's heard this part before, but Ford hasn't. They lean in a little as my story progresses into the time after Wade. "I was in my last foster home and the father"—I stop to snort—"tried to come into my bedroom and touch me a few times. And believe it or not, even after all those foster homes, the crack ones, the single moms with scummy boyfriends, the ones who collected foster kids just so they could make the mortgage every month, this was the first time one of the grownup guys tried anything. And I figured I'd had enough. I was sixteen, I already took my GED, so I never went to school, and I was just done being someone's problem. So I left and lived on the streets for a while with a girl I knew from a previous foster home. Then she got busted for drugs and I was all alone. And then Jon found me in a diner, scarfing down a sandwich that I bought with my beg money.

"And he had everything, you guys. And he was handsome. He was just like Ronin. He had a college degree, he had an apartment in Lincoln Park. It was small, and not all that nice, but it was still an apartment in Lincoln Park. He had a job and a car and food." I shrug my shoulders and look between Ford and Spencer to see what they think of this but they just nod, like they get it.

"So I stayed with him. He never touched me at first. Not for a long time actually. I was only sixteen and he waited months before even kissing me. It lulled me into a false sense of security. Like he was a gentleman or something.

"But he wasn't. He was a predator who knew exactly what he was doing because I wasn't the first girl he took in and I definitely wasn't the last one either. He liked the kinky sex, that *Fifty Shades* shit. Except... not sweet." I stop and look directly at Ford. "He liked it rough and mean."

Ford's jaw clenches and he downs his shot and pours himself another one. We all stop to drink. Me because I know what comes next, them because they can take a good guess.

"So one day, before we even slept together, he came to me with this piece of paper. It was a sex slave contract. And even though I realize now that it wasn't legal, I really thought it was back then. I feel so stupid, but I just didn't know any better. And he said this was what he needed from me in order to allow me to stay with him, so I signed it."

"You couldn't have known, Rook," Ford says. "It's not something a child should ever know about. It's not your fault."

"I know, Ford. But I just accepted it. I was so dumb. So after that he started having sex with me and it started out bad right away. I was a virgin and the things he was doing to me... they were just *weird*. I was so confused, and it was just too much for me. I—*God*, I'm so fucking embarrassed to tell you guys this."

"Rook," Spencer says, "we're not judging, OK? We just need to understand how we got to this day, you know? We need to know so we can make the right decisions going forward."

I get that part, but it's still so embarrassing. I take a deep breath and continue. "Well, to cut to the chase, even though he tried his hardest to make me... come"—I look away and blush as I say the word—"I just, it just... it never felt good. You know?" I look up and they're both nodding at me, somber frowns on their faces. "And this made Jon very angry. And one night he took me to his BDSM club to do a scene and I didn't... get off. And his friends there realized he wasn't able to get me ready, and they all talked about their girls and how they should trade us off, see if that might improve our... responsiveness."

"Oh, fuck, Rook," Spencer says.

"No, Jon didn't agree. He was possessive of me. But

he did agree to help those guys with their girls. By this time we had already moved out to the country in the serial killer house, that's what I called it. So these girls would come stay with us and he... *trained* them in the basement. He liked them a lot better than me, to be honest. He stopped fucking me so much after that. I sorta just became the house slave. Which I could definitely live with, but he got more and more violent.

"And then, I'm not sure how it happened, but somehow he became involved in like, matchmaking. Selling, I guess, since there was money exchanged. They had auctions in our barn, I kid you not. Girls showed up, willing, money was exchanged, and at first I'm pretty sure the girls were the ones getting the money wired to offshore bank accounts. Their contracts had expiration dates. Six months, a year, that sort of stuff. But later, those girls were not there because they wanted to be. They were kidnapped."

I look over at Ford and he's slumped over, his elbows on his knees, his head in his hands. Spencer's got his hand over his eyes, like he's picturing the scene and wants it to go away.

"Jon came to me one night soon after this started. I'd just found out I was pregnant."

"Pregnant?" Spencer and Ford say at the same time.

"Yeah, I had just found out I was pregnant and things sorta got better. Jon seemed happy about it, and by this time we were already married, so in a rare moment of trust, he came to me and asked me to help him hide some stuff. In case these partners of his ever decided they wanted to get rid of him or turn him in for what he was doing. He told me it was in my best interest since I was his accomplice. So we went down to the basement where his uncle had already made the hidey-hole underneath the laundry room drain grate. Jon knew about it but he was too big to do anything with it, he needed me to squeeze down there, dig it out and make a safe spot where he could keep me and the important things he had in case anyone ever came to mess with him. I would be his ace in the hole, he said."

"What happened to the baby?" Ford asks quietly. He's still got his head in his hands.

"I lost it. Miscarriage." I continue quickly before they start asking too many questions about my son. "Things got pretty bad after that happened. Jon was angry and I mean constantly. He started beating me. Violently, much worse than any of the stuff he ever did sexually. And then he almost killed me. And that's when I ran away and ended up in Denver."

We sit in the silence for a few minutes and I take the opportunity to down my beer and take a shot.

Spencer is still pinching the bridge of his nose and covering his eyes at the same time.

It's killing me to know what they think of me right now.

"Rook." Spencer blows out a long breath of air and then opens his eyes and stares straight at me. "You are the bravest fucking chick I've ever met."

I realize I was holding my breath and I let it escape in a rush.

And then Ford straightens up, leans back in his chair and starts talking. "Those drives contain the names of everyone involved in that little trafficking ring Jon was part of. There are seven FBI agents, twelve Chicago cops, a mayor of a small Illinois town, a state senator, two US House members, and a shitload of well-off businessmen.

One of whom"—Ford raises his eyebrows at Spencer for this—"is our friend Cooperson Smyth from Boulder."

Spencer sits up for this bit of news. "No."

"Yes," Ford says. "He was part of it so you know what, Spencer? You can stop with your own guilt about that now. He was even dirtier than we could ever have imagined. I never heard about this, did you?"

"No, I knew about the money crimes and what his daughter told Ronin about him…" Spencer trails off as he looks over at me.

"His name is all over these documents. And it makes you wonder, right?" Ford looks over at me now, shaking his head and huffing out a breath of incredulity before continuing. "If this was fate after all."

Our conversation all those months ago at Coors Field floods back. When I told Ford that I got off the bus because of the film department at CU Boulder. 'Fate,' he'd said. 'Weird,' I'd replied.

But maybe he was right.

These guys have always been my future.

"That's just the US people. We have several dozen international men as well. Including one particularly nasty cartel head from Columbia. We have signatures, wire-taps, which are probably not admissible in court, video, which probably is admissible, phone records, bank account numbers and transaction records, passwords, and a complete list of girls—both the ones who were traded by mutual agreement and those who were kidnapped and sold. Jon kept very, very thorough records."

"Great, so we're good, right? We can use that to bargain for Ronin, can't we?"

"Well, Blackbird," Spencer says from the couch. "Yeah, it's damn good stuff. Almost airtight, in fact. But the problem is, we might be killed for exposing it. This is high-level shit. People will not take kindly to us barging in on their well-planned crime ring, guns a-blazing, making demands."

"So what do we do?"

Spencer blows out a long breath of air and pinches the bridge of his nose with his fingers, staving off a headache or trying to beat one back down into submission. "Take them all down at once, knock them out before they see it coming. But we're down a team member. We need a front man, and it's gotta be you. Because Ford and I do not, let me make this clear, we *do not* get involved in the public side of things. We've got too much history, Rook. We can't do it. Ronin is like a brother, but we can't risk being the face of these crimes. And just so you know, you're a nobody now. Next year, if we never get involved in this, you'll be a minor curiosity with the show and the modeling.

"But if you do this you'll be famous whether you want to or not. People will dig up your past, smear your name, probably send you hate mail and stand outside wherever you live with giant signs telling you you're going to hell.

"They'll call you a whore, find every last foster home and get them to talk shit about you, and you'll never be invisible again. Say goodbye to grocery shopping and say hello to your own Wikipedia page complete with editors fighting over how to portray you publicly for years to come. Your children will grow up knowing you were a sex slave for a sadistic man and watched human beings being auctioned off in your barn. And that's just for starters, God only knows what could happen. So, Blackbird…" He sighs deeply. "It's your call. You lead, we follow."

I chew on my nail a little, thinking it over. I'm so

ashamed that I was part of what happened back in Illinois. And if I'm honest with myself, that's why I always want to run from things. I have no guts. I'm so weak. Ford was right. And I have done so many stupid, stupid things that I'm not sure I can even make up for it.

But I can try.

Even though it will be difficult and I'll have to admit all these things to the cops and reporters, and God only knows who else—shit, maybe they'll even put me on trial for not turning them in sooner—I still have to try.

I look over at Spencer and swallow down the fear. "Can you come up with a plan that will make sure the cops believe me? Might they just blow me off? Maybe the person we tell is involved? I mean, I know how far-fetched that is, but there are a lot of names on that list, Spencer. What if that's not all of them?"

"That's your risk, Blackbird. This is most definitely not all of them. You can bet that Jon's whole part in this scheme was small, it's international. Even if we get all the names on this list, this is probably a small fraction of the people involved."

"Will they come after me?"

He shrugs. "Maybe. Look, we're not gonna just leave you to deal with it alone, OK? We'll be here behind the scenes, but we won't be fielding questions in front of cameras. You're the one connected to these people through Jon. Ford and I will just make it more complicated. They'll start looking into our pasts, they might even try to pin it on us."

"I might throw up."

"I already have a plan buzzing around in my head and we'll just kick back here for a few days and figure it all out. I'm certain I can set it up so at the very least Ronin will get out of jail for the comments about getting him arrested. And we can probably get some of the people on this list arrested, but beyond that, Rook..." He throws out his hands. "I have no idea. They could all walk in the end. That's just how the system works."

CHAPTER FORTY

Ronin

On day three, rule one and I are no longer on friendly terms. Maybe because orange is not my color or maybe because this shit is like wearing burlap, or maybe because it smells like it was washed in armpits.

I'm not quite sure, all I know is that I'm done embracing the orange jumpsuit.

On day four condition number one is out in full force. Only now I'm talking to Ford in my head, practically begging him to find Rook and figure this shit out.

On day five I break down and call Antoine collect to ask about her. He denies the charges like he's supposed to and saves my ass.

One day six I stop eating. All I do is think about her. Where is she? Did they find her? Is she safe? Hurt? *Fuck, fuck, fuck!*

On day seven I'm getting ready to admit to everything because I'm not very good at obeying rule three right now.

But my lawyer stood me up today, so luckily, my temporary insanity cures itself and I come back to my senses.

And this is just about the time I admit I suck at this jail shit. One week without Rook and I'm insane. I know now for sure—not that I ever doubted it, but now I have proof—I am addicted to Rook and this is my withdrawal.

It fucking hurts.

I let out a long sigh just as my door buzzes signaling someone's on the other side and wants me to come out.

"Finally, fucking lawyer shows up."

But when the door opens it's not my lawyer. It's a big black dude in a suit. "Flynn, come with me," he says, waving me out of the cell.

Gladly, I think to myself. But now that I'm working I'm all business, so that shit stays tucked. We walk past the door to the visitors' hallway. We walk past the door to the rec area, which I hardly ever see since I'm in solitary. Another door buzzes and then we enter a large room filled with more guards. "What's this, beat-the-shit-out-of-Flynn night?"

"It's ten AM, Flynn."

"Oh, well, no windows in the cell, how am I supposed to know?"

"You're not, now just shut up and watch the fucking TV. Hit play, Lenny."

And just as Lenny hits play I glance up at the screen and see Rook standing at a podium with a shit-ton of microphones in front of her. "What the—"

"Just watch," black suit guy says.

She looks a little nervous as she begins, swiping at a stray piece of hair that whips across her face in the Denver wind. The crawl at the bottom of the screen says Denver County Courthouse. I listen as she tells her story. Mostly calm, mostly strong, but a few moments of hesitation and eye-wiping to thwart off the tears. She describes what she's been doing for the past week. The trip to Chicago, Jon, the secret stash, the fire, the rescue.

She tells of corruption in the FBI, calls that bitch Abelli out by name as being one of them, then rattles off a list of people that has the crowd gasping, time... after time... after time. She ends with a name everyone who lived on the Front Range three years ago recognizes.

Davis Cooperson Smyth. The guy we killed in that last job.

Only that's not how Rook tells it.

Because this guy's name is on record as being part of the major human trafficking ring Rook just blew up with her statement. And Jon, the guy who tried to "kill" us last summer, was part of this whole thing from the beginning. She uses the word *assassin* as she holds up thumb drives and an iPhone that contains a video of Abelli—the network shows this video in-screen as Rook talks—beating the shit out of Jon and then ordering him shot and the house set on fire.

Rook's house in the Chicago burbs. While she was inside. Trying to save people and put the bad guys behind bars.

She even flashes a bit of leg to show what's left of her burns and the cameras can't zoom in on her skin fast enough.

Yeah, she's gorgeous, you assholes, and she's mine, so back the fuck off.

And then Rook goes in for the kill shot.

"The FBI set up Ronin Flynn and his friends as the murderers of the wealthy Boulder businessman, Davis Cooperson Smyth, because they found out he was part of this disgusting crime ring and the other men involved wanted to neutralize the threat. Ronin Flynn, Spencer Shrike, and Ford Aston tried to stop the buying and selling of women and girls years ago, and they almost went to prison for their troubles. They've been badgered repeatedly by these criminals and the general public, constantly threatened and shunned in the community. And this past summer these bad men sent my abusive ex-husband to assassinate us. But he failed and I shot him in self-defense."

Ho. Leee. Shit.

Rook just flipped that whole case on its head.

I laugh and when I look around every one of these guys laughs with me. The suit pokes me with his elbow. "She's good, man. We know she's full of shit, you know she's full of shit, but hey, she's still damn good. And I guess no one cares that one less sadist who was buying and selling humans in the hills above Boulder is dead. Your lawyer's here too, by the way. This presser was outside the courthouse because the charges were just dropped and you're gonna walk out of here just as soon as we process the paperwork."

The guards let me hang out in their break room for the duration of my stay. They even give me back my clothes and feed me donuts and coffee.

And I can't stop fucking smiling.

My little Gidget just saved my ass.

Shit, who am I kidding. My little Gidget just saved a whole bunch of people's asses. Women and girls who were kidnapped and those who might've been in the future. She blew open a crime ring that spanned more than a hundred and fifty people.

Even after Rook leaves the podium we all sit and watch as the different news personalities discuss what just happened and run down the timeline.

At seven AM Eastern this morning the State Department was tipped off that a private jet traced to a Columbian drug cartel had landed at the Fort Collins airport with a known representative on board. At the same time, bank records from an account attached to Agent Abelli were also mysteriously forwarded to the same authorities, documenting a transaction the night before out of the Cayman Islands.

A half a million dollars was transferred from the drug lord to Abelli and that little money move has Ford written all over it. He set that sale up with the cartel guy and Abelli probably had no clue it was even going down.

The screen switches to the video Rook talked about in her statement. The one where Abelli tells Jon he plans on selling Rook to a Columbian drug lord for half a million dollars.

All three of the women sitting on the news panel on screen do a collective "mmm-hmm," complete with neck roll, because Abelli is guilty as sin in their eyes.

Enter the court of public opinion.

Abelli has been tried and sentenced. And we're only an hour into the bust.

On top of that, the network states that sources inside the State Department confirm that Abelli's Cayman account can also be directly tied back to the money stolen from "that dirty bastard"—the woman anchor talking actually calls him this on camera—Davis Cooperson Smyth when he was killed three years ago.

Enter nice tidy noose hanging Agent Abelli by his own FBI-issued tie.

I can barely hold down a snicker because this little move proves that Spencer really is a genius. According to Rook, Abelli killed Cooperson Smyth for reasons unknown, but presumably related to this whole crime ring, looted his bank accounts, and stuffed it into a Cayman Island bank. Then used that account to accept money from a Columbian drug cartel so he could sell Rook

Corvus into a life of sexual slavery.

One by one, people are arrested on live TV. The state senator in Illinois, the two US House members right out of their DC offices, several high-ranking FBI members including Abelli here in Denver, and on and on. Even the Columbian drug rep is held.

After the specifics are dissected the news people talk book deals and then the personal stuff comes out. A Japanese erotica cover flashes on the screen and they discuss Rook's recent stint as a body-painting model on a post-production reality TV show.

I think Spencer Shrike is negotiating a new contract with the Biker Channel right fucking now.

They leave the Japanese book cover up on screen as they talk and this makes me smile. Because it's the sweet one in the pink dress where she looks like Gidget, not the one with my hand between her legs where I look like the devil.

The whole country goes wild over Rook.

The mayors of Denver and Fort Collins almost come to blows trying to claim her when they do an impromptu news conference.

And every major news channel has a van outside the jail waiting to get a peek at us when they set me free. The tragic girl who swoops in against all odds to save a local golden boy from being the fall guy for an international crime ring.

When they say that shit, I really do laugh.

It takes DPD almost all day to process me out and at the end of it all black suit guy, whose name is actually Detective Carl Murphy, is riding down the elevator to the garage with me. I'm so ready to see my Rook I'm actually nervous.

She's waiting where they keep the cop cars in order to foil the reporters. The elevator doors open and I hold my breath until she comes into view. She's stopped mid-stride, like she was pacing. And then she is nothing but blurry motion as she runs toward me and flings herself at my chest. I catch her and pull her tight, cupping her ass and copping a feel at the same time.

Life beyond Rook's face ceases to exist.

I kiss her. Not hard and desperate, no. I kiss her softly. I kiss her like the precious thing she is. I kiss her gently. And passionately. And carefully.

And when our tongues are tired of the kiss and we need to come up for air, I dip my mouth into her neck and whisper, "What did you do?"

She leans back in my arms, but her legs are still wrapped around my middle and my hands are still cupped under her ass. "Fiona, it's me, Shrek. I rescued you from your tower to prove I'll fight for us. I'll fight for us every single time. You'll never even have to wonder if I'll be there, because I'll show the fuck up before that thought can even cross your mind. I want you, Ronin, and I'll risk everything for you. I will never walk out on you."

I squeeze her. I just want to make her part of me, pull her so close that we merge together and become one soul. "I love the fuck out of you, ya know."

She smiles and then gets a little more serious. "I hope you still have it," she says.

"Have what, babe?"

"My heart. Because it's the only one I got and I don't want to lose it."

I pat my chest. "I put it right here, Gidget, right next to mine. I'm gonna hold on to it for you. Keep it safe forever."

Antoine throws us a huge party. Everyone shows up.

And relief washes over me for the first time in a long time. Relief that says things are gonna be OK now.

Rook didn't drink even one beer tonight. Not even one. I noticed this early so I stopped drinking too. She's perceptive, but so am I. It's part of my training. Usually I watch so I can imitate later, bring those feelings and emotions out in modeling or lying to the fucking cops during an interrogation. But with Rook I watch because I want to learn more. I want to find her secrets and uncover her soul.

What she said at the press conference revealed a lot about her, but I know there's more. And if she's getting ready to tell me tonight, the last thing I want to be is drunk when she finally gets enough courage to say it.

I'm already in bed, waiting for her to come out of the bathroom. The water shuts off as she finishes brushing her teeth, then the door handle jiggles and she appears wearing some lacy pink boy shorts and a white tank top.

Just Rook.

But she's got something in her hand when she gets in bed and I know this is it.

"I have something to show you, Ronin."

I look at the paper clenched in her fist and then up at her eyes. Tears are already flowing down her face. "What is it, babe?"

She wipes them away and then thrusts the crumpled paper towards me. I take it and realize it's a picture.

My world stops.

When she'd told me she'd lost a baby, I'd figured it was early in the pregnancy. But in this picture she is very pregnant. And she looks young in that peach dress. Her expression says she's happy, her hair is pulled back, and her bare feet and ankles are so swollen I almost start to worry about pregnant Rook. When I look up she's got her hands over her mouth, trying to stifle the sobs. I hug her close and we sink down into the covers a little more. "What happened?" I ask in a soft voice.

She opens her mouth to speak, then stops and shrugs her shoulders. "It was an accident." She nods her head and says it again. "A terrible accident and I lost the baby. I do want kids, Ronin, but this"—she taps the picture with her finger—"this feels like it happened *today*, that's how bad it still hurts. I almost had him, Ronin. My son was two weeks away from being born." And then she breaks and rivers pour down her cheeks. "I'm sorry I'm so emotional and indecisive, but I'm just not over it yet." Her eyes peer up to me, her dark lashes heavy with tears. "That baby..." She stops and chokes on a sob and my chest is suddenly filled with sadness. An aching that pours into me and makes me hold her tighter. "I was gonna name him Jake." She looks away and takes a deep breath. "And his crib was white."

"Rook, I'm so sorry, babe." I feel like total shit dragging her to that baby store.

"It's not your fault, Ronin. I tried to forget about it, to pretend it never happened." She looks up at me again. "But it did happen. And I can't be over it yet because I never took the time to just... experience it. But I'm gonna do that now. I'm gonna make an appointment with a counselor. And one day..." She stops to sniff and wipe her face, taking her time until every last tear is dry and her breathing is slow and calm. She turns those bright blue eyes up at me and nods. "One day, I'll be ready."

At that same moment I give her what she needs, I tell her what she wants to hear and what I need her to understand. "I'll be here waiting. I will wait forever. If that's what it takes. I'll wait for you until the end of time."

She takes the picture and places it gently on her bedside table and then snuggles down into my chest. "You saved me, Ronin."

"And you saved me, Rook."

"So I guess we're even."

"I guess we are."

"And I'm still Shrek because I'm the one who thought of it."

I laugh and kiss her on the head.

My world will never be the same. This girl blew in like the spring wind and whipped me around like a hurricane. She took over my life, she got Spencer to commit to her, and she made Ford feel things. Antoine and Elise love her so much they want us to be godparents and she got an entire city to cheer for her and set me free.

She is a force.

And she's not done yet, I can feel it.

Hurricane Rook is just picking up speed.

EPILOGUE

Ford

The Chaput New Year's Eve party is famous in Denver. I'm not a party person and for me New Year's Eve is a time to be alone, so I've only ever been once besides this year. I wouldn't even be here tonight if we weren't filming for the season finale of Shrike Bikes, but Rook disappeared almost the entire month of December with Ronin. First the GIDGET runway show in LA, then a week in Cancun, then Christmas.

So, here I am, trying to pin her ass down and get this over with.

I'd rather be anywhere but here. I'd rather talk to anyone but her.

The entire studio has been cleared of equipment and replaced with tables and a dance floor. The band is playing, the lighting is moody and atmospheric, and there are almost three hundred people here all dressed in black. I've finished the exit interviews for everyone except Rook, but she's conveniently made herself scarce.

A waitress walks by with a tray and I tap her on the shoulder as she passes. "Have you seen Miss Corvus?" I ask politely. I creep her out, I can tell, because she immediately pulls away from me and then points wordlessly over the crowd to Antoine's office.

She's gone before I can thank her.

It's quite difficult to be polite and when I'm handed rudeness in return, it makes me want to morph back into the old me.

I drop that thought as I make my way through the throngs of people and spy Rook standing just inside the door with Veronica. They are thick as thieves these days. If I were Spencer I'd watch out. They will be into trouble soon, if they're not already.

Ronnie is wearing a short black dress with very high heels. Her look says she takes her fun seriously.

Rook, on the other hand, is dressed like a dark princess. Her dress is not a dress. It's a gown. A long midnight-blue gown that breaks the black only rule, but no one cares because she is stunning. The dress has a tight strapless bodice and elaborate skirts that touch the ground. Her hair is flowing down her back in long waves and atop her head is a shiny blue cardboard tiara.

Just as she turns and spies me, the light catches the blue of her eyes and her crown at the same time. It's like a flashbulb and my mind takes a picture.

"Rook," I say loudly and with a smile. She winces and it's official. She's been avoiding me. "It's your turn, let's go." Veronica pats her on the shoulder like she needs her sympathy and that makes me angry. But I strike through that emotion and beckon my friend with a finger.

"Ford," she starts. "I'm not in the mood. I'm tired of talking. I'm sorta drunk. I'm not ready for this. I'm—"

She goes on and on like that but she follows like a good girl and I just tune it out. We exit the studio and walk down the hallway to the room where I've set up the camera. When I wave her through the doorway she's still talking about waiting guests and Ronin missing her if she stays too long.

I nod. *Yes, yes, yes, I get it*, that nod says. I motion for her to sit. She sits. She always does as she's told when I'm the one asking.

It should make me feel good, that I have this control over her. But it doesn't.

I sit across from her and sigh.

And it's only then that she notices. I'm surprised it took her so long, her skills at reading body language are astute.

"What?" she asks. "What's going on? Did something happen?"

"I'm not going to tape an exit interview of you, Rook. We have so much footage of you from the news, there's no need."

She smiles and the knife slips in. She gathers her dress in her fingertips and rises out of the chair. "Good, then I'm not needed here and I'll just be going," she says, twisting the knife just a little.

"I'm leaving," I say quickly.

"What?" she asks, halting her fleeing feet mid-stride. "But it's not midnight yet."

"I just want you to know I did it all for you," I say, ignoring her statement. "And I'd do it again if that's what makes you happy. I only ever wanted what's best for you."

Her whole body softens at my words. "Ford…"

"And I understand why you wanted to stay in community college and finish your general ed classes and not transfer into Boulder just yet. Online classes are better. The weirdoes and haters are thinning, but they're still out there, so that keeps you safe. I'm proud of you, I want you to know that. Whatever makes you happy makes me happy."

She sits back down, rests her elbows on her knees and props her chin up in her hands. Surely she knew this would have to end eventually.

"If it were anyone else, anyone but you who wanted me to give them so much for so little in return, I would've walked away and never looked back a long time ago. But you make it so, *so* difficult to turn away. And I couldn't let the sadness and pain touch you. It drives me mad when you're unhappy. I lie awake at night wishing I could bring Jon back to life and torture him myself. I wanted to kill that Abelli asshole for even entertaining the thoht of selling you. I want to pull you into my chest right now and keep you for myself. Because, Rook, I just want you." I stop to study the shock on her face for a moment before continuing.

"I. Fucking. Want. You," I say, my voice a deep rumble in my throat. "If I'd found you first instead of Ronin, you'd be mine right now. And I'd never let you go. I know what you think of me, of the girls I have, of my"— I look away for a fraction of a second, then drag my heated stare back to her slumped shoulders and sad face— "idiosyncrasies. But I am nothing like Jon. I have never been anything like those men on that list."

"I know that, Ford," she says softly as she reaches out to touch my arm.

"Don't." I pull away before she makes contact with my suit coat. "You can*not* touch me. If you touch me…" I shake my head, unable to continue.

"If I touch you what?" she asks with an air of challenge.

My own mother hasn't even touched me as many times as Rook has, so this probably does deserve an explanation. "If you touch me I'll touch you back. I'll cup your face and kiss your mouth. I'll hold you close and make you choose me." I stop and swallow hard and then lean into her space and whisper, "I'll ruin everything if you touch me. I'll ruin us. I'll ruin this. I'll ruin you, just like you said. I'll ruin you and I'll ruin your life. And I love you too much to ruin you. So I'm leaving."

Her shoulders slump a little more. "I don't want you to leave, Ford. I'm not sure life without you is possible."

"And I'm not sure life with you is possible. I can't watch you with him, Rook. I'm seething with jealousy. It infuriates me that time and time again he gets what he wants. Ronin pulls love towards him like he's gravity." I stop to laugh. "He only has to ask and love appears in his life. And me? I beg for it. I want love more than anything, yet everyone thinks I'm insufferable." I kneel down in front of her and shake my head. "Everyone but you, Rook. You are the only person on this entire Earth I care about. And you belong to someone else. And if it were anyone but him I'd just take you and say fuck the consequences. But you chose one of two people who will stand by me no matter what I do. And even though these days I count Ronin as a friend, and I would never betray him, I'm so fucking jealous. His life since Antoine has been one long string of lucky breaks. And every day I ask myself, why? Why does he get you? Why does he deserve this luck and I'm always left with nothing?"

I shrug and stand up and her eyes follow me, making her head tilt.

It takes every ounce of willpower not to slip my hand across the milky white skin on her throat, grasp the back of her neck, pull her towards me, and claim her mouth. "This isn't even me talking right now. I don't feel these things, Rook. Ever. When did I become capable of jealousy?" I huff out some air. "Well, it's not really a mystery. It was the day I met you, that's when. You've changed me, Rook. You make me weak, you make me stumble, you make me fall, and even though I know you'll pick me up if I ask you to, it's not enough. I want you to make me stronger, just like I made you. I want it all or I want nothing. And since I can't have it all, I'll take nothing."

She stares up at me in silence, the shock of my words displayed on her face.

I can't stand to see the hurt in her eyes. I can't stand to see her fear and sadness as the realization of what's happening finally sinks in.

So I do what I have to do. I make it worse.

So she's left with no more doubts about what kind of man I am. So she will release her hold on me. So she will stop looking at me like she cares.

So I can let go and move on.

I turn away.

I walk out.

And I never look back.

End Of Book Shit

Welcome to the EOBS. If you're reading through this series then you already know that this is the brand new End of Book Shit edition with the new covers. :) And you already know that I don't edit these final thoughts, so you will excuse any typos. And you already know that I'll pretty much say anything I want.

So... I remember the reactions when this book came out. The twist at the end was... nope, it wasn't Jon. I mean, yeah, he counts as a twist since he was supposed to be in jail. But the twist at the end was learning that Rook was full-term when she lost her baby. People... really reacted to that. And I don't think I knew how much it would affect them until I started looking at people's updates on Goodreads. (Which should tell you how long ago that was, since those assholes banned me in 2015 and I haven't looked at that site since!)

There were comments like, "No, no, no, no..." And "OMG, I'm a crying mess right now." Stuff like that. So it wasn't until then that I realized what I had done. And I say "done" meaning, written. I didn't know it was going to be powerful like that. I didn't expect it, either. I mean, I know losing a baby at any stage in pregnancy is traumatic and horrible. I've had several miscarriages in my life.

But losing one at full-term is quite a bit worse than that. It changes you in ways you might never imagine. And for Rook, this was both bad and good. It devastated her but also gave her strength. She would've stayed with Jon a lot longer—possibly forever—if she had not lost that baby. She saw her pregnancy for what it was. Both the good and the bad. A child. A beautiful little human she would love. And a death sentence. A trap that would hold her in this bad relationship until one of them died.

And no. For Rook getting out of Jon's hold wasn't worth the life of her baby. She would've stayed and found some kind of happiness, even if it was only through her child. But it happened. And she realized there was a gift given when the baby died. The gift of a second chance.

The other twist, was of course, Ford. Learning that he was in love with Rook was shocking. To her, to me—even though I wrote it—to him, even though he knew. And to you, the readers.

That epilogue in Ford's point of view changed my life even more than the release of the first two books. Ford is the character who propelled me onto the scene of "big time" romance authors. It was Ford who brought in my first fans. It was Ford who captured hearts and minds and yes, quite a few of you told me about how much you wanted a Ford of your own.

My fan group on Facebook (Shrike Bikes) was formed just before the release of Taut and that's where you can still find me every single day hanging out with my fans. So Ford the character was a major turning point for me. My whole life really.

The other surprises are typical of what you find in a romantic suspense novel. And by this time I had fully embraced my genre. If I couldn't write SF thrillers and pay the bills, then romantic suspense was my new thing. I love it. This one was plenty suspenseful. The FBI on Ronin's tail. Rook taking off to get that file. The Team finally coming together to get Ronin out of jail. Yes. I had the suspense down.

But there was plenty of romance too. Ford, again, was awfully romantic even though it wasn't his romance. And now Rook & Ronin knew—they were meant for each other. And they would prove it.

In the last EOBS I mentioned a book called Braving The Wilderness by Brené Brown and I talked about how art touches people and changes them. Well, that book was really about belonging. And finding your way to the place you fit in.

This was the entire trilogy, in my opinion. This theme of belonging. Even though the guys were a team once, they'd drifted apart after they messed up and almost went to prison. Each went their separate ways, doing their best to leave each other behind and move on into something new. So it's almost ironic that this one lost girl, with enough regrets for all three of them combined, would be the overpowering force that actually brought them all back to where they belonged.

Knowing where you belong, and how you fit into your "team" is something you can't just go *get*, ya know? You can't buy belonging. You can't even go search for it. It's something that just happens, or doesn't, and it's all beyond your control. You can either go out and look for your people or stay home and hope they find you instead. And even though Rook wasn't looking for anyone when she met Ronin, she took a risk. The took that business card, showed up for a modeling job that wasn't hers, and she let others into her life at a time when she was just about done with belonging to anyone.

So... ironic? That she belongs to Ronin now? :)

Maybe. Or maybe it's just fate.

I think belonging is what brought people to this story in the first place. The desire to read about people who are so fiercely loyal, they would give their life for their team. Loyalty, as a virtue, is undervalued I think. People might think a kind heart has more value. Or generosity. Or love.

But to me loyalty is everything. It's all those things, and more, because to be loyal is to be generous, to be kind, and to love those you are loyal to.

So if you're still looking for that place of belonging... take a moment and ask yourself... Who is loyal to me? And if you've got one or two people in your life that you would call loyal, there... that is where you belong. No need to look further.

I hope you go on to read the rest of the story. Because the journey isn't over yet. Not even close. Ford will be back, and Spencer will be back, and a whole bunch of new characters will join them and spin off, taking you on new romantic adventures and into new sexy stories.

There's more lessons to be learned.

More regrets to get over.

More good times coming.

Books four and five in this series are called Slack and Taut, respectively. They're about Ford Aston, who you haven't met yet, but if you read book two, you will pretty quick. And books six and seven are called Bomb and Guns and they're about Spencer and Veronica.

Guns is the complete ending of the story arc of Rook, Ronin, Ford, Spencer, and Veronica. And a few new characters too—Ashleigh, Sasha, James, and Merc. All of whom intersect in the book called The Company and standalones called Meet Me In The Dark and Wasted Lust.

So if you're looking to enter a WORLD. If you're looking to meet characters so real, you feel like you know them. If you're looking to go on the ride of your life with Rook and her friends, keep reading, bitches.

I got you.

Thank you for reading, thank you for reviewing, and I'll see you again in the new EOBS of Manic.

Julie
JA Huss

About The Author

JA Huss never wanted to be a writer and she still dreams of that elusive career as an astronaut. She originally went to school to become an equine veterinarian but soon figured out they keep horrible hours and decided to go to grad school instead. That Ph.D wasn't all it was cracked up to be (and she really sucked at the whole scientist thing), so she dropped out and got a M.S. in forensic toxicology just to get the whole thing over with as soon as possible.

After graduation she got a job with the state of Colorado as their one and only hog farm inspector and spent her days wandering the Eastern Plains shooting the shit with farmers.

After a few years of that, she got bored. And since she was a homeschool mom and actually does love science, she decided to write science textbooks and make online classes for other homeschool moms.

She wrote more than two hundred of those workbooks and was the number one publisher at the online homeschool store many times, but eventually she covered every science topic she could think of and ran out of shit to say.

So in 2012 she decided to write fiction instead. That

year she released her first three books and started a career that would make her a New York Times bestseller and land her on the USA Today Bestseller's List eighteen times in the next three years.

Her books have sold millions of copies all over the world, the audio version of her semi-autobiographical book, Eighteen, was nominated for an Audie award in 2016, her book Mr. Perfect was nominated for a Voice Arts Award in 2017 and her book Taking Turns was nominated for an Audie award in 2018.

She also writes book and screenplays with her friend, actor and writer, Johnathan McClain. Their first book, Sin With Me, will release on March 6, 2018. And they are currently working with MGM as producing partners to turn their adaption of her series, The Company, into a TV series.

She lives on a ranch in Central Colorado with her family, two donkeys, four dogs, three birds, and two cats.

If you'd like to learn more about JA Huss or get a look at her schedule of upcoming appearances, visit her website at www.JAHuss.com or www.HussMcClain.com to keep updated on her projects with Johnathan. You can also join her fan group, Shrike Bikes, on Facebook, www.facebook.com/groups/shrikebikes and follow her Twitter handle, @jahuss.

Made in the USA
Columbia, SC
10 February 2018